# FIGHTING BLIND

## E. MARIE

Please feel free to send me an email. Just know that my publisher filters these emails. Good news is always welcome.

E. Marie – e_marie@awesomeauthors.org


Sign up for my blog for updates and freebies!
e-marie.awesomeauthors.org

### About the Publisher

**BLVNP Incorporated**, A Nevada Corporation, 340 S. Lemon #6200, Walnut CA 91789, info@blvnp.com / legal@blvnp.com

### DISCLAIMER

# Fighting Blind

By: E. Marie

BLVNP

ISBN: 978-1-68030-884-6

# Table of Contents

*I want to dedicate it to my mom, my biggest supporter and critic.*

# FREE DOWNLOAD

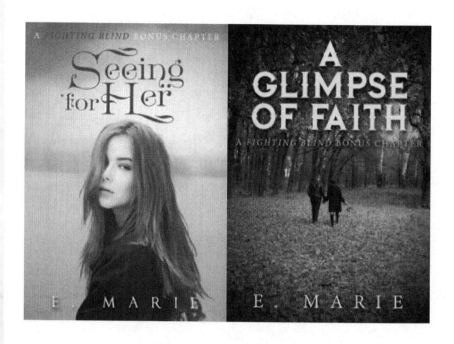

Get these freebies and MORE when you sign up for the author's mailing list!

e-marie.awesomeauthors.org

# Prologue

You would never really appreciate something until you've lost it. The same went for me. Losing my sight felt like the end of the world—the end of my world. Plunged into darkness without any warning made me realize how unfair fate could be. It was as if I was now all alone in a dark room with no one to help me escape from the monsters that hid in the shadows.

Of course, I had my parents. They helped and supported me, as I was only a child and scared to death. Yet, soon, they too were gone, just like my sight. Now, alone and wandering the woods blindly (literally) and with nowhere to go, I prayed that the rogues that had attacked my pack and killed my family won't come for me next. As I trudged alone, a heavy darkness hovered over my head. Heck, black was the only thing that I could see. Yet, I clung to the hope of living. I clung to it so hard I felt all my other senses heighten. And that's when it happened.

My world suddenly had color again.

I was so ecstatic to see something other than black, the darkness that had taken over my life. What I didn't notice at first was how everything seemed to emanate a soft glow, comforting me in its brilliance.

That's when I noticed my surroundings. I couldn't see objects but, instead, see only their color or auras in other words. I never knew this until I was older years later, and I continued to learn much more about my gift, or gifts, I could say.

I didn't die in that forest that night. Instead, I got out with a new determination, and that was to become stronger to help the weak.

And that's how my story began.

# Chapter 1

*Kei Valancia*

I stood there bored, waiting for the man to unknot his panties.

"How do we know we can trust you? You're just a filthy rogue," the man before me said with a snarl, and I simply sighed. Looking closer, the colors swirling around the man were red and blue, meaning anger and uncertainty. To be honest, I'm sick of seeing those two colors. Of course, I couldn't see the man himself, but I imagined him to be a straight-laced kind of guy.

"First off, I'm not a rogue. There's a complicated process for that, and I really don't want to get into it. So, can you just *please* take me to your alpha? I kinda really want to talk to him." I sounded bored even to my own ears. He only growled in response, and I sighed. "For the love of goddess, just take me to your freaking alpha. What can a girl like me do anyway with a pack full of wolves?" *Probably, annihilate all of you without breaking a sweat, but that's just evil and totally not me.*

The man was silent before I heard him let out one more low growl.

"Fine, but if I see you do anything suspicious, then I will—"

"Yeah, yeah, you'll kill me without a second thought. Been there, done that. Now, let's go." I waved my hand in a dismissive manner just to annoy him a little more, and it worked. I was suddenly lifted up into the air by my neck, his grip tightening with his anger.

"I would watch your attitude if I were you, rogue." He spat at me. I rolled my eyes and gripped his wrist.

"Sorry but no thanks. That's just not my style." Lifting my leg and folding my body in a lawn chair sort of way, I planted one foot on his chest and kicked off. He let out a grunt in surprise while I flipped back and landed neatly on my feet. Dusting my pants, I looked in his direction, making sure it looked as if I could actually see him.

"Come on, the night is still young, and I actually have a schedule to stay on. Now, let's go."

"Cocky little—" I growled loudly, and he shut up real quick.

"I dare you to finish that sentence," I smirked smugly when he was silent and began walking away. Following his loud stomps with my own silent ones was the only sound in the woods.

I was currently in the Red Moon territory, and I'd been hearing stories about how rogues have attacked this place five times in the last three weeks. To be honest, I'm surprised they aren't all dead yet.

As we continued to walk in silence, I began to observe my surroundings a little more. I smiled a little in content as the familiar presence of colors swirled around me like a colorful blizzard.

What I actually "see" was something sort of like energy or, in a simpler term, auras. Every living thing emanates an aura. Either it's dim or bright, it still has energy. Of course, energy may be transferred to an object if the owner of that object has strong enough feelings towards it. It's like giving a piece of oneself to an object.

But I love plants the most; every single one seemed to have a unique color all on its own. Same goes for humans, vampires, and so on.

Usually, though, each species have their own mark. Let's say if I touch a rose or look in the general direction of it, I would know it was a rose because I would see a light pink glow coming from the object.

Of course, a plant's energy is dimmer than a person's, but it's still there, nonetheless. It's almost as if walking through pitch darkness with the occasional flashes of colors but maybe ten times more intense.

Kind of the same concept goes for someone's aura. A person emits very bright colors, and each color tells a type of feeling someone has at the moment. And as for a person's soul, let's just say they are the most beautiful things I have ever seen, but I usually have to look a little harder if I want a little peek into someone's innermost person. So, I usually don't for privacy reasons.

It's true that I love what I can see, the energy of the things around me, but I also miss how I can't see what the auras actually looks like in the real world. But I don't usually like to dwell on such things when I know I can't fix it.

Sounds weird but I'm the epitome of weird, so it only makes sense.

I stiffened when I began to hear other sounds, like children's laughter in the distance becoming louder along with the chatter of stressed conversations. Listening closer, I could even hear parts of the conversations going on.

"How will we keep the rogues back? We can't take another attack without being destroyed." The voice was strained, and I felt a pang of pity for this pack.

"I don't know. However, I heard that another rogue was sighted on the west border and was being brought in." I smirked slightly when I heard this. It's about show time.

I knew we were spotted as everything went silent, and I tilted my head up with confidence. I knew they were tense due to their auras; plus,

I could even smell the tension in the air. It was like a salty sea breeze filling my nostrils, and I really couldn't blame them.

I wore a long cloak with a thick hood over my head covering most of my features with the help of dark sunglasses covering my eyes. I pulled the cloak closer, the fabric soft against my skin. I darted my eyes around catching glimpses of all kinds of colors. Dark brown mostly as it represents tension, and I even caught a glimpse of yellow for curiosity.

Judging by all the auras, I could tell that there were twenty adults along with ten kids in what seemed like a large yard.

Cocking my head to the side, I stared at my guide when he stopped and turned to me.

"You will wait here while I get the alpha," he ordered, not giving me time to reply before he was gone. I shrugged and simply continued to "look" around.

I manipulated my powers outward, the blackness of my sight taking shape as I could now see distinct outlines of objects. I couldn't see the details but, more or less, the shape. As I did this, I noticed a large structure emanating a feeling of grief and anger. The feelings of the people living here were influencing the energy of the house, which can happen. The atmosphere says it all, and I knew that inside it would hold a certain heaviness in the air that would sit on your shoulders until it felt like you would be crushed.

I could hear all the whispers, but I decided to ignore them; so used to this treatment it didn't have an effect on me anymore. Instead, I tapped my foot with impatience and kept my face an emotionless mask. Finally, in what seemed like ages, I saw a swirl of power finally enter my vision.

I made a noise of approval as the alpha stepped in front of me, his power quite impressive as I watched it surround him and his pack in a protective cocoon. Each alpha I have met seems to always have a unique color in their power. This alpha was beautiful swirls of dark red and glittering purples.

"Alpha," I said respectfully.

"Rogue," he replied in a dark tone. I rolled my eyes knowing he couldn't see.

"Sorry, alpha, but I'm not a rogue, just an innocent passerby," I said.

"You look like a rogue to me," he replied in an even tone, and I shrugged in return.

"I may look like one, but do I smell it?" This made him pause before answering.

"No," he said shortly. I smirked and nodded.

"I know it's not going to fully convince you, but I don't necessarily care at the moment."

"Then what are is your purpose here," he demanded. I noticed at the corner of my eye of the sparks of browns and other colors identifying their owners with their uniqueness.

"Well, first off, I'm not going to attack you or cause any of you harm. Secondly, I actually want to help you." I imagined him to raise an eyebrow at this.

"And how would you help?" he sounded skeptical as he asked this. I smiled, and it may have come off as frightening, but it was supposed to come off as more friendly.

"I want to train your warriors into some of the best fighters in the world." I made my voice sound self-assured, which I was. I couldn't help it. I was just a very confident person in general. This caught everybody's attention, as I knew it would. I smirked and waited for his response.

"Who are you?" My smile widened, and I spread my hands out, palms facing forward.

"I'm just here to help," I replied, shrugging and trying to look as innocent as I could, which may not have been much. He was silent. The only noises were the distinct sounds of nightlife, and a faraway hoot of an owl pierced the tense air around us. Two minutes of silence passed, and he finally came to a decision.

"Fine. To prove your skills, why don't you fight one of my best warriors?" I stood there for a moment. He must have mistaken this as hesitance as when he spoke, I could hear the smugness in his tone. "Unless you're all talk. Instead, I can have you escorted off of my land with your tail between your legs." I barked out a laugh.

"I wasn't hesitating but more like debating whether how much I wanted your poor warrior to be hurt." I would admit. I did sound rather cocky, and when I saw his power flared with annoyance, I knew I had pushed his buttons. I couldn't help but grin a little. Pushing buttons was one of my specialties, and it was one of my favorite pastimes.

"Fine." He growled. "Mark."

Almost instantly, a man appeared by his side. Electric green surrounded him completely, and I found it surprising. He was just full of excitement.

"Mark, I'll let you have full reign with this one,"

"Yes, Alpha." I could hear the grin in the man's voice or Mark, I now knew, and I couldn't help but let my own smile grow also.

"All right, pup, better get ready 'cause you're going to get your butt whooped," I taunted to him, and in return, he didn't say anything but scoff. I stood still and watched as his colors swirled around him, a mixture of steely gray of concentration and the same bright green of his excitement. I cocked my head to the side and waited for him to make the first move.

I could hear the quiet crunch of grass beneath his feet, smell the salty sweat coming from the other nervous wolves around us, and taste the bitter sweetness of the alpha's confidence. It was intoxicating.

I inhaled deeply and felt myself relax even further, a knowing smile on my lips as the wolf charged at me. I kept still, waiting it out until the last second had almost passed too late. When I did move, it was when I could feel his warm breath on my cheek as he snarled, the heat of his body searing onto mine.

With reflexes that never ceases to surprise even me, I sidestepped while subtly sticking my foot out as he whizzed passed me. A second later, I heard his body thump against the ground. I chuckled as I heard gasps surround us. Their reactions were pretty predictable at this point. I've visited many packs, and I could practically play out all of their reactions by now. The wolf before me snarled loudly, probably flashing his canines at me. I rolled my eyes. Too bad, it wouldn't intimidate me.

"Come on, I don't have all day." I huffed with impatience. That seemed to spur him on as he jumped and changed in midair. I watched as the air rippled around the colorful mass, and I mean ripple. I can see how it seems to shimmer before the mass in front of me becomes larger. By the way the air rippling around him, he was a decent-sized wolf but nothing I couldn't handle.

Letting out one loud growl, he charged once more. I quickly went into a defensive position and prepared for the impact. He was a lot heavier than I had predicted as he slammed into me with full force. Letting out a grunt, I wrapped my arms around his neck tightly while I was pushed back several feet. I heard the snap of his teeth as he tried to bite my face off while his body trembled violently with his growls.

"Dear Goddess, you need to lose weight." I gritted out before falling down onto my back, using this momentum to kick the wolf over my head. He whined from the impact, but I didn't give him a chance to recover as I stood and kicked him in the stomach. He yelped, and I knew just from the sound of a crack, I had broken a couple of his ribs. I jumped back to let him recover for a few seconds, his heavy pants filling the silent air around us.

He snarled viciously, and I yawned in return before shooting him a wide grin. He circled me all the while snapping towards me every few seconds, testing the waters I presume.

I almost ended it as I was starting to get incredibly bored, but he decided to kick the excitement up a notch. As he jumped towards me a second time, he surprised me by changing back into his human form and tackled me to the ground. He elbowed me in the gut, knocking the air out of my lungs.

He straddled my waist as he threw a punch to my right cheek. My head whipped sharply to the side, and I felt my sunglasses fly off somewhere. Pain flared on my face but instantly dimmed and went away. I barked out a laugh once I was hit again. I felt his body freeze above me, and the sharp intake of his breath told me he caught sight of my eyes. I stared straight up at him, a grin once again on my face.

"Good job, pup. Not only did you land one but two punches. You even managed to surprise me. I gotta say I'm impressed." I grinned wickedly. "But sadly, I must end the fun."

"What are you—" He was cut off by his own grunt as I threw my own punch, a solid right hook might I add. His weight was lifted off of me, and I jumped to my feet without a moment to spare, crouching low. He let out a groan before I noticed his outline showing him stumbling to his feet.

I attacked him one last time, running at him and jumping, my feet landing on his chest with a solid thump. His body flew back several feet, hitting what sounded like a tree. I noticed his colors dim, meaning he was unconscious. If he were dead, there would be a lifeless, dull gray, and the smell of death would reek throughout the air. Nodding in satisfaction, I brushed my hands together as if dusting them off and turned to look at the silent crowd. Gasps and soft curses surrounded me, and the color orange of surprise zinging around me. The bright color held my attention until a booming voice brought me out of my reverie.

"Take him to the pack doctor."

"Yes, Alpha," a couple men responded instantly, their own colorful shaped figures picking him up and hurrying him away. I turned to face the alpha and noticed the color orange mix in with his power. I smirked once I saw it. I guess even the big, bad alpha can be surprised.

"What are you?" he demanded. I lifted my hand to run through my hair but was surprised to see my hood was still up. Wow, that was magic all on its own.

"I'm a werewolf," was my short reply.

"But what else?" I shrugged and made the show of darting my eyes around before landing back onto him.

"I think it's best told in private." He was quietly debating my answer, and I was waiting once again.

"How about you pull off that hood to show your face more clearly?" He rumbled, and I shrugged.

"Fine, not like I'm hiding my identity, anyway." Reaching up, I pushed my hood back to reveal my face. I felt my hair roll over my shoulders and down my back. More orange colored my vision, my appearance surprising everyone around me, unsurprisingly. I felt my hair spill over my shoulders and down my back. I've asked many people about my appearance as I became blind when I was young, my memories too faded for me to remember what I looked like. From what they described, I had shifting eyes that would change between the colors bright emerald and ruby red, with a head of silver hair that looked as if the moon poured its silvery light onto the strands itself. Of course, I also joked that they were implying that I was the Moon Goddess, which is sort of a religious figure in werewolf standards. However, she is not an all-powerful being like the one the humans have with their God. The Moon Goddess is simply the first female werewolf to ever be created, along with her mate. But that's a story for another day.

"You are not only werewolf." His voice brought me out of my thoughts, and I gave him a wolfish smile.

"Like I said, let's talk in private." And with confident strides, I walked passed him and everybody else. Displaying a sure step and cocky smirk, I knew he would follow. And he did.

# Chapter 2

*Kei Valancia*

Following the alpha's scent, which was a mysterious musk that I couldn't really put my finger on, I found myself where the scent was strong. Stopping in front of a door, I reached out to softly touch the wood. It was smooth under my fingertips, and I could almost smell the earthy scent as I envisioned the tree that it came from.

"How did you know where my office was?" His voice growled behind me. I tilted my head and moved aside.

"I'll spill my secrets once we're alone." I grinned cheekily at him, and he only inhaled sharply before letting it out slowly. I felt his body brush past me and the sound of the doorknob turning squeaked between us. He walked in first and didn't even seem to care if I followed or not.

"I guess chivalry is dead," I mumbled and walked in after him, shutting the door behind me.

"Only with you," he retorted dryly as I heard the sound of a squeak as he sat in what I assume would be a chair. I pretended to look around but only saw darkness. The only color I could see was from the alpha himself, but everything else was just black. I let out a quiet sigh. It would be nice to see a flower or something.

"Take a seat." Obeying his orders, I walked over smoothly, pushing my senses ahead of me until I could picture the outline of the room in my mind. There were two plush chairs in front what seemed like a large wooden desk, the alpha of course sitting behind it in a massive chair. A table was off to my right along with a couch facing me.

Striding over, I sat in the chair with ease and felt myself slightly relax. It's been a while since I've rested on a piece of furniture like this. I let out a small groan and tipped my head back. This was definitely a little piece of heaven.

"Now, explain to me what you are and what you plan to do here." Cracking my neck, I lifted my head and faced him.

"I'll start off with my name." I cleared my throat dramatically and heard him tap his finger impatiently. I mentally grinned and finally spoke. "My name is Kei Valancia, and I like to think of myself as a traveler of sorts. For a few years now, I  weaker packs to teach them everything they need to know to protect themselves from other packs or rogues. Now your question as to what I am, I'll let you try and figure that one out yourself." His finger tapping stopped as I finished.

"Your features are too bizarre even for a witch nor do you have the air of a vampire," he mused. "My only guess would be that you are half fae, the one species that is cloaked underneath a cloud of mystery." I smiled slightly at his words.

" I know much about them if I was being honest with you," I admitted to him. "Knowing this, I would love it if you wouldn't advertise it as well. I know rumors are bound to swirl around, but it would be helpful if you don't say anything about it." He was silent for a minute, feeling his eyes scanning my face.

"What are you benefiting from helping us out?" he asked in a serious tone. I crossed my legs and made myself comfortable.

"Nothing really. Maybe it's for my personal reasons, but I genuinely do want to help you. Already, I can tell you have some strong fighters in your pack, and all you need is a little help with training them."

"Are you talking about Mark?" I grinned at him.

"He's definitely strong. You're lucky to have him." I noticed the alpha emanate a glittering gold for pride.

"Yes, he is," was his only reply.

"So will you let me help you?" I asked seriously, knowing that this wasn't the time to joke anymore. He was quiet as he contemplated his thoughts, and I began to braid my hair out of boredom.

The room was quiet as I did this, looping one strand of hair over the other, and soon, I found myself in a soothing rhythm.

Over, tighten.

Over, tighten.

Over...

"All right." My hands froze, and I cocked my head to the side with a smile plastered on my face.

"So we have a deal?" I guess he nodded as he didn't say anything, and my smile widened. Finishing off my braid quickly, I tied it at the end and stood.

"I promise; I won't let you down."

"I hope not." He rumbled deeply, and I outstretched my hand for him to shake. After a moment, a large warm hand engulfed mine, and we shook one solid shake. Once we parted, he asked me one last question.

"Is there anything else I should know about you?" I had stopped in front of the door just as he asked, and I turned to look at him with a devilish smirk.

"I'm blind."

* * *

I laughed at the man walking beside me as he grumbled grumpily.

"What? Still mad that I kicked your butt and by a girl, no less?" He grumbled some more before speaking up.

"And it doesn't help that you're blind. I got whooped by a blind, little girl!" I looked in his direction mockingly.

"Aww, did I hurt your precious ego? I would say sorry, but you probably know that I'm not." I felt Mark cross his arms over his chest, and I laughed as he continued to sulk. Turns out, I did break his rib, but he still managed to get up without breaking a sweat. I'll give him credit for his toughness.

"Don't worry, Marky, you'll get your time to shine again."

"Don't call me, Marky." He growled, and I just smirked at him as we walked in the middle of the clearing in the backyard from earlier. We stopped, and I saw many auras surround us, all their colors blending together and looking like a messed up rainbow but still beautiful, nonetheless. Becoming serious, the two of us faced the crowd.

"All right, people. As you can see, we have a newcomer. Her name is Kei Valancia, and she's here to help train our warriors to be the best." Almost instantly, the air around us was filled with angry chatter, dark red splattering across my sight like spilled blood.

"How can we trust her?"

"She's only a filthy rogue!"

"She's only going to kill us all!" I stood there with a stoic expression, not surprised by their accusations. Actually, I even mouthed along with them. Seemingly seeing this, Mark nudged me with his elbow.

"What are you doing?" he whispered in my ear.

"I've visited over a hundred packs and have heard over a hundred of the same lines that I hear now. I could practically recite it in my sleep," I whispered back with a chuckle. I didn't know what his response was, but I decided to calm the crowd myself. Putting two fingers in my mouth, I blew out an earsplitting whistle. This got everyone to shut up real quick.

"Okay, listen up! I get you're all kinda cautious about letting a strange she-wolf just waltzing in and training you, but I'm going to say this only once so you better listen." I waited for anyone to interrupt but was mildly surprised when no one didn't. "I'm here for one thing and one thing only: to train you." I let my eyes wander over the blurry colored masses, not letting my gaze stay still for a moment.

"On my travels, I have heard of the rogue attacks that have happened. And frankly, I'm surprised you're all not dead," I said bluntly. This caused a few angry mutters, but overall, they were calm. "So, I thought if I could help you become stronger, this pack may be the best and strongest pack in the world. 'Cause let's face it, not many packs could hold off five rogue attacks and make it out alive. You can hate me, love me, wish for me to burn in the deepest depths of Hell, I don't really care. Just let me help you feel safe to be in your pack. Let me help you become feared instead of stepped on. That is all I ask of you." I sucked in a deep breath and waited for their response, watching as their auras all flickered with flashing colors, but one of the main colors I had spotted was blue. They were still uncertain, but I noticed one color that was also becoming common.

White—brilliant and pure—white was hope. They finally had hope. And it was riding on me to make sure that I didn't let it burn to ashes.

"Fine, we'll listen to you." A man stepped from the crowd, and I caught his scent of pine trees. I tilted my head and examined the man before me. His aura was a calming light blue tinged with a neon orange. I smirked at his calming aura, but at the same time, he was brimming with confidence—my kind of person.

"I'm so glad you'll listen," I replied casually.

"But that doesn't mean I'll go easy on you when kicking your ass." At his comment, I threw my head back and let out a gut-deep laugh. It was the only noise echoing around us as if I was the only person here. Facing him once more, I grinned almost manically.

"I wouldn't have it any other way."

\* \* \*

I sat ramrod straight, gasping and sweat dripping down my face. The nightmare was already fading away, leaving only bits and pieces of the gruesome images that have haunted my mind for years now.

Swiping a hair out of my face with a shaky hand, I took a deep breath to calm my nerves.

My dreams are the only things that I can actually see visual objects. Yet, I would prefer not to dream at all. The nightmares that plague my conscious haunt and torment me, making me feel as if I'll never get away. What's worse? I could never remember them nor could I decipher the images that cause me so much stress. Groaning, I hid my face in my hands. There's no way I'm going to fall back to sleep now.

Growling in frustration, I got out of the bed. The bedroom that I was currently occupying in the pack house was almost empty except for the bed and a dresser pushed against the wall across the medium-sized boxed room.

Earlier when Mark had dropped me off here, I immediately went into action by running my hands all over the place and pushing my powers out to get the layout of the room. The walls hung bare of anything, and a rug covered some of the cold wooden floorboards.

Stretching, I leisurely walked over to an old ransack on the dresser where I held all of my belongings. Opening the top, I reached my hand in and found a pair of yoga pants and a t-shirt. Changing quickly into my new attire, I slipped on a pair of extra tennis shoes lying beside the door that the alpha was kind enough to give me.

Digging my hand through the sack blindly, my fingers finally found what I was looking for. Smiling slightly, I pulled out the elastic and put my long hair into a bun.

"Come on, I need to run." I chuckled at my wolf's impatience.

"Chill, Rei, I'm going."

"Well, go faster."

Rolling my eyes, I opened the door and walked out. Power buzzed around me as I kept my sense on the alert, the dark outline of the hall taking a dim form in my mind. It was empty of any other souls, and I walked down with silent steps and entered the kitchen.

I was lucky enough to get a room on the first level, so I didn't have to bother sneaking down the stairs. Opening the back door, I shut it behind me with a quiet click and felt myself relax slightly.

Inhaling the crisp night air, I let out a small sigh. Without hesitation, I walked with long strides across the damp lawn and stopped at the edge of the woods. Finally, I let go of the powers flowing through me, and everything in my mind went back to black.

I had a moment of panic as the familiar feeling of energy didn't register in my mind, but I soon calmed when a small spark of green flashed at the edge of my vision along with other small flashes, signaling all the different kinds of plant life. Popping my neck, I could feel the restlessness of my wolf begin to affect me.

"All right, all right. I'm going," I said before running at a full sprint through the woods. I just let my body move on its own accord, dodging any obstacles without even seeing. I wouldn't be able to explain how I do it, but it's just that I know that I can. Makes total sense, right?

I suddenly felt myself jump, and I had in that one second of being suspended in the air the feeling of being weightless until gravity reminded me it was still there and began pulling me down. Just as I felt myself nearing the ground, Rei decided to take the reins.

Transforming in mid-air, I landed on the forest floor with four feet instead of two. I yipped in excitement as I felt like I was breaking free from a tight dress I had worn too many hours. Though I still couldn't see, as my wolf, it sucked a little less. Actually, everything was sharper. My powers were more tuned into the energy surrounding us.

Now, full of happy energy, we ran at full speed through the woods. I heard the whizzing of trees passing us by inches, the smell of the sweet honeysuckle and fresh pine mix to make a heady concoction. I was on a high that I never wanted to come down from.

We ran like that for hours until I had circled and was now just a couple miles away from the pack house. However, I was stopped by an overbearing presence that dripped with power.

Halting immediately, I swiveled my head around, and my ears perked up high. I froze when I caught sight of the source of my caution.

The power that seemed to reach the morning sky waved in a hypnotic dance, a glittering black that consumed anything in its path. I felt my breath catch just from the beautiful sight.

This type of darkness was different from the cursed blindness that I have. No, this kind of black glittered. It wasn't suffocating or heavy. Instead, it was light and free. It was beautiful. Entranced by this phenomenon, I took a step without even realizing it but stopped when a vicious growl ripped throughout the early morning air.

"Stay where you are." The power from this source increased even more, spreading out even further. I looked and saw what I assume would be a man. His form was outlined by his dark power, catching a glimpse of his form. The funny thing was he wasn't big like his power suggested. No, he was lean and sinewy with his long limbs, but he would loom over my human form easily. That was the only thing that I could really define as everything else on him was covered in darkness. I felt myself sigh.

Too bad, I bet he's hot as Hades.

"Shift," he demanded, his deep voice filling me with contentment which I found strange.

"Hmm. He smells heavenly," Rei said dreamily and I agreed. He smelt of dark chocolate and a certain masculine musk that called to us.

"Maybe it's that Axe cologne that is popular among humans," Rei suggested.

"Rei, I don't think that's quite right," I told her in amusement.

"I won't say it again, shift." He growled, and I knew he was beginning to become irater. I changed back into my two-legged form, my clothes magically reappearing. A tint of orange floated around him, and I heard his breathing momentarily stop. Violet enveloped his form like a blanket, and I furrowed my brows. I would like to think that it was my supernaturally good looks that made him go all lusty or something because I haven't seen this much violet from a man in quite a while. Yet, how could his desire grow from simply looking at my rumpled clothing and sloppy hair?

"He's obviously not seeing the same thing as I do," I snickered to Rei.

"You are so childish nonetheless," I could still hear her hidden laughter in her words.

I cocked my head towards him with a small frown on my face. It doesn't seem as if he's the only one having some major hormonal issues, however. The strongest urge to leap into his arms and devour his face was beginning to fill my mind. Not only that, but I could smell his scent from where I was standing, and pray for my soul, it was absolutely mouthwatering.

I took slow steps towards him, seeing the familiar color of dark brown surround him. He was tense. Why, though? He seemed to be a grown man while I am only a small girl or woman, I guess.

"Who are you?" This time, his voice held an edge that could have cut the hardest stone on earth. I didn't answer as I kept creeping my way even closer to the source of sexiness.

"Answer my question." The mystery man growled, but I simply continued to ignore him. Following where the powerful presence was coming from, I stopped when he was right in front of me. Reaching out, I felt my hand touch a prickly cheek. What I wasn't expecting was the sudden explosion of colors and electricity zip through me. Gasping, I pulled back, but a large calloused hand gripped mine in a tight hold.

The one word that I never dreamed of ever hearing was suddenly spoken.

"Mate."

# Chapter 3

*Ryker Dare*

"I allow you to come to my lands, Alpha Dare."

"I, along with my men, will search the area of any rogues before meeting you." I rumbled into the receiver.

"Thank you." No more words were exchanged as we hung up the phone at the same time. Sighing, I stood up and set the device inside a desk drawer. I rolled my shoulders trying to loosen the tense muscles before three terse knocks were rapped on my door.

"Enter." Almost instantly, the door swung open to reveal a tall man with dark blond hair. Clark Davis, my beta and second in command, stood and bowed his head before meeting my eyes.

"Alpha, the men are ready to leave anytime." I nodded, and he bowed one more time before leaving. Cracking my neck, I was about to take my first step when I heard my phone go off in the drawer, the buzzing muffled. Pausing, I was going to retrace my steps before my wolf surprised me.

"No! We must hurry." He almost sounded as if slightly panicked causing me to frown.

"What's the big rush?"

"Let's just go," was his tense reply, and I stood contemplating if I should answer the call anyway. Shrugging, I decided to just leave it. Walking out of the room, the long hallway was dim. Making my way through the winding corridors, I finally made it to a staircase and descended.

"Hurry," Axel, my wolf, was pacing around in my mind, agitated beyond belief. Rolling my eyes, I made the last step and entered a spacious living room.

Walking on the plush carpet, I walked over to the front door and pushed it open to reveal the backyard of my house. Everybody's voices ceased, and ten of my best men bowed their heads.

"Alpha," ten synchronized voices echoed around me, and I simply nodded in acknowledgment. Walking past all of them with long strides and stopping at the edge of the tree line, I heard my men shift and stand beside me. I stared into the dark forest with a blank expression.

"Go," and with that one word, they all pushed off of their haunches and disappeared among the trees, not once making a sound. Standing one moment longer and Axel pacing with agitation in my head, I took a running start and jumped, shifting in mid-air. I landed swiftly and shot off like a bullet into the trees. I could feel my men already miles ahead of me, keeping alert of any signs of rogues.

Axel didn't relax in the slightest as we got nearer to the Red Moon pack. Instead, he seemed even more restless.

"What is your problem?"

"You'll see," was his only reply, and I growled lowly before becoming silent. After a few minutes of silence between us, I could smell the air around us change telling me that we had crossed territories. Slowing down, I sent a command through the link.

"All of you keep guard outside. I'll go in myself."

"Yes Alpha," was the instant reply. My wolf hummed in satisfaction with their obedience, and I rolled my eyes. His controlling personality was more suffocating than mine was and, some days, gave me the urge to throttle him even though it was physically impossible to do so since we were one and the same. Suddenly, I felt my wolf growl not in anger but desire as we caught a whiff of a scent that sent tremors through me. I immediately stopped and stood erect, my head held high looking at my surroundings trying to find the source of this scent.

"It's her." He rumbled, and I felt myself freeze. Shifting abruptly, I stood in my faded dark blue jeans and button up navy blue shirt. I was still as my eyes scanned the surrounding woods, searching for something that I wasn't exactly sure about, but soon, I found what I was looking for. My breath caught in my throat as a beautiful silver wolf stopped a few yards away, the fur glittering in the moonlight that escaped from the thick trees above us.

"Go to her!" Axel practically screamed in my head, but I stood still, not quite trusting this wolf yet. What really caught my attention were the wolf's eyes. I watched silently as the vibrant green irises suddenly melted and turned into an electric red. I watched as the ethereal wolf took a step forward towards me. A growl suddenly ripped through my throat in warning.

"Stay where you are," I commanded. The wolf studied me for a long moment, warming my skin under its gaze.

"It's her," Axel said, and I frowned.

"How do you know"? He never answered, and I sighed quietly in annoyance. Turning my attention back to it — her, I noticed how she was looking around me instead of actually at me.

"Shift," I demanded, seeing her body shudder slightly. She didn't, and I was becoming impatient. "I won't say it again. Shift." I growled. After one more second, the she-wolf shifted and what I saw left me shocked and breathless.

Standing just a few yards away from me was a beautiful woman, her silver mane of hair tamed in a bun and glittered just like her fur. My eyes traveled down her form slowly, noticing how the black yoga pants hugged her legs and as well as the white tank top that she wore, a pair of worn tennis shoes completing the look. I watched as she cocked her head, a few strands of loose hair falling on her face. As I inhaled, I tensed. The sweet smell of lilacs and cotton filled my nostrils, making my wolf rumbling in delight.

"Who are you?" I asked tersely, trying to understand why this woman was affecting me this way. She didn't answer but, instead, crept closer with smooth movements. I stood frozen, watching as she walked closer until finally, she stood before me. With a slender hand, she reached up and touched my cheek.

My eyes widened once I felt the electricity dance across my skin and sending pleasure throughout my body. I watched as her expression matched my own, and she let out a gasp. She started pulling her hand away, but I reached up and gripped her soft hand with mine without thought, feeling the tingles of electricity that meant only one thing.

"Mate," I growled, my wolf howling with happiness. We stood frozen, staring into each other's eyes. I couldn't help but marvel how her eyes kept changing from green to red and back again.

She's not just a werewolf, I thought.

"No, she isn't. But she's absolutely perfect," Axel purred. I stared down at my mate.

"She is," I said out loud. The woman stared up at me with awe and wonder, her perfect teeth grazing her bottom lip.

"No way," she said softly, her voice husky yet strong. I found it absolutely irresistible. I smiled and cupped her cheek gently. "I can't believe it." To be honest, I couldn't believe it either. I've gone over two hundred years and then some without a mate, and now, I've finally found her just by accident.

"What's your name, mate?" She smiled a little at the name before answering.

"Kei Valancia," she said in a quiet murmur.

"Kei." I rolled her name on my tongue, already loving how it sounded off of my lips. It seemed she liked it too as she shivered. Smirking, I took a step closer, not so close that we were touching but close enough that I could feel her heat seep into my skin.

"What's yours?" she asked as I bent down next to her ear.

"Ryker Dare," I whispered, and her body froze. I pulled back to see her reaction.

"Ryker Dare, as in the Alpha King Ryker Dare?" Her voice held disbelief and slight awe. I chuckled before tucking her hair behind her ear.

"The one and only." She laughed, and I was once again left breathless. It was if I was hit in the face with a bucketful of sunshine, the tinkling sound sweet and soft.

"You're cute," she said. I frowned and growled.

"I am not cute," was my quick response. She smirked and tapped my nose.

"Of course, you are." She suddenly slipped from my grasp to which Axel, and I growled.

"Where are you going?" I reached for her, but she simply danced away with a giggle.

"I have to get back to the pack I'm currently staying at," she answered.

"And where would that be?"

"The Red Moon," she said without missing a beat.

"Good. That's where I'm heading as well," I told her. She cocked her head as she looked at me.

"Really? Why?"

"I'm here for their rogue problem." She smirked and took a couple of steps back.

"Funny, that's exactly why I'm here also." I raised an eyebrow.

"You're not actually part of the pack?" I questioned.

"Nope, in fact, I should be getting back now." She looked behind her as if she had heard someone call her name before she turned back to face me with a smirk. "But a quick game wouldn't hurt." She turned on her heel and shifted, her skin sprouting silver fur and her wolf bigger than the average one. She was almost the same size as I was.

Turning her large head, she looked at me playfully, daring me for a race and she shot off into the dark woods. I smirked and started running.

"Fine, I'll play along," I said out loud, shifting and chasing after her. I heard her yip ahead of me, and I felt my wolf smile. Letting our childishness come out for once after so many years was like breaking through a suffocating box.

I pushed myself until I spotted her just ahead of me. She turned her head to look back at me and winked before sprinting even faster. I growled and pushed myself harder.

I got close enough where I nipped her tail. She yipped and looked at me with a glare, and I chuckled. Rolling her eyes, we continued on like this for a couple of minutes until I could sense we were approaching the pack.

Slowing down, I was about to shift when a dark blur suddenly appeared from our right and rammed right into Kei. I heard her yelp, and my vision became red.

No one messes with our mate. I just got her and like hell will I let anyone take her from us.

Letting out a vicious growl, I got ready to pounce on the wolf when I was rammed in the side. The impact left me skidding until I finally regained my balance. Spinning, I growled even more loudly than before.

"I need everyone here now!" I snarled into the link. I felt my men instantly become stiff before my beta replied.

"We're on our way."

Snarling, the rogue and I circled each other. I quickly glanced over to see how Kei was doing but widened my eyes when I saw her lift the wolf with one hand and slam it down, making the ground around us shudder. My attention was snapped back to the wolf in front of me, however, as the snarl ripping through the air gave the only warning before he lunged towards me. With no hesitation, I sidestepped and clamped my jaws around his neck, tightening as he struggled and howled. I growled as he kept struggling between my teeth but relaxed as I felt a slender hand pat my head. I looked over to see Kei standing beside me, her eyes focused on the wolf trapped in my jaws.

"Can you let him go for a second? I need to have a little chat with him." My response was instantaneous as I shook my large head as if I would let go of the rogue who would attack the moment I let him go. "Come on, I'll be fine. Just let me talk to him for a minute." This time as I stared up at her, I inhaled sharply as I took in the sight of her eyes. The colors kept switching from swirling reds and greens, a golden glowing ring surrounding her iris while her hair even seemed to emit its own light. I couldn't move even as she bent down, took the scruff of the wolf, and pulled him out of my slackened jaws. She grinned at me while the wolf in her hands struggled.

"Don't worry about me. A small fry like him won't do me much damage." Almost nonchalantly, she tossed him off to the side with ease, and all I could do was stare, completely dumbfounded. The rogue shifted, and as he did, Kei put her foot on his chest, pushing down to keep him in his place.

"Hey, half-blood freak, long time no see," the man said with a sneer.

"Shut your pie hole, rogue. What are you doing here?" Kei asked flippantly. The rogue barked out a laugh.

"You have the audacity to call me a rogue when you are one also. Seems hypocritical to me." I stiffened and stared at her back. She was a rogue?

"Rogue? My pack didn't banish me nor did I betray them like you did yours. No, mine was attacked and killed, but you already knew that, right, Christopher?" The rogue snarled in return, his brown eyes flashing red.

"Don't you dare say my name!" He snarled, his hands reaching up to grip her leg.

"Oops, must have poked a sore spot. Sorry, but a little doggie like yourself should just stay put." As his hands gripped her ankle, I growled and got ready to pounce, but Kei beat me to it. Lifting her other foot, she sent a hard kick to his stomach. I mentally cringed at the impact, and I wasn't the one getting kicked. The rogue grunted, and his body flew twenty yards in the air before hitting a tree and landing on the ground with a loud thump.

"Alpha!" Just then, my men came hurtling at us, their forms tense. I shifted, and I noticed Kei looked completely unperturbed. Instead, she pursed her lips in a thoughtful manner. I nodded to my beta to shift, and once he did, I growled. His eyes darted over to me, and he bowed his head.

"Everybody, keep your eyes off of her. She's mine," I growled, letting my power seep through my words. Everybody's heads mirrored my beta, and I felt a small hand touch my arm.

"Now, now, big bad King. No need to be so jealous," Kei teased, a smile on her lips.

"I will not have other men look at you while you're in front of me, not any time for that matter," I said in a guttural tone. She smirked.

"We'll deal with the trivial stuff later. Right now, I think you have some rogues to capture," she said, sounding as if this was a regular occurrence that happens every day. With a wink, she strutted past me while nodding towards my men. "I'll see you guys at the pack house." I heard her chuckle quietly to herself before she shifted and disappeared into the trees.

"I can already tell she's going to be trouble," I grumbled to Axel. He only laughed.

"Alpha." I turned to Clark who had a quizzical expression. I chuckled lowly before raising an eyebrow.

"What do you think of your soon-to-be Luna?" His eyes widened.

"You found her?" I nodded, and a smile broke out on his face. "Congrats, man. Adeline is going to be ecstatic." I chuckled lowly before becoming serious.

"Bring those two rogues with us," I commanded. My men bowed before detaining the unconscious men. Without another word, we began to head our way to the Red Moon pack.

# Chapter 4

*Ryker Dare*

As my men and I entered a yard to a dreary looking house, fully clothed and still on high alert for more rogues, two men stood tall waiting for us. I noticed with slight disappointment that Kei was nowhere to be seen.

"Alpha Dare," a man with light brown hair said while bowing his head slightly.

"Alpha Hale, it seems your rogue problem has gotten worse." He frowned deeply when he caught sight of the two unconscious men.

"Who are they?"

"That's why I brought them here instead of killing them. I thought it would be a nice present to greet you with." I smiled sardonically at him before he continued to frown while letting out a gut-wrenching sigh.

"All right. I'll have my men bring them to the cellars." He nodded his head over his shoulder, and two young men appeared from the shadows, throwing the rogues over their shoulders and disappeared

back from where they came. "Let's discuss further matters in my office."
I nodded, and he turned with me following behind him into the house.
Everybody took this as a sign to disperse and to get into his or her own
position guarding the pack house.

The two of us were silent as we made our way through the back
door, entering the kitchen. We walked through the dim room before
going out into the hall with a staircase at one end and another room at the
other. I followed with silent steps as we went up a staircase before going
down another hall. He opened the wooden door to the right and walked
in before stopping with an annoyed growl.

"Why are you in here?" He growled to the person that I couldn't
see. I walked in and stood beside him but stopped. Kei grinned from the
couch, her shoes kicked off while her sock covered feet dangled off the
side of the couch that she was lying on.

"Come on, Brad, aren't we the best of friends already?" I
stiffened at her familiarity with him as he shook his head, but his lips
turned up in a small smile.

"I swear, you're going to kill me instead of actually saving," he
remarked dryly. She smirked and fluttered her hand in a dismissive
manner.

"You have to be near death for me to save you," she pointed out,
her eyes twinkling. He grunted, and I stood to the side watching silently
as the two exchanged a few more words before I had had enough.

"Alpha Hale, we have some business to attend to," I said rather
roughly. His shoulders straightened, and he nodded.

"Kei, I think you should—" She held her hand up to cut him off.

"Save it. I know why the Almighty King is here, so it won't hurt
for me to stay." He growled at her slight attitude, and my wolf snarled in
my head.

*"How dare he?"* I shook my head just barely but didn't answer
him.

"You know I'm going to have to tell him," Hale said rather abruptly. This put me up on alert immediately. She shrugged, but her gaze filled me with heat as she gazed at us.

"Then why don't you two sit down so I can tell him." It wasn't a question but an order. My wolf didn't like her commanding us at all.

"I would watch who you're ordering around, my little *Lune*."

"Is that some fancy word meaning Luna?" she questioned. I walked over and sat beside her on the couch, Hale watching us with amusement.

"More or less," I told her vaguely.

"Hmmm," was her only response.

"I'll let you take the stage," Hale finally said. She shook her head before looking at me, but like earlier, I noticed her attention wasn't on me but around me.

"So, King, I assume that you have figured out, by now, that I am not a full-blooded werewolf, am I correct?" I nodded, and she cocked her head to the side. A stray silver strand brushed her cheek, and she swatted it away with annoyance. "Of course, this is only part of what I wanted to discuss."

"Come on, just spit it out," I said with impatience. She winked and wagged her finger at me.

"Patience, my adorable King, patience." I growled at the word "adorable," but she kept on as if I did nothing. "The point is, I'm blind." Blunt and straight to the point, I see. However, that didn't make the news anymore less impactful.

"What?" She grinned and poked my arm.

"I am blind, King." I stared at her for a few moments. She's blind? My mate and soon to be Luna is *blind*?

"So you can't see me," I said, more of a statement than a question, but she nodded anyway.

"In a sense, I can't. But I do see other things." I stared at her to continue when she paused. She grinned right at me while staring me right in the eyes. How could she do that if she was blind? "The thing is, I see auras."

"The things that surround people?" Hale piped in. I gave him a look, and he shrugged. "She never told me this, either." The two of us turned back to Kei who was braiding her hair.

"Yes. Granted it's a bit more complicated than that, but that's the general idea," she explained.

"So what do these auras mean?" I asked, keeping my tone even. I watched as she finished her braid and tied it off with a hair tie before answering.

"Hmmm, let me start with the basics of it." She tapped one slender finger to her bottom lip. "Everything gives off energy unless it's an inanimate object like this couch for example. That's when I don't see anything unless something living influences it."

"Influence it how?" Kei shot Hale a glance as he asked this.

"This house is a prime example of this." Hale raised an eyebrow.

"Oh?" She raised her hand up palm upward, and a dark swirling ball appeared. We froze at the sight, and Kei's expression turned solemn.

"This is the kind of energy surrounding this place; dark and angry yet full of absolute terror and grief." She brushed her fingertips along the surface, the ball swirling more erratically before calming. I watched with rapt attention, the twirling sphere seemingly palpitating with its own angry energy.

"The cause of this is from the occupants inside. I can't really blame all of you, though." With a flick of her wrist, the ball of energy dissipated. "Enough of me. Tell me something about you, King." I studied her for a moment, her expression relaxed and seemingly carefree.

"My name isn't King, *Lune*." I tapped her nose, and she frowned at me.

"Well, *Dare,* my name isn't looney."

"It's Ryker, love, not Dare nor King, and it isn't looney, it's *Lune.*" She quirked an eyebrow.

"It sounds like the same thing to me."

"Am I missing something here?" Hale looked between the two of us with suspicion.

"Oh, I forgot to mention, Brad, we're mates," she said with lazy grace. Hale's eyes turned to me sharply.

"Is this true?" I nodded and wrapped an arm around her waist, pulling her to my chest.

"It is. So tell all of your male pack members that if I catch them looking at her, I'll rip off their heads—" The rest of my words became muffled as a small hand covered my mouth.

"Now, now, no need to be violent about it. I get you'll be extremely possessive with you being an alpha and all, but you need to just stay chill. M'kay?"

"What else do expect me to say?" I said as I bent down and stuck my nose in the crook of her neck, inhaling deeply.

Lilacs and cotton, such a strange but pure smell. I wrapped an arm around her waist and hugged her close, feeling her melt against me. I heard the door shut with a quiet click, leaving the both of us alone.

*"Keep it clean, got it?"* Hale said through a mind link.

*"No promises,"* I replied and cut off communication. I peppered light kisses up her neck, the electricity shared between us almost too shocking. I felt her become rigid beside me as her hand came up to grip one of my shoulders.

*"Mark her,"* Axel demanded.

*"Not a bright idea,"* I replied. *"We can't rush her."* He grumbled with annoyance but agreed with me. I looked up at her to see her watching me with furrowed brows and biting her lip with a small amount of vulnerability in her eyes.

"Ryker." My name was just a breathless sigh on her lips, and I pulled back. I knew that my eyes were black as I stared at the beauty before me, her eyes hooded but bright.

"Yes, *Lune*?" I smirked at her flushed cheeks. I stiffened when her hands cupped my face in a soft caress, her fingertips trailing the planes.

"It's times like these that I hate that I can't see," she whispered. I sat still as she continued to trace my face, lingering on my lips. "I feel like a lot of arguments will be started by the words that leave your mouth. The same goes for me as well." I raised an eyebrow at her.

"Why do you say that?" I asked. She smirked and let her hand fall while I instantly began to miss the softness of her touch already.

"Oh, if anything from earlier gave me any clue, we are going to butt heads like two stubborn adult bulls that have nothing better to do," she said with a light laugh. "And King, you do not know yet how annoying and thickheaded I can be. I think it's a gift."

"I guess you will get to see my pig-headed side as well. I think that should be interesting, wouldn't you agree?" She laughed, and it made me soften at the sound.

"I have no choice but to. Now—" I had to blink as one moment she was sitting beside me, and with incredible speed, she was suddenly standing in front of the door.

"I would really love to stay and chat, but a girl like me has a very busy schedule." I couldn't even utter a sound as she disappeared with a wink. I stayed in the exact same position for a whole minute, letting my mind finally catch up to what had happened. I grinned wryly.

She was quite the sly one, and it was making everything only the more interesting, the longer I was in her company. Standing up with a quiet sigh, I walked with long strides and opened the door. Just as I took the first step out into the hall, an earsplitting scream pierced the air.

Without hesitation, I sprinted down the hall and back into the kitchen, bursting out of the back door. I, however, stopped dead in my tracks at the sight before me.

My mate stood tall before a looming rogue, his eyes blood red and his canines bared in a snarl. I didn't notice the girl lying on the ground beside Kei, whimpering with fear. Before anyone could move, I appeared beside Kei and let out a ground shaking growl. I knew without a doubt that he wasn't alone as I caught the scent of five others in the woods behind him.

"I do not take kindly to rogues setting foot upon my territory so freely." I didn't turn to look as Hale came barreling towards us with fury. The rogue shifted and stood before us with a snarky smile.

"Alpha Brad Hale, I'm honestly surprised that you're still up and kicking." Hale snarled, and I tried to push Kei behind me, but she wouldn't budge.

"What is it that you want?" Kei asked calmly. The man gave a roguish smile before turning his attention to Kei. I let out a threatening growl and wrapped an arm around her. He saw this and surprise fluttered across his face until it burst with delight.

"Well, well, if it isn't the Alpha King and it seems he's found his mate. Oh, what fun that he will have," he said gleefully, and I had to resist the urge to roar and rip him to shreds.

"What is it you want, Will?" Kei said with an icy tone and cold eyes. Hale and I turned to look at her sharply, but she ignored us. He let out a low chuckle.

"Oh, little Kei, do you think he doesn't see what you're doing? He has let you have your fun for years now, but it seems he's about ready to collect his dues." I was surprised as a vicious snarl ripped through her, her body trembling with anger.

"Go tell him to put a sock in it and die." The rogue *tsk*-ed.

"I would rein in that attitude of yours. You know how he hates disobedience." The rogue seemed absolutely delighted as he watched my furious confusion with this conversation.

"Do I look like I care? No, now, go before I actually put your head on a stake," Kei retorted. He barked out a laugh at her response.

"So feisty. But I suppose that's why he wants you. I guess he still sees you as a valuable plaything." I noticed with growing anger as his eyes raked up and down her body. I've finally had enough. With a loud roar, I charged and shifted midair. The rogue's eyes had widened before I landed on him with all of my weight.

"What are you all doing? Help me!" He screamed pathetically to the woods behind us, but no one came to his aid. I growled and bit into his shoulder, his blood tasting of spoiled fish.

I leaned back and spat it out on the ground beside us. The man lay underneath me white as a sheet and eyes full of terror, no longer filled with the cockiness he had seconds ago.

"Please," he begged. "I'm just the messenger." I snorted and gave him one last glare before baring my teeth and ending his life with ease. His face was frozen in a silent scream as he bled to death onto the ground, the air around us deathly still. Once I was satisfied that he would never get back up, I felt the presence of the other rogues leave.

*"Should we follow them Alpha?"* Clark asked. I shook my head.

*"No, just let them go for now."*

"Ryker." I turned and watched as Kei looked at me with a distant expression. I shifted and hurried over to her.

"*Lune*, are you all right? He didn't touch you, did he?" I looked at her worriedly for any injuries, but she shook her head and smiled.

"I'm fine. But I need to get her back home." That's when I finally noticed the small girl clinging to her leg, burying her face into her jeans.

"I'll come with you," I told her, and she shook her head.

"I am capable enough to take a little girl home. But with you, however, it may seem to others that you would be a creepy pervert walking with a little girl all alone in the dark with something else in mind." She smirked as I stared down at her, stunned. In my moment of surprise, she took that chance to take the hand of the little girl and walk away.

"Oh, Goddess, she is going to be the death of me," I mumbled while Clark suddenly appeared beside me and had a similar smirk on his face as my mate.

"That was sure a blow to the ego." His eyes twinkled as I frowned at him.

"You better hope I'm in a good mood when we get back," I growled back at him, jogging to Kei's retreating back.

"But it's true!" he yelled at me, and I simply ignored but gave a silent promise that I would get him back at some point in time. I followed her as she made her way to the front yard and walking down the gravel driveway. As I glanced back at the main house, I noticed how it still looked as dreary and sad.

*"They wouldn't have made it without any longer without help."*

*"Well, it's a good thing that we came in the nick of time, isn't it?"* I said.

*"Yes, however, if Kei was here just by herself I feel that they still would have been fine without us,"* Axel commented. I stared at her back as I noticed how she chatted to the little girl in her arms, the early morning sun just peeking over the horizon and lighting her figure.

*"Yes, that is true,"* I said gently. Feeling my eyes on her back, she stopped and looked over her shoulder.

"Aren't you coming or what? I want to get back before the day truly begins."

"Don't worry, I'm right behind you. Actually, I guess you could say I am just enjoying the scenery better from back here," I called after her.

"Your pervy side is showing, King. I don't find that very attractive at all." She faced forward once more and trekked along the driveway.

*"Oh, way to go. Now, she thinks that we are some old creeper,"* Axel scolded me.

*"I think she was just joking,"* I said drily. I hurried my strides to catch up to her, and when I did, it was when the driveway met the main road. The layout of most packs consisted of the main house or what is commonly known as the pack house, located at the end of the main road. This is where the alpha and his family stay and where most of the pack business takes place. Surrounding it is where the pack members in the pack live and are all connected by one strip of road.

"Do you know where she lives?" I asked her.

"Yeah, Brad told me." I stiffened at the mention of the other alpha but made no comment as we continued walking the street. "So how old are you exactly?"

"Old enough where it could classify me as a pervert I suppose," I mused. "But my look is stuck at the age of twenty-five at the moment." She raised an eyebrow and tilted her head towards me, the sun rising higher in the morning sky.

"Wow, you must be old. Let me guess; are you a thousand years old?" I grunted and shot her a look to which she didn't react to, and it hit me once again that she was blind.

"Not quite that old. I am still in the hundreds." She stopped and fully faced me this time, the little girl asleep in her arms.

"In the hundreds? I mean, I figured you would be old, and I was teasing about the thousand thing, but I didn't figure that you were in the hundreds." I looked at her calmly.

"Kei, I've been alive quite some time now, and it is widely known as well."

"Look, I'm only twenty, and I've been living under a rock. What do you expect?" Now, it was my turn to gape at her. She was twenty?

*"For some reason, I pegged her to be eighteen, not twenty. Now, I feel a little less like a creepy old man."*

*"Axel, twenty is still considered young."*

*"But not as young as eighteen,"* he pointed out. I rolled my eyes and stared at the young woman in front of me.

"Well, then it should come as a surprise that I am two hundred and fifteen years old. One hundred and ninety-five years your senior might I add." I waited for Kei's reaction, but instead, she took a step towards me and lifted her free hand to my face, poking it and rubbing her fingers down my cheeks.

"It feels wrong that you have a smooth and perfect face while I am picturing an old, withering man with wrinkles that can be seen for miles."

"Like I said, I am stuck at the age of twenty-five." I gently took her hand as she continued to rub my forehead and held her hand in my own. "I'll tell you later about the aging process, but I imagine we should get her home." Kei sighed but nodded.

"You're right. I imagine her parents are worried sick." She made a move to pull her hand away, but I held it tighter, and she didn't resist. Instead, we walked down the road with our hands woven together between us. It was only a few minutes, but it was one of the most peace minutes of my life, walking beside my mate with the morning air filling my lungs while the birds chirped their morning song. You could even say it was one of the happiest moments of my life.

"It's up ahead," Kei said abruptly, disturbing the peace. I gave her a sideways glance, a question on my lips, but before I could speak it, I saw a couple standing up ahead in front of a medium-sized white house, holding onto each other with identical worried looks. Once they caught sight of us, though, the worry turned into relief and joy.

"Blaire!" The little girl's parents came rushing over to us, taking her from Kei's arms. "Thank you so much for protecting our little girl. We can't thank you enough." The woman had tears streaming down her cheeks as gratitude shined brightly in her eyes. Kei shook her head and smiled at her warmly.

"You don't need to thank me. That's why I'm here, to begin with," she told the couple.

"Still, if you need anything, you can come to us for help." This came from the man, and Kei smiled at him before nodding.

"Thanks, I'll remember that." He nodded before his eyes slid over to me. He bowed his head, as did his mate once they knew that their daughter was safe.

"Thank you as well, Alpha King." I simply nodded in response.

"It was nice meeting you, but I suppose we should be off. I hope to see you around," Kei told the couple. They nodded and smiled brightly at her.

"Of course. Goodbye, Kei Valancia." Kei seemed slightly surprised to hear her full name, but she smiled one last time, and we turned and began the trek back.

We walked in peaceful silence until questions began to appear in my mind, nagging at me to ask. Finally, I couldn't contain any of them any longer.

"Who was the man that the rogue was talking about?" I finally asked. She sighed heavily.

"Let's start that story for another day. What do you say?" I glanced at her before nodding.

"If you want, then I will wait." In response, she gave me a small smile.

"Thanks, King." She reached down and gripped my hand. I didn't comment but only tightened my hand around her smaller one, letting the morning stillness be the only thing between us.

# Chapter 5

*Kei Valancia*

I pinched the bridge of my nose, feeling a slight headache forming and the few hours that I could sleep were slipping away.

"Would you please get out?" I growled at the man lying on my bed. He chuckled before patting the space beside him.

"I promise I won't touch. Now, get in." I let out a groan until an idea popped into my head. I grinned evilly before turning my back to him. "What are you doing?" He sounded quizzical as I grabbed the hem of my shirt.

"Do you promise that you won't touch?" I asked evenly. He was quiet for a moment.

"I promise."

"On your life?"

"On my life," he repeated.

"Good. Because if you break it, I'll break you." That's all I said before whipping the shirt over my head and letting it land on the floor beside my feet. I heard him inhale sharply as I began wiggling out of my skinny jeans.

"What are you doing?" His voice was terse, and I imagined his whole body tense.

"Getting ready for bed," I replied casually. After a moment of undressing, I began rummaging through the drawers of the dresser and searching for my old sweats and shirt. Once my hand felt the familiar material, I pulled it out and dressed once more. I sighed in content once I felt the loose shirt settle around me.

"Nothing beats a good old pair of sweats and a ratty t-shirt. Honestly, it's like a piece of heaven. Now, scoot all the way over. I can't get in because your fat body is taking up all of the room." Thankfully, he slid over without saying a word, and I shot him a smile. Climbing under the covers, I let out a sigh as I snuggled deeper. I closed my eyes and silence filled the room. I counted down from ten and smirked as I finished.

I felt him snuggle closer, his hand lightly brushing my face. With an even tone, I said with my eyes still closed, "What did I say about touching?" I felt his hand brush across my cheek and play with a strand of my hair.

"I can't help it. You're my mate, and I am extremely possessive. So let me just enjoy this." I chuckled before yawning.

"Fine, but if I feel your hands wander below the neck, you won't have any hands to get a feel." He just laughed at my threat before getting up. I opened my eyes and saw his black aura shimmer in front of the bed before he slid under the sheets with me. I grabbed an extra pillow and shoved it between us before scooting slightly further away.

"I didn't peg you as the shy type," he mused. I rolled my eyes.

"I'm not shy. I'm just not willing to get hand-sy under the sheets with a man I just met." He sighed but kept to his side.

"I'll let you have your space now. However, don't expect it to last long." I didn't reply but smiled into the pillow.

"Night, Ryker." He was silent for a moment.

"Good night, Kei," he replied softly. We laid there in peaceful silence. Soon, I felt comfort in the heat radiating from him and fell asleep.

* * *

Gasping, I awoke with a start. I sat up and gripped the comforter with tight fists.

"What's wrong?" A deep voice tinged with sleep startled me.

*A stupid nightmare that has haunted my dreams for years woke me up earlier this morning, and then I have the same dumb dream to which I woke up again,* I ranted in my head. But out loud, I said, "Nothing. What time is it?" I asked trying to change the topic. He let out a grunt.

"It's 10 AM, and it doesn't seem like nothing," I groaned as I turned away from him, letting the blanket fall. I felt the cool air hit my sweaty skin like a splash of cold water, and I just wanted to crawl back under the covers and never get out. Getting only three hours of sleep will do that to a person.

"You know," I blurted out. "You don't seem as intimidating as I thought." He was quiet as I stood and strode over to the dresser with confident steps.

"And you don't seem as blind as you say." I gave him a dry smile before pulling out some clothes.

"I am part werewolf you know. I have all of the heightened senses to help me out." I didn't see, but I knew that he shook his head.

"But that still doesn't explain how you know how to fight like the way you do." He was quick to point out. I sighed and turned to face him, placing my hands on my hips.

"Let me put it this way. My senses are more heightened than that of a regular werewolf. My reflexes seem to be quicker, and my hearing is very acute."

"Now that I think about it, you never told me what else you are." I let out a quiet grunt as I pulled down my warm sweats before slipping on my jeans, balancing on one leg.

"It's because you never asked," I told him. He let out a dark chuckle.

"At the moment, I was getting hit by the news that you're blind." I finished buttoning my pants before sighing.

"Yes, and let me tell you, it sucks." I had just taken off my old tee before there was a sudden knock on the door. I didn't think twice before answering, "Come in."

"Kei, I was thinking—" A man's voice was cut off by a loud growl. I turned sharply to face Ryker whose aura was filled with an angry red and a crackling silver gray of possessiveness.

"Hey, King. What crawled up your butt and died?"

"Get out," he rumbled deeply, and I quirked an eyebrow. I, then, began walking towards the door but felt a strong arm wrap around my waist stopping me from going any further. "And where do you think you're going?" His warm breath tickled a strand of hair against my neck.

"You told me to get out, so I was only granting your wishes, King." I heard a scoff to the side and looked over to see a familiar aura tinged with a soft amber.

"Mark, what brings you here?"

"How did you know it was me?" he asked, sounding dumbfounded.

"One, your scent," I said, counting off on my fingers. "And two, you have an amber color around you."

"What does the amber mean?"

"How about you get out and ask your questions later?" Ryker snapped. I slapped him on the chest.

"Don't be rude. He just wants to know."

"Then maybe you should get dressed." I frowned and tried to face him, but he simply held me tighter to his chest.

"What are you talking about?" I questioned. He let out noise between a groan and a sigh.

"Love, you don't have a shirt on." I stilled and finally realized that he was right. My upper body was bare for everyone to see, showcasing my bra which wasn't really much to see. I tilted my head in the direction of Mark, who was still standing in the doorway, and sent him an apologetic smile.

"Sorry, but could you give us a minute?" I didn't hear him respond. "Was that a yes or a no?" I finally spoke, and I heard the floor creak underneath him as he jerked as if shocked.

"Oh, uh, yeah. Sorry." He then turned and left, shutting the door behind him with a quiet *click*. Chuckling, I tried to pull away but seemed to be stuck.

"Could you let go of me now, please? I have to finish getting dressed." He didn't say anything but, instead, picked me up abruptly, cradling me against his chest. I let out a small squeak as he threw me on the bed and trapped me beneath his body.

"King, down, boy. Don't make me use the spray bottle on you," I said teasingly. He didn't even budge from my threat. "You may think that I am kidding, but I will literally get a spray bottle, fill it with water and use it on you."

"Don't worry. Even if we just met, I would believe anything that you told me," he said with a chuckle. I smirked and tapped his cheek with my index finger.

"There we are. Your adorable side is peeking through once more." He groaned and fell on top of me with all of his fat weight lying on top of me.

"Dang it, King. I have stuff to do today, and you using me as your mattress is not going to help anyone." I managed to gasp out, his weight compressing my lungs. After a moment, he still didn't move, and I thought that I was going to get crushed. "All right, you're not adorable. You're amazing, macho, and the hottest guy alive. Better?"

"Now, I am," he said while getting up simultaneously.

"Oh, thank the Goddess, I can breathe." I lied there, trying to get my breath back. "Dang, King, what do you eat?"

"Girls who keep calling me King," he replied flatly. I smirked and sat up.

"Well, lookie here; King has a sense of humor." He groaned before flopping next to me, making the bed bounce slightly.

"You're killing me," he said exasperatedly. I laughed before sitting up.

"But my beautiful looks make it worthwhile," I teased, poking him on his hard stomach. He laughed, and I felt myself hum at the sound.

"Your purr is so cute," he said with mirth. I rolled my eyes and pushed myself off of the bed.

"Sweet words aren't gonna get you in my pants and to get technical, it's not really a purr. I mean, we aren't cats. It's more like a rumble," I said with a smile. I walked over back to the desk and found my shirt that I had earlier. Pulling it over my head, I straightened my clothes and pulled my hair up into a tight bun. I bent down, grabbed my combat boots and sat on the edge of the bed, slipping them on. I could still feel the dip of the bed where Ryker was lying.

"Purr, hum, it's all the same thing." He said as I tied the laces and stood back up.

"I don't know if it's really the same thing," I called over my shoulder as I walked over to the door and reached out to open it when a loud slam echoed beside my head.

"Aren't you forgetting something?" His deep whisper was right beside my ear, and I felt my wolf start to stir.

"Sorry, you're going to have to tell me what I'm forgetting," I murmured, staring straight ahead and only seeing black. I felt his other hand come to my front and laid his palm across my shirt covered stomach. He leaned close and nibbled my ear, sending shocks throughout my whole body.

"A goodbye kiss," he whispered, kissing at a sensitive spot on my neck.

"I'm not saying goodbye. And besides, you are going to have to woo me some more to get access to these virgin lips. Right now, however, there is a locked gate blocking your way," I said breezily, gripping onto his forearm that was now wrapped around my waist.

"But you're leaving the room and away from me." He tangled his hand with mine, intertwining our fingers into a knot that I wasn't sure that I could untie. "And I'm glad that I get to steal away your first kiss." I laughed lightly at his words.

"Such a charmer, King. Really, your words are full of magic," I teased him.

"It seems I am already learning from the best," he retaliated back, his words equally joking. I chuckled one last time before trying to squirm free from his grip. He didn't budge, and I groaned quietly in exasperation.

"All right, King, I have training to do, and you restraining me here all day is not going to help."

"Hmmm," was his simple reply and he only buried his nose in the crook of my neck, his warm breath brushing against the sensitive skin and leaving butterflies in my stomach.

"Dang it, King, stop it."

"I will when you stop calling me King," he growled against my neck.

"I'll give you a choice, Dare. Either move or end up on the floor." He chuckled but didn't move.

"Babe, you're my equal, but I don't think you could actually get me to move." I stiffened, and instantly, all of the happy feelings I had earlier were gone. Poof. Bye-bye, your mate ruined it.

"Oh, *darling*," I said with a sickly sweetness.

"Yes, love?" he murmured. I turned so that I was facing him. I wrapped my arms around his neck loosely and smiled lazily. I gripped his thick locks and pulled his head closer to mine.

"I have something to tell you," I whispered in a conspiratorial tone. He leaned in even closer.

"What is it?" His voice was so soft I almost didn't catch it. I leaned in close and brushed my lips against his ear. I felt a shudder go through his body and I couldn't help but smirk.

"Never underestimate me, *babe.*"

He didn't even know what hit him as I took his arm and twisted, using my momentum and second of a surprise to fling him over my body and slam him onto the floor. It almost felt like an earthquake as his body hit the wooden floor boards with a loud *thump*.

He cursed loudly as he lied on the ground, and I simply turned and yanked the door open, darting through the opening. "KEI!" His roar shook the walls, and I laughed. I heard footsteps echo through the hall as people came rushing to see what was going on.

I didn't pay them any mind as I started to span my power out, and my surroundings started to take a black outline in my mind. I saw the familiar doorway leading to the kitchen, and I ran harder as I heard him charging after me.

"You're only making this worse for yourself," he called after me. I only increased my speed until everything was only a blur as I darted through the kitchen, catching the attention of several others as I burst out of the door. I could tell by the colorful masses that some teens were already outside training at the edge of the woods as I came barreling towards them.

"All right students!" I yelled, their heads whipping to look at me, the color orange of surprise discolored their auras. "Watch and observe your marvelous teacher have an awe-inspiring fight with the one and only king." I grinned widely before twirling around to face the house. Just as I had turned, the King himself made his appearance. And good Goddess was my dear darling King beyond furious if the angry pulsating red energy was any indication.

"Kei, I wouldn't run anymore if you knew what's good for you," he rumbled loudly. I simply smirked and crossed my arms over my chest.

"Oh, I wouldn't, *Dare*." I put emphasis on the last word making him even more agitated.

"Kei," he growled, prowling even closer. "You are making it so hard not to put you in your place." My features hardened at his words.

"Here's the thing, King. I won't be put in *place*. I'm not some dog that you need to punish."

"But aren't you? You have gone long enough without a leash." I bared my teeth and snarled viciously even Rei was beginning to get ticked off at our dumb mate.

"Listen here, mate. You may have been the one in charge, but now that I'm here, you either treat me as your equal or don't even bother at all." Just as the words left my mouth, I instantly regretted it.

*"He's going to take it the wrong way,"* I thought.

"What? You're going to reject me?"

*"He totally took it the wrong way,"* Rei groaned. I sighed and shook my head, the air around us deathly still. I knew I was going to have to choose my next words carefully. Right now, I could see many colors swirl around him. The two most prominent being blue and a very bright neon yellow.

*"Great, not only did I hurt him, but I also made him uncertain about us now."*

*"That's what you get for talking without thinking,"* Rei said scolding me. I ignored her and instead focused on our mate who was hurting. Because of me.

"Look, Ryker." My tone was considerably softer than it was before. "I'm not going to reject you even if there was a gun put to my head."

"I'm not going to let anybody be near enough to you to allow them to do that," he snarled. I chuckled.

"But anyway, the point is, I just want you to recognize me as your equal. Someone who you can trust to fight with."

"You are my Luna. You shouldn't be fighting." I shook my head and frowned.

"See! Right there! Ryker, there will come a time when I will have to fight alongside you, and when that time comes, you're just gonna have to deal with it."

"I will tie you to the bed if I have to." He took a few more steps, his body now just a few feet away. I shook my head but smirked.

"Fine, you stubborn King. But"—I opened my arms in a grand gesture—"I want you to fight me."

"No," was his immediate answer. I rolled my eyes and put my hands on my hips.

"What? The big bad King scared to go up against a little girl like me? I didn't know you were so shy." I smiled as I threw his words that he had said earlier right back at him. The black glittering of his power flickered even higher as he recognized my words as a challenge.

As he was silent, I finally noticed the swirling of emotions around me. I cocked my head and noticed Alpha Hale in the crowd, his aura a calming light blue.

"Fine," he finally growled. "But if I win, then you will have to obey me without a fight." I puffed out my cheeks in thought before nodding. This was just more motivation for me not to lose.

"Okay, I can agree to that. However, if I win then you'll include me in any plans you have about anything. Deal?" He was quiet before agreeing. "Oh, and one more thing, you'll have to obey me without a fight as long as I see fit." I grinned devilishly, adding the last tidbit just for my amusement. Quiet murmurs broke out through the crowd. He was silent a while longer than earlier, but finally, he agreed to that also.

"Fine, but I swear. Don't start crying when I hand your fine ass on a platter." I grinned lazily at him.

"We'll see, King."

# Chapter 6

*Ryker Dare*

"So you're really going along with this?" Clark stood in front of me with his arms crossed. Before the fight could begin, Alpha Hale had pulled Kei off to the side, and the two were whispering among themselves about Goddess knows what.

"Yes, Kei challenges my authority too much, and she needs to be taught a lesson." Clark frowned at me.

"Is this you actually speaking or your wolf? We both know that you're not usually this thickheaded unless Axel is involved," he told me. I growled low in warning.

"Even so, I wouldn't be bad mouthing at this time, Beta." Immediately, he bowed his head, knowing not to push me even further.

"Yes, Alpha."

Nodding in satisfaction, I turned my gaze back to my mate who was staring at Alpha Hale with a bored expression. I took this moment to admire the beautiful young woman.

A few silvery strands of her hair that had escaped from her bun flowed along with the gentle breeze passing through. The skinny jeans she wore was plastered against her long, slender legs as if made like a second skin.

*"Just imagine her without any clothes."* Axel practically purred.

*"I don't think envisioning our mate naked is a good idea right now,"* I replied with annoyance.

*"Why not? Just look at that figure. And those never ending legs are just so—"*

*"Enough!"*

"Hey, King! Are you ready to get your butt kicked?" I didn't give any indication that I was just talking to my wolf about imagining her with a lack of clothes. Instead, I quirked an eyebrow.

"You know, if you wanted to get a piece of this, you could have asked," I called over to her. She scoffed and rolled her eyes.

"Puh-lease. We both know who the hotter one in this relationship is." She grinned at me brightly. This time, it was my time to roll my eyes, but I didn't say anything.

I began taking lazy strides towards her in the middle of the yard, the afternoon air crisp and clear while the sun was warming the earth.

I stopped a few yards away, spreading my feet in a defensive position.

*"We need to go easy on her,"* Axel said. I agreed and waited for Kei to get in a defensive position also, but she simply stood there with her hands loose at her sides. I didn't say anything about it as I watched her eyes shut, and she inhaled deeply.

"King, I know I look like a weak little woman and it doesn't help that I am your mate, but I am going to show you that I can handle myself. So please, try, at least, to get serious for just a little bit." Gasps were emitted around us as she opened her eyes again, the colors switching from red to green. However, what really made her eyes even more abnormal was the golden ring surrounding her irises. "You ready to play, King?"

"Always when it's with you, *Lune*." She scoffed and cocked her head as I began circling her.

"Get ready. I won't go easy on you," she said.

She didn't even finish the sentence when she came charging at me. I didn't falter however at her abrupt advance. I took one swift step back just as she reached me and gripped her arm, using her momentum to flip her over. The plan backfired when she landed on her feet and twirled, lifting her leg up and kicking me right in the stomach. If I were any normal wolf, it would have broken all of my ribs on impact, but being who I am, it would simply leave a bruise. We both jumped back and circled each other once again, her eyes still retaining that eerie golden ring.

"I will say, your power is quite impressive." Her eyes darted above me before coming back down.

"I'm glad you approve," I said with a smirk and pushed off of the balls of my feet into a sprint, my form only but a slight blur. I suddenly appeared behind her and wrapped an arm around her neck. She didn't move, not even tense at my sudden appearance.

"Just give in," I muttered into her ear. She didn't say anything but only laughed instead.

"Oh, my dear King, your naivety is almost breathtaking." My arm involuntarily tightened even more.

"What—" I couldn't even speak the next word before I was flying through the air and hit a tree with a *crack*. Surprise stilled the air around us, and not even Axel could utter a word. I coughed and felt the pain in my back pulsate dully. I stood up and brushed the dirt from my pants.

"That was one hell of a throw," I finally said, watching Kei stand in front of me with a teasing smile.

"Thanks. I've had plenty of practice." She gripped her right shoulder and wound up her arm.

"What, tossing fully grown men into trees?" I asked quizzically.

"You'd be surprised." She suddenly became somber. Shaking her head slightly, she took one more step in my direction. "Fighting is a part of my life that I can't let go." Her words caught me by surprise, and I stood still, studying her stoic face.

*"She's been through things that we can't imagine it seems,"* Axel said a little sadly.

*"It seems that way, doesn't it?"* I murmured back to him.

"Fine then. I'll get serious just for you," I said to her, and just as I finished off the sentence, power crackled around me like furious whips. People around took several steps back while Alpha Hale and my men stood still in their spots.

"Ooh, you're so hot when you're serious." She sent me a wink before materializing out of sight. I immediately stiffened and let my senses take over. Instantly, I felt her presence behind me. As I whipped around, I found that we were now face-to-face. Before I could make the first move, her hand darted out and gripped the collar of my shirt, pulling my head down so she could speak into my ear. Instantly, her scent filled my nostrils, and I had to concentrate my attention on her words.

"Guess I'll get serious as well. I'll apologize in advance for your loss. Don't worry. I'll be there to comfort you," she commented to me cockily. I felt her wet tongue dart out to lick the edge of my earlobe, and instantly, pleasure filled my limbs like a heavy drug. She giggled and pulled away, sending my wolf and me into a frenzy.

"Goddess Kei," I said through clenched teeth, trying to reign in Axel. "Why are you such a tease?" She wiggled her eyebrows and pranced back.

"It's just so fun, King. Why wouldn't I want to do it?" I clenched my fists and knew that Axel was going to break through any moment.

"Kei, do you really want to meet Axel so bad?" Her lips tilted in a smirk, and the golden ring suddenly bled through her eyes, making the whole iris a glowing golden.

"Oh, yes. Yes, she does, my King." She purred at me, and I knew Kei was no longer with us but her wolf instead. "And Goddess, dark chocolate just became my favorite food." She grinned and took off into an abrupt sprint towards me, her hair glinting in the early light.

Cursing, I put one foot back to embrace the impact. I was taken by surprise as her slight frame rammed into me, feeling as if I was rammed by a bull. I let out a quiet grunt and gripped her arms, using her momentum and my body weight to roll onto my back and kicking her over my head. She laughed as she simply landed on her hands and pushed off the ground, landing with fluid grace back onto her feet.

*"Why is it so hard to get her down?"*

*"She's our mate after all. She's going to be strong just like us."* Axel sounded humorous as I got back onto my feet and made a move to restrain her. She simply slipped away out of my reach.

"King, you're going to have to try harder than that if you want to defeat me and put me in my place." She winked and laughed as I growled at her.

"You are having too much fun with this—" I muttered. "—prancing around while I'm being serious." She raised an eyebrow at that.

"This is you being serious? I highly doubt that, King. Even now, I can see you restricting your powers, and at this rate, I'll be the winner if you don't step it up."

"You sound so sure," I said to her. She shrugged and smiled slightly.

"You're not the first to underestimate me, King. Now, let's get this show on the road. I think we've done enough talking." Shaking my head, I got ready.

"I couldn't have said it any better," I said. Smirking, she faced me and took one step, appearing in thin air right in front of me. This time, though, I was ready. I dodged her right hook and maneuvered myself behind her, kicking at the back of her legs. She bent onto one knee, giving me precious moments to grip her arm, and twist it behind her back, pushing her front into the ground.

"That was easy. From all of your talk, I thought that you would put up much more of a fight." She giggled underneath me before, suddenly, the world blurred, and I was on my back, blinking up at the clear blue sky.

*"Goddess, she's hot."*

*"Can you for one moment stop thinking about how attractive Kei is and focus on beating her in this fight?"* I said in annoyance.

*"Ha! You should know me better than yourself, and yet you ask me that question? I am disappointed with you, Ryker."*

*"I knew it was futile, yet I wanted to give it a shot, anyway."* Jumping to my feet, I rolled my shoulders to ease the tense muscles.

"This is going on longer than I had anticipated," I said to Kei.

"You're right. I guess it's about time I ended this, don't you think?" She grinned mischievously, and before I could open my mouth to retort a reply, she had taken two strides to close the distance between us with her fist pulled back, letting it swing before I could react.

"Have a nice nap, King." The last thing I felt was her fist connecting with my jaw, a surge of energy so great it made my vision go black, and my consciousness left me like a fleeting thought.

# Chapter 7

*Kei Valancia*

I watched in amusement as Ryker's aura dimmed as he went into unconsciousness.

*"I can't believe you would do that to our mate!"* Rei screamed at me. I chuckled.

*"Oh, chill. He's the freaking King, he'll be all right."* She only huffed and stayed silent.

"Kei Valancia," Brad's booming voice surrounded the clearing like a heavy blanket. I turned to face the crowd.

"Yes?" I felt a grip on my arm, not rough but firm enough that he meant business as he began pulling me across the yard and back into the house as we made our way towards his office. When he shut the door behind him, I pulled away and sat in the chair.

"So what's all this about? I think I should be with Ryker when he wakes up or he'll freak when he doesn't see me." He didn't say anything as he walked over and sat behind his mammoth of a desk.

"Would you like to tell me what the hell you just did?" I shrugged and looked at him innocently.

"I won a fight against the Almighty King? Pretty explanatory all by its self." I smirked at his low growl.

"Kei, I'm serious." I could hear the power behind his words, but it had no clear effect.

"I'm completely serious too," I said keeping a straight face. He groaned and pounded his fist lightly on the desk. I could see the steely blue of irritation entwine with his powers.

"Why must you be so difficult?" I opened my mouth to speak, but a roar that rattled my bones interrupted me.

"It seems the beast has awoken," I muttered. The two of us were quiet, waiting for the man that was my mate. Right on time, his familiar black power instantly filled the room as he slammed the door open, making it recoil from hitting the wall. "King, have a nice nap?" I smiled cheekily in his direction. I didn't hear his footsteps before I felt his presence right in front of me.

"How did you do that?" He growled. "What are you to have that much power?"

"What? You talking about little ole me?" I smiled innocently.

"Kei, be serious. You're not some ordinary wolf half-breed." I pursed my lips and crossed my arms.

"You haven't told him?" Brad asked sharply.

"Told me what?" At this point, Ryker was sounding fed up by everything.

"Ah, well, I guess you could say that there was never really a good opportunity to tell him." I chuckled to myself quietly.

"Now would be a good time I would think," he said.

"Yes, it would be a perfect time to tell him actually," I replied casually.

"Both of you, stop this and tell me what is going on." Ryker finally couldn't take it any longer, and I finally answered his ever nagging question.

"I would just like to inform you, King, that I am half fae, the one race that everybody can't seem to figure out." He was surprised all right, stunned even, as the bright orange around him was the brightest that I had ever seen on him.

"I guess I shouldn't be too surprised, given how all signs pointed to it," he finally said. "Though, it is still quite a shock to find out that my mate is half werewolf and fae."

"I guess you could say that I am as unique as they come," I told him with a grin.

"However, I do not see how you could have that much strength even being part fae."

"That's funny, I can't see it either." I laughed at my own joke, and I heard Ryker growl at me in response.

"Alpha Hale, do you mind giving my mate and me some time alone," Ryker said. It wasn't a question.

"Do I have a choice?" I heard him mutter before I heard his chair squeak slightly from him standing up. His muffled footsteps on the carpet were the only thing that could be heard as he walked across the room and shut the door behind him with a quiet click. I leaned my head back and sighed, my eyes closed.

We didn't say anything for a long eternity. He could be mad all he wanted that I handed him his butt on a shiny platter. I'll just be off in my own little corner laughing off my own. I felt the heat of his arms as he caged me in between them, blocking my escape. I didn't react as his fingers trailed down my neck, leaving a fiery blaze even though it surprised me more than I would have liked to admit.

"I am your mate, it's kinda my job to keep you on your toes." My voice came out raspy, and I felt his warm breath tickle my cheek as he leaned down to whisper in my ear.

"Say that again," he said in a guttural growl. I lifted my head and opened my eyes, his comforting presence surrounding us in a protective cocoon.

"Say what?" I felt one of his large hands cup my cheek, his warmth seeping into my skin, burrowing deep until it was ingrained into my memory.

"Tell me that you're *my* Luna, *my* mate… *mine.*" I chuckled and tugged his soft hair playfully.

"All right, Tarzan, I'll be your Jane any day." He groaned and stuck his nose into my neck.

"You just ruined the mood." I quirked an eyebrow.

"And that mood would be…" I trailed off, and he pulled back with a sigh.

"You're insufferable." I grinned cheekily at him as he stood, gripping my hand firmly and pulling me up along with him.

"I think you meant adorable. Let's face it. Who wouldn't love this pretty little face?" I batted my eyelashes and smiled sweetly. He laughed, a deep, husky sound that had my wolf howling in my head.

"You're pretty hard to resist," he mused, pulling my body flushed up against his.

"I know. My magnetic personality is just too hard to resist," I said dramatically. If I could see, I imagine him to be rolling his eyes at my ridiculousness.

"Come. We need to begin training." I followed after him dutifully, hand in hand.

"We? As in, you and I?" I questioned, letting him lead me through the room and out into the hallway, the air turning slightly cooler than the office.

"No, you and Santa Claus," he replied with sarcasm.

"Ooh, I've always wanted to meet Santa. I picture him to be gorgeous and not at all like the fat jolly guy that everyone depicts him to be." I sighed dreamily just to get a rise out of him. Which worked of course. We were in the middle of the hall when all of the sudden I felt the wall pushed up against my back, the vibrations of his low growl reverberating through him to me.

"No, you aren't going to meet Santa. And if I hear another word of him, I will hunt him down and put his head on a stake. Got it, love?" I remained relaxed as he took in deep breaths to calm himself down, inhaling my scent.

"You do know Santa is a fictional figure, right? And even if I was able to meet Santa…" I ignored his sharp growl. "I wouldn't be able to see if he was gorgeous or not, so the point is kinda moot. Besides, jealousy looks so hot on you." Deep indigo surrounded his tall for, the color glittering brightly. I chuckled at the idea of him being jealous of a man that wasn't even real. He stayed silent and seemed to be taking in my words.sights are only on you." He didn't laugh. "Oh, come on. It was sort of funny. You know, me being blind

"So, don't worry 'cause my sights are only on you." I poked him in the chest. "Get it? My and some men do." I paused for a quick second.

"By the way, why do men do that? Is it a language shared among men to just grunt in response to all." Still no response, I pouted and crossed my arms. "You're no fun."

"Do you always talk this much?" I frowned and stuck my tongue out at him childishly.

"Only when I am in a good mood." I smiled and leaned up so my lips could brush against his lightly. The orange of surprise and violet of desire mixed together to fill my vision. "But I'm also a bigger tease."

"Kei." My name was a sigh, and I smiled at his breathlessness and took this chance. Slipping from his loose grip, I pranced away as I left him dazed. I simply laughed as his words roared behind me.

"Damn you, vixen!"

# Chapter 8

*Ryker Dare*

"Curse that sly woman," I mumbled angry words under my breath and watched from the sidelines as she instructed her peers who now looked at her with newfound respect.

Her face was in a serious mask, calling out commands with her back ramrod straight all the while giving off the air of authority and power. Goddess, she was so alluring.

"King." Her voice was cool and calculating, making me straighten.

"What is it?" I began walking towards her.

"I need you to train with this group over there." She jutted her chin in the direction of a group of teens, their eyes becoming wide at the sight of me.

"What exactly do you need me to do?"

"I need you to give them the basics of fighting. They're quick learners but are still clumsy in some areas." I nodded but quickly remembered that she couldn't see.

"All right. What are you going to do?" She suddenly smirked and pointed her thumb over her shoulder to another group of men who were checking out her figure.

"I need to teach these bimbos a lesson. You can watch before you start your own training." She whipped around and sashayed over to the group before I could answer. I glared at the men as they raked their eyes up and down her form.

"King, stay calm. I'm the one who needs to show the discipline if I'm going to be the trainer here." With a wave of her hand, she walked up and stood in front of one tall man, in particular, his eyes burning with hunger that made Axel and me angrier the longer we watched.

*"Rip him apart,"* Axel snarled, and I had to grit my teeth to keep him in check.

"So, Cole, I couldn't help but overhear your earlier words," Kei said with a casual smile. I was stiffer than a brick wall as I watched the man smirk.

"And what about it? I don't know if we should let a little girl like you be in charge of training us." He looked down at her, and I snarled, making a move to strangle the guy before Kei raised her hand, making me still.

"Is that so? Well then, I guess we'll just have to do this the fun way, eh?" She chuckled before her hand darted out, gripping a fistful of his shirt and throwing him onto the ground. His loud grunt was the only thing that filled the air, as everybody was shocked into silence.

"Now, boys, you may all think that just because I'm a woman, I can't fight. I think you are being sexist idiots, but hey, maybe you all just hate being one up by the opposite sex. Goddess knows how you all need to inflate your egos like a bunch of hot air balloons." The man, Cole, stumbled back to his feet.

"It's not because you're a woman. It's because you're a *rogue.*" He spat. I couldn't hold Axel back any longer. Letting out a loud roar, I suddenly appeared in front of him. His face paled, and his eyes widened with fear at the livid expression on my face. Gripping his neck, I slammed his body back to the ground and held him there.

"How *dare* you say that to your future Queen? If I were you, I would keep your mouth closed, pup." I snarled, tightening my hold on his neck. I almost turned and snapped at the person who dared to touch me but instantly relaxed as the familiar buzzing of electricity warned me of who it was. Shooting one darker glare at the man, I let go and straightened. Just as I turned, I was met with two furious eyes that were currently bright angry red.

"Oh, Alpha Dare, would you mind coming with me for a moment? I need to have a little chat with you." The way she actually acknowledged me as an alpha with a sickly sweet voice caused alarm bells to ring through my head.

*"She's mad at you,"* Axel commented.

*"Thanks for stating the obvious. And don't pretend that you aren't involved with this as well,"* I replied dryly.

"Oh, and do tell your wolf he needs to listen extra carefully." She turned her back and began making her way to the woods. "Everybody, do two hundred laps around the yard. Do not go into the woods until I get back." She called over her shoulder, and instant groans and mutters followed right after but obeyed. I took long strides after her and finally caught up right as she entered the tree line.

We stayed silent as we walked, the tall trees providing cool shade while the summer wildlife created a song that could only be replicated in real life. Finally, she stopped. I waited patiently as she turned and glared at me viciously, growling lowly with her eyes flashing with fury. Stunned doesn't even cover what I felt from her reaction. Not even a nun cursing during prayer could have made me even more surprised.

"What did I do?" I growled, glaring down at her. She met my eyes with a steely one of her own, her lips turned down in a scowl.

"What are you doing? If I want your help, I would have asked for it." She glared at me, livid beyond relief. This reaction caused many emotions to flutter through me, annoyed that she dared to growl at me, furious with the pup called Cole, and lastly, emotionally stressed by my infuriating hormones that go into overdrive every time I'm near Kei.

"Praise Goddess, my patience is already wearing thin, and we just met." I gritted out before shoving her against the nearest tree, caging her in between my arms. "You are mine, Kei, *mine*. And because of this fact, no one gets to speak to you like that. So get this through your pretty little head, *Lune*. I will rip anyone into shreds who dares disrespect the future Luna and Queen as long as I live." I ended my mini-rant with a soft caress on her cheek, my eyes softening.

"I did not spend half of my existence without a mate to let others badmouth you. Yes, I'll probably infuriate you off beyond belief. Yes, I'll make you want to wrap your hands around my throat and throttle me, but know that I'll still be by your side. Nothing will ever change that because Goddess knows I've waited too long." She was silent as I finished, staring up at me with calming green eyes. They seemed to twinkle with something that made her even more beautiful.

"You know," she finally said. "What if I was a horrible candidate for a Luna? What would you have done then?" I smirked before kissing her lightly on the forehead.

"You're the mate of the Alpha King; of course, you're going to be strong. I just never imagined something like you, however."

"Thank you?" I chuckled and pulled back, tucking a stray hair behind her ear.

"Take that as a compliment, *Lune*. You're better than my wildest dreams." She grinned up at me.

"Why does that sound a lot more perverted than I am thinking?"

"It's probably because your dirty mind is stuck in the gutter," I said with the roll of my eyes.

"I guess not being a virgin doesn't help," she said bitterly with a sardonic smile, but as soon as she said those words, both of us froze.

"What did you just say?" My words were slow and sharp, careful to keep them even. She cursed under her breath and tilted her face away from me.

"When did I become such a blabber mouth?" she muttered, but I didn't have the patience to wait for her answer. I reached up and gripped her chin, forcing her to face me. "What… did… you… say?" Each word was ground out through clenched teeth, the feeling of rage starting to fill my body like lava.

"It was something that I never wanted to happen," she finally murmured, and I pulled back as if scalded. She looked up, and her eyes held hurt, but I couldn't make myself feel for her. Even Axel was hurt and didn't say anything in her defense.

"So what? Did you just jump into bed with any man on the streets?" This time, as she flushed red, it wasn't from shame.

"What? Because I'm not a virgin that instantly classifies me as some harlot?"

"Well, it looked as if you weren't going to save yourself for someone special," I said with a sneer, ignoring the pang of pain in my chest. She looked at me as if I had struck her, anger and betrayal shone clear in her eyes, and I instantly wished I had kept my mouth shut. She maneuvered around the tree and away from me, her eyes becoming blank.

"I'm not going to justify myself to you if you aren't even willing to hear me out. You're being an absolute hypocrite. And right after what you just said earlier, how can I believe you? You, who not only minutes ago, told me that you were going to stay by my side, but after you find out I'm not a virgin, you instantly just assume the worse of me?" She laughed, but it wasn't the sweet sound that I was beginning to love. No, this was full of hurt and disbelief. And my heart clenched at the sound.

"Kei—" she moved away from my outreached hand and gave me a venomous look.

"I guess I'm going to be collecting my winnings earlier than anticipated." I was silent with apprehension. "Alpha Dare, I want you to stay away from me unless it's anything about the pack or any business-related to the pack until when I deemed fit will you have been punished enough, got it?" I went tense as the words finally registered in my mind.

She brushed past me, and I didn't make a move to stop her. Even though everything in my being wanted to reach out and pull her against me. Axel was screaming to go get her and demand that she take back whatever she said, but a deal is a deal, and I would respect her wishes. I stood there and finally let what happened to sink in. Digging my fingers roughly into my hair and pulling did nothing to relieve the sting of her words and the guilt gnawing at my chest.

*"She's right. You're just one big hypocrite, and now, we could have potentially lost our mate because of you,"* Axel growled at me.

*"You were thinking the same things as me, Axel. That doesn't make you any less guilty."* I snarled. He didn't reply. I ground out curses and tilted my face up to the sky, letting the rays of sun that peeked through the dense leaves blind me until I brought myself back to the dark shadows.

*"I need a run. Clark, you're in charge."*

*"Yes, Alpha."* I cut off the link and shifted, forcing my legs to go the fastest of my ability, knowing that staying away will make me want her more.

# Chapter 9

*Kei Valancia*

I ignored the angry growls and screams of Rei inside my head. Instead, I focused on the task at hand.

"Everyone, stop," I yelled. Everybody heeded my demand and slumped to the ground, panting hard. The only one who didn't seem winded was Mark who strolled over to me.

"What happened to you and the Alpha King?" I shrugged and scanned over the array of colors spread across the yard.

"He and I had a little disagreement. Let's just say we won't be conversing much for a while." I saw him become yellow with curiosity, and I decided to ignore it and continued today's training. I gathered them all into groups of two and had them begin fighting, "watching" with a critical eye.

"Laci, keep your arms up more! Garett quicker steps." I watched their auras outline their bodies, putting all of my focus and power into every detail as they fought. Their black forms were the only things I could see as their bright colors illuminated the air around them.

"How can she even tell what we're doing?" I heard a boy mutter. Turning my gaze in his direction, he became silent almost immediately.

"Harold Jay, come here." I noticed him stay rooted in his spot for one moment before coming towards me with slow steps. I let out a quiet sigh before speeding up the process. I used my freaky speed and sprinted in a quick burst, gripping his arm while twisting it behind his back. He let out a cry of surprise and pain before I pushed him down onto his knees.

"Now, my Harold boy, when I say to come here, I expect you to be in front of me as if the hellhounds were on your heels, not this slow poke crap 'cause in a real battle, you can't afford to be a freaking turtle, or you'll be dead. Of course, there is always a chance that you'll get caught and tortured." His fear was almost more palpable than what I could see of the coppery brown emotion.

"So, Harold..." I leaned down so I could whisper in his ear. "Test my patience again, I dare you." With a smirk, I pulled away and let him go. Immediately, he scrambled to his feet and began backing away.

"Y-yes," he stuttered. I gave him one lasting stare before nodding. His aura was a deep coppery brown but was now filling with the color of a pale turquoise. He better feel relieved that I let him easily off the hook. Usually, I was stricter, but I felt that the boy was scared enough, for now, at least. Clapping my hands, I made everyone look at me.

"Now, on that note, please continue training." Groans erupted around me, but the familiar thuds filled the air once more.

"You're such a demon," Mark teased me. One corner of my lips tilted up as I faced the group.

"I can't make you the best if I wasn't," I responded to him.

"That's true I suppose." I heard him chuckle before he went back to his own partner. I crossed my arms and began studying them all once more until two hours had passed before I nodded in satisfaction.

"All right, everyone, you're done for the day." Cheers and cries of relief made me chuckle, and I was honestly surprised at everyone's quick learning skills. They're gonna be a formidable force if they keep going like this. Turning, I started to head back inside but stopped when the all too familiar silhouette of my mate filled the doorway leading back into the house.

Mentally steeling myself, I squared my shoulders and continued walking, becoming even tenser as I got closer. We didn't say anything as I brushed past him, my shoulder barely touching his upper arm. Before I could even comprehend what was happening, I was pulled into a hard chest and dragged into the cooler room of the empty kitchen. I remained calm as he held me, trying with all of my might to ignore the dumb sparks.

"King, what are you doing," I said in a low voice, keeping my composure. He didn't say anything as he bent down and put his nose in the crook of my neck. I couldn't help but roll my eyes. *"Men and their weird obsession to sniff."*

"I understand your need for space, but if I'm going to stay away for a long period of time, then please let me enjoy this small moment of bliss," he murmured, hugging me to his chest. I was still and knew that my resolve along with my anger was beginning to fade.

"Here." Gripping his hand, I began pulling him towards my room. He didn't object and, instead, followed me until I had pulled him inside my room and shut the door behind us. We didn't say anything for a moment, our connected hands hanging between us like an old bridge barely holding on to connect the path over a chasm, a chasm that seemed to have been created by the little trust that we had in each other. In me.

"I'm sorry." Ryker broke the silence with those two words, and I fought to keep my resolve.

"Sorry for what?" I knew it was a low move for me to ask, but I got the feeling that he had never apologized in his life, and I wanted to see what his response would be. I felt his grip on my hand tightened.

"I'm sorry for accusing you of such things when I don't even know the whole story. I'm sorry for being such a bad mate and for not trusting you," and he did sound apologetic, that is, and I felt myself soften. I pulled him closer and reached up to brush my fingers against his scruffy cheek, the prickly hair tickling my fingertips.

"I guess I can't really ask for you to trust me when we just met each other, mate or not. However, it hurts that you think so lowly of me." His arm suddenly wrapped around my waist and pulled me closer while his other hand cupped my cheek. I closed my eyes, not just from the feeling, but also I couldn't bear to look up at the spot where his eyes to be but only see black.

"*Lune*, I don't think lowly of you, not at all. You're beautiful, strong and, in every sense, perfect. Don't ever think differently." I fisted his shirt and put my forehead against his chest, taking in a deep breath. His musky scent made me shudder, and I was suddenly hit with something. Pulling back slightly, I tilted my head.

"Wait, are you a virgin?"

His breathing seemed to pause before he let it out slowly. "Yes." I felt my body freeze. Oh, Goddess, he was a virgin, and that single thought made my heart break. He had waited for me, his one mate, but circumstances on my end ruined that for me. I suddenly yanked out of his grasp. "Kei?" Surprise was heard in his voice and seen in his aura with the orange glaring at me, but I ignored it. I felt empty, angry, and full of hate. All three emotions that could consume me at any given moment.

I pressed myself against the door, feeling every ridge and plane through my shirt. Darkness began creeping through my mind and my emotions, just like my sight, and I was on the verge of going back to my past self. Memories began to fill my head, the feeling of another's touch that sent disgust up my spine.

I didn't notice I was trembling until I felt large hands gripping my shoulders, slightly shaking me. Almost on automatic, my hand whipped out and gripped the assailant's wrist, twisting it to its nearest breaking point before I twisted around the man and flipped him onto his back. The man cursed, and I noticed I was still shaking. Letting go, I backed away and stared at the air blindly, the darkness of my vision bringing me to the point of panic.

"Kei! Snap out of it." Fear, absolute and pure, shot through me. Some part of me knew that it was Ryker, my mate. Yet another part of me was being pulled back to the past that I prayed would go away.

"Ryker, I don't deserve you." I suddenly sobbed, hiding my face in my hands. He tried to turn me, but I didn't budge. I wouldn't let him see me so vulnerable, not caring if he was my mate at the moment. No, my mind still thought that he was the enemy, and I couldn't bring myself to do anything about it.

"Kei." His voice was broken, and I bit my lip, the pain in my chest intensifying, as I knew that I was the cause of the pain.

"Ryker, I am going to tell you something that you are not going to be happy about, but I just need you to listen, okay?" His silence was the confirmation to continue, so I breathed in deeply to control my emotions. "There are things that I am not ready to discuss with you, and it's my turn to be hypocritical in this matter, but I would really appreciate it if you could give me some space to sort out my feelings. I don't want you to be around me to fog my thoughts because, let's face it, we distract each other to no end."

"So you won't even hear my feelings in this matter at all?" he asked lowly. I shrugged and smiled at him wryly before pulling away, his arms letting me move.

"No, I will not. And I would like you to respect my wishes." I became cold and stoic, almost business-like, as I regained my composure. His body was surrounded by such an angry red. I was amazed by its intensity.

"Fine," was his clipped reply, and he simply turned and walked out of the room, the door shutting behind him with a quiet click. Almost instantly, I fell to my knees and let out a choked cry. The suffocating feelings came back, and my skin itched at the phantom fingers. The sound of distant laughter filled my ears, and I knew it was all in my head.

*"Kei, it's in the past,"* Rei said, but she too was shaken up.

*"I know, but it still seems as if it was yesterday. And I hate it. I hate it so much,"* I cried, the silent tears dropping onto the rug beneath me.

*"Yes, but we have our mate now. He'll protect us,"* she said with conviction.

*"Rei, do you really believe that?"*

*"Yes."* I smiled weakly but didn't say anything back. I knew that Ryker couldn't protect me from everything, especially not from my own demons that I harbor.

*"I'll see you soon, darling."* The blood in my veins froze, and I felt my world stop. The voice was only a quiet whisper, but I heard it all the same. I shut my eyes and leaned against the bed, my body emotionally and physically spent.

"Come and get me, I dare you," I whispered into the empty room, knowing that he heard me. However, the voice never answered back, and I felt myself relax; now noticing how tired I was.

I was already half asleep when I noticed I was being lifted up and being tucked in. A kiss was planted on my forehead, a scent of dark chocolate teasing my nose as I swore I heard the words, "I'll wait for you forever," before I was pulled into the all-too-familiar black abyss.

# Chapter 10

*Ryker Dare*

"How the hell am I supposed to deal with this?" I let out a loud grunt as I punched the punching bag with violent swings.

*"Just let her have her space, for now."* Axel sounded pretty damn calm given that we were just told to leave our mate alone.

"You know what alphas get after they find their mate, especially when she's going to go into heat any day now?" I sent a roundhouse kick right into the bag, the chains groaning from the pressure. "And let's not even start about your possessive ass. Goddess only knows how long you'll last before marking her."

*"All right. This situation is a bit direr than I had hoped."* I let out a scoff.

"This situation is a mess." With one final kick, the heavy sand-filled bag broke from the chain and slammed against the concrete wall twenty feet away. I panted as I stood in the middle of the room, glaring at the floor.

*"It would be easier to just find her and mark her,"* Axel said with a huff. I let out a harsh laugh.

"See. Right there. That's the kind of idiotic thoughts that will get us in trouble."

*"Maybe she's mad that we're still a virgin."*

"I don't think that's necessarily the case," I said dryly. I walked over to the bench pushed up against the wall, sitting down roughly. Sighing, I placed my elbows on my knees, leaning forward and entangling my hands in my hair. I was silent as I recalled the look in her unseeing eyes. At that moment, it was as if she was truly blind.

"She flinched away from me as if I was going to hurt her," I murmured, recalling the way her body recoiled from my touch.

*"Something bad has happened to our beautiful mate. It's only a matter of time before she tells us."*

"Unless you go all crazy and demand answers from her." Axel made an annoyed snort.

*"I'm not the only one who would rather go and strip our mate bare and mark her."* I sat up and thwacked my head against the wall gently.

"No, I guess not," I muttered. I left Kei in her room alone for the rest of the day, sleeping in another room located on the side of the house. It was pure torture, knowing that I left Kei by herself, but I was trying my hardest to follow her wishes. I sat in silence for a long time, not caring about anything at that moment. However, the peaceful moment was broken by the door slamming open.

"Alpha." I frowned before standing up.

"Clark, what's wrong?" His face was grave, and I felt unease stir in my stomach.

"Alpha, three bodies were found just on the edge of the border." I didn't waste any time after that. Grabbing my t-shirt from the bench, I slipped it on and followed Clark.

"Rogues were reported being seen twenty minutes earlier at the same location. It became even more suspicious as they simply ran when they were spotted."

"Where are the bodies now?" We walked at a brisk pace through the halls, passing the door that was my mate's room. Some part of me, about ninety percent, wanted to stop and demand she tell me. However, the last ten percent was my hard ass restraint that took all of my willpower. I deserved a damn applause.

"Alpha Hale had them brought into the infirmary to be examined," Clark reported. I nodded, and we began our way towards the destination. We had finally stopped in front of an open doorway, the room inside a blinding white with beds lining the wall adjacent to the door. Alpha Hale along with two other men stood before three beds occupied with the lifeless bodies. As I let my presence be known, the men stiffened and turned. They bowed their heads, other than Alpha Hale who inclined his head in respect.

"What seemed to be the cause of death?" I questioned, taking long strides to examine them.

"Tortured with Black Roza." His tone was grim, and I stiffened slightly. The Black Roza, the name originating from Russian which literally just meant Rose, was not an easy flower to get. The Black Roza was mainly found in the middle of the equator where most of the tropical forests were. It was first discovered by a Russian traveler, who happened to be a werewolf, and noticed its dangerous qualities and decided to use it for his own desires. Let's just say his own discovery was his own destruction.

I stopped beside one of the beds and examined the corpse. It was quite a gruesome sight as the deceased man's skin was clawed and torn as if he had gone through a paper shredder. Around all of the cuts that were all over his body, the skin was black as if he was burned. A sign that Black Roza was used. And the smell—the air had the strong, disgusting scent of burnt, decayed flesh.

I glanced over at the other two bodies, all male, to see them in the exact same condition.

"Do you know their identities?" I turned to look at Hale. He shook his head and looked at the bodies with a hard look.

"Their bodies are too mangled up to tell, but we can only assume they are from here." I raised an eyebrow.

"Are there men missing from here?" His lips were pressed into a thin line, and he nodded. "How many?"

"Ten." I gritted my teeth, anger flashing in my eyes.

"And you didn't tell me this in the very beginning because…" I trailed off, trying hard to reign in my annoyance. He looked at me before settling his gaze on the bodies.

"We didn't know they were missing until just last night." I shut my eyes and pinched the bridge of my nose.

"Well, ain't it a fun tea party we got going on in here?"

All the men in the room spun to see who had spoken, but I stayed still, the voice caused me to freeze. "No need to look all surprised. Don't I usually turn up when crap is going down?"

"Kei, go back," Hale said in a clipped tone. I wanted to turn and rip his head off for it. Kei just *tsk*-ed, and I heard her quiet footsteps enter the room.

"Now, now. You should know that I never listen. Besides…" Her tone became more serious. "I can help you." I finally opened my eyes and dropped my hand, turning to stare at her. She looked as if what had happened yesterday never occurred. Her eyes were their usually bright shade, melting into green and red. Her hair sleek in a high ponytail, dressed in her normal black skinny jeans and tank top.

"I don't see how," Hale argued. She smiled and shook her head.

"Ah, my young grasshopper. There's still a lot about me that you don't know."

*No kidding,* I thought to myself almost bitterly. She didn't acknowledge my presence at all as she walked in and stood on the other side of the bed, her eyes downcast and a stoic expression on her face.

"What are you going to do?" My voice came out low, making her finally lift her head.

"I'm going to need an article of clothing from each missing person." She reached out and brushed her hand against the ruined flesh. Her brows were creased in a deep frown, and a look of sorrow and pain filled her features before it was gone. Hale had that distant look in his eyes before they cleared.

"You'll have them in the next ten minutes." She nodded absentmindedly before pulling up a chair and sitting down beside the bed. I gave them all a look, and they seem to get the message. "We're going to go meet up with the families and tell them what's going on. Alpha Dare, tell me if you discover something." I nodded, and the three men bowed their heads and left, leaving the two of us alone. I stared at her, while she kept her eyes downcast.

"So what? Are you just going to ignore me?" I tried to keep my voice level, but a hint of anger could still be heard. Her shoulders visibly tensed under my gaze, and she looked up.

"Would you be mad if I said yes?" She smiled slightly, and I felt my earlier anger wane.

"Depends if you tell me why you are." I strode over and stood beside her, clenching my hands as to not reach out.

"I want to." I felt myself become hopeful. "But I can't, not now." And that bubble of hope popped right into my face. The two of us were quiet for what seemed like forever but was only a minute while I looked at her, and she kept her eyes towards her limp hands in her lap.

"Fine, I'll let you have your space. But..." I leaned down, placing one arm on the back of the chair and one in the bed and leaned close, my breath disturbing a stray hair against her cheek. "When the time comes to take you as mine, I won't be holding back." I kissed her cheek tenderly before pulling away.

"You, sly King," she muttered, but I noticed her cheeks blush red.

"Think of it as my punishment for you." She looked up at me with an adorable pout, her bottom lip slightly pushed out.

*"Those cursed lips look so good."* Axel groaned. I laughed quietly before finding a chair and pulling it up beside her. I sat down and stretched my long legs out.

"What's so funny?" Kei questioned. I glanced over at her.

"Axel is an untamable beast of sexual needs," I told her. She stared at me before going into fits of laughter. I smiled slightly at the clear sound, still amazed that this creature was my mate. I was frozen as she looked at me with a dazzling smile, her eyes an ethereal red.

"He seems like an interesting character," she teased. I rolled my eyes.

"He's the biggest knife in my side."

"He is your other half, so it's only natural," I growled at her half-heartedly. She simply grinned, and we lapsed into comfortable silence. I stiffened as I felt a presence behind us. I immediately stood to face the person but had to hide my surprise as a young woman stood in the doorway with a hesitant look in her eye, a black bag in her clenched hands.

"Alpha Dare." She bowed her head.

"What do you want?" I felt a sharp jab in my side and noticed Kei give me a menacing glare. The woman looked at us with a nervous look.

"What this big sack of meat meant was... is there anything you need?" The woman coughed and looked at Kei with wide eyes.

"I, um, well, I came here with the clothes you requested." Kei smiled before walking towards her.

"Thank you. It'll really help," Kei admitted. The woman smiled and handed her the bag.

"Your welcome." She faltered. "May I ask you a favor?" Kei cocked her head to the side but nodded. The woman breathed in deeply as if mentally preparing herself. "Is it all right if I stay?"

"No, I don't have a problem. Do you have someone you're looking for?" The woman fidgeted with her hands.

"Yes. My brother." Her voice became quiet. Kei, instead, didn't say a word but nodded. She turned, and her eyes had a faraway look in them. Without a word, I moved out of the way as she walked passed.

I watched silently as she sat the bag down beside the bed, unzipping it and pulling out a handful of men's clothes. She held a dark green shirt in her hands, her eyes slowly closing. I noticed but didn't look at her as the woman walked up beside me.

"Alpha, if I may ask, do you know what she's doing?" she asked timidly, and I glanced down at her. She was a small woman, reminding me of a glass china doll with her small figure and her light brown hair. Her hazel eyes were wide and doe-like as she stared at Kei. I turned back to face the scene before me.

"I don't know," I finally replied. She didn't say anything, and together, we watched Kei unravel the mystery.

# Chapter 11

*Kei Valancia*

*"Something is wrong with this,"* Rei sounded uneasy as I gripped the material in my hand.

*"What? The shredded bodies or the weird smelling shirt?"*

*"I'm serious,"* Rei snapped.

*"I'm serious too. If this is really his doing, then he's escalating quicker than we had originally thought."*

I bit my lip and frowned. The shirt smelled like a werewolf, but another scent was on it. I grabbed another article of clothing from the bag. It was a different scent, but it still had that smell. I checked all of the clothes in the bag, each having their own trademark smell but they all had that one thing in common.

*"It has to be him,"* Rei hissed venomously.

*"We can't be sure."* I could feel her anger grow.

*"Well, who else could it be?"*

*"I'm not sure,"* I admitted. I went back to identifying each body to a piece of clothing. When I was sure, I placed each shirt to its

matching scent. Of course, the room reeked of the heavy stench of death, a thick cloak filling my nostrils. After I had finished, I stood back.

"Do you know who these are?" I turned to look at the small form standing beside Ryker. I noticed with curiousness that the energy around her seemed off. I frowned as the murky brown shifted to an ugly yellow.

"Are these right? They can't be." Her voice came out in a quiet whisper.

"They are." Something was incredibly wrong with this woman. Her energy bubbled angrily, the grotesque two colors swirling up and down her body almost like a snake. My eyes widened when it dawned on me. She didn't see me coming as I wrapped my fingers around her slender neck, slamming her body against the wall.

"Kei!" I ignored Ryker and, instead, narrowed all of my attention to the current problem.

"How the hell did you manage this?" I hissed in her ear. I felt the malice roll off of her in waves, this all-too-familiar bottomless black tried to envelop me, but I clenched my jaw and fought it off.

"Please... you're hurting me," she whimpered. I growled.

*"Oh, that lying little—"*

"Kei, that's enough!" Ryker roared, and he gripped both my arms in a painful grasp. He practically threw me across the room, and I landed on my feet in a defensive position. I snarled viciously at him while he in return roared back.

"What the hell is wrong with you?" I saw him go to the aid of that *thing*, her pitiful whimpers followed by the quiet reassurances of my *mate*.

*"I may know your reason for attacking, but to others, you look like a crazy wolf gone wild,"* Rei sounded amused, and I sighed.

*"You're right."*

*"Of course, I'm still irritated that our own mate is consoling that thing."* I chuckled quietly, and Ryker turned to me with disbelief. I think I hated the light yellow.

"Kei," he spoke cautiously as if not wanting to spook a frightened animal. "I think it's best you go blow off some steam." I quirked an eyebrow and scoffed.

"I don't think me taking a run will change this situation."

"Sweet Goddess, Kei. Will you just listen for once?" I glared at him.

"I will only listen if I think it's best. Right now, me leaving this *thing* alone is the worst possible outcome," the woman inched her way behind Ryker, and I would bet my life that she had an evil smirk.

"I-I'm sorry for whatever I did wrong." Her voice was timid, but I heard an underlying sound of giddiness underneath her stutter.

*"Just let me kick her ass."*

*"Chill. This woman has been here a lot longer than us. Therefore, she has a butt ton more of influence than we do, and she knows it too. By the end of this, she'll probably have me in a chokehold."*

"Look, lady. You can't hide that energy from me."

"I don't know what you're talking about," she instantly replied. Suddenly, the dark green tint in her aura caught my eye, an idea dawning on me, and I had the strong urge to facepalm.

"Oh, I bet you do. Have you ever heard of the name Draven?" She jolted as if I had shocked her.

"No." Her voice came out sharp, and I smirked.

"Oh, but your reaction tells me that you do." I smiled slowly. "And with the state that your aura is in, you've been hanging out with him for quite some time, haven't you?" She was silent, but that answered my question. However, I had my doubts, though, as the colors warped even more. Draven may be involved with her, but I had a reason to think that he wasn't actually involved with the main problem. I knew Draven was just not an evil man. He was more like damned Casanova from what I could tell.

*"He has got to stop with his playboy ways, or else, he's going to get himself in trouble."* I groaned to myself. So now, the question left unanswered would be what happened to her? Whatever it is, these people had a rat, and I'm more than happy to exterminate it.

"Kei, explain what is going on." Ryker was beginning to sound livid at this point.

"Hmmm. Let's just say that I've found the reason to how these men were captured." I walked over with slow, deliberate steps, a smile growing as I noticed her increasing unease.

"And what would that be." I shot Ryker a sideways glance before putting my attention fully on the woman before me.

"You're standing right next to her," I said. The room was silent; the woman's ragged breathing the only sound.

"And what's the evidence," he rumbled. I cocked my head.

"The evidence is her horrible color. I mean, jeez, woman, what in the world happened to you? Did Draven make you do some freaky stuff under the sheets? Wait. Don't answer that. I do not want the details." I shivered with disgust. "The question is, why?" She was silent. But then something happened. And that something would be me being slammed against the wall with a hand wrapped around my throat.

"Totally called it." I choked out and smiled crookedly.

"Kei!" I tilted my head and noticed with slight confusion that Ryker's body and power seemed muted, but then it dawned on me.

"You have some freaky magic shield thing going on." Her laugh was sounded almost like a dying deer but underwater. It was quite the laugh.

"To be honest, I didn't believe Draven when he kept going on and on about your powers. But I guess he was right after all." Her voice was a sneer; the colors around her were all mashed up into a dark, ugly mess, showing how unstable she actually was.

"I am slightly horrified that Draven would mention me to someone as crazy as you. Correction, I am *immensely* horrified that he mentioned me at all." Wow, she had a powerful right hook for such a petite woman, but the pain quickly subsided.

"He loves me. Besides, Draven isn't the one to do this." Her grip on my neck tightened, and I simply rolled my eyes. Seriously, it was like a child trying to choke me. *No wait, that's offensive to kids.* But then her words only confirmed what I knew.

"Man, this conversation became so boring. Oh wait, it was always boring. Now, why don't you turn yourself in like a good little psychotic girl or we can play? I would choose the second choice." I grinned wickedly, and she just snarled in my face.

"I'm the one in control. Your boy toy won't be able to help. Same goes for that dumb fleabag of an alpha." I shook my head as if I were disappointed.

"Oh, dear, you're not only psychotic but an idiot." I raised my arm and patted her on the shoulder comfortingly. "Well, maybe a good beating will fix you right up."

"You—" I cut her off by reaching up and gripping the collar of her shirt, throwing my head forward and head butting her hard. She let out a cry before her grip loosened, and I pushed her away.

"Kei, how the hell do we put this thing down?" I noticed that to be Brad's voice, and I didn't look up.

"Oh, don't worry. I'll bring down justice upon her like a freaking tsunami." I cracked my knuckles as I stood over her.

"We don't know what she can do. Kei, just get this thing down." This coming from an angered Ryker. Why is it so fun to push Ryker to his limits with his temper?

*"Maybe because it's hilarious, and he sounds so irresistible when his voice gets all deep,"* I had to agree with Rei on this one.

*"True, true. Now, let's have some fun."* I smiled evilly.

*"You are going to enjoy this way too much."*

*"Probably."* I reached out and gripped her leg, pulling her towards me. She screeched like a banshee as her clawed hands swiped at my face.

"Woah, there. You're quite feisty, aren't you?" I remarked, staring at her in amusement.

"I'll kill you," she hissed, leaping up onto her feet. I popped my neck.

"Didn't Draven tell you anything? Sweetie, you're just an annoying fly to me." She roared, and it shook the room around us. I watched her ugly form bend and charge right at me. I dodged her attack, causing her to blow past me and rammed into the wall instead. "Too slow, sweet pea." She shrieked, and crimson spilled around her. That sure was a lot of hate coming from such a small body.

"Aww, I hate you too!" I cooed at her, blowing a kiss and a wink in her direction.

"Kei, be serious!" I heard Ryker pound against the invisible wall.

"I *am* serious, sort of." His loud growl made me sigh. "Fine," I muttered in a pout before striding over to the woman. She hissed and spit, crouched down into a defensive position. I stood just a few feet away, my legs shoulder apart and my arms crossed.

"Since it seems like I can't have my fun, I might as well make this quick," I grumbled grumpily before holding my hand out and forming a ball of power in my palm. It glowed in the darkness, an electrifying white orb that would stun her into a deep sleep for a while. "All right, doggie, it's time to play catch." She only growled and made a move towards me. Unlucky for her, I already "saw" this move, pulled my arm back as if I was a baseball pitcher and chucked it right at her face. She didn't even see it coming.

I watched as the ball made contact with her blobby form, little white electric bolts spreading through her body. She stood rooted to her spot, her aura a now peaceful soft white before it dimmed, and she collapsed onto the ground. I made a clicking noise with my tongue before turning to face my audience. I spotted Brad's familiar reds and purples, along with Mark's soft amber glow that was uniquely his own. However, I did notice a new silvery gray aura standing in the background, but I couldn't examine it further as Ryker was becoming more agitated, his power filling the whole room except for the part that was closed off by the invisible shield.

"Dude, calm your furry butt. I'll get this thing down in no time." I rubbed my hands together. "I would recommend that you step back a bit." They did, and I closed my eyes. I took in a deep breath and probed the wall with invisible tendrils, trying to find a weak link. Of course, I didn't, and I knew whoever helped sleeping psycho over there was quite powerful to make such a barrier.

*"She must have gotten help from a witch,* Rei concluded.

*"I don't know, but I'm going to strangle Draven when this is over."*

"He's such an idiot, bedding any woman that he can get his eyes on," I muttered out loud.

*"He doesn't seem to change,"* Rei mused. I chuckled quietly and with ease, overpowered the wall. I watched as the colors on the other side brighten once more, Ryker's power filling the space like a flood.

"You know, I think it's time I and my dear old friend Draven have a long chat about his suitors," I mused, looking towards the unconscious woman. Two large hands suddenly gripped my shoulders, and I was pushed into a hard chest.

"Who the hell is Draven?" Ryker said in a clipped tone.

"Like I said, he's an old friend of mine. We go way back." I chuckled at the memories of the goofy man, more like a brother than anything else. His mind could be perverted, but he usually meant no harm unless you did something to make him mad. Ryker growled possessively, and I patted his chest.

"You don't need to feel threatened. He's honestly like a brother to me," I said soothingly. His arms didn't loosen around me, and I sighed. "Anyhoo, I think you need to keep that woman contained. I have a feeling that she's the main reason as to why these men had disappeared."

"And what makes you think this?" Brad stepped beside us, dark brown of tension tinting the air around him.

"One, her energy is seriously all wacky. It's all gross and warped-looking. Two, she made a pathetic attempt to try to kill me. And three, I just hate her guts." I shrugged at the last part and smirked. The room was silent, and I could hear the peaceful breathing of the woman. Oh, how I wished I were in bed sleeping the day away.

"Alpha Ryker, I would like to discuss something with you in my office. Jett, take her to a room. Have guards posted outside the door," Brad commanded. I noticed the silvery aura from earlier bow, and I observed the tall, broad form walk over and pick the woman up and walk out of the room without saying one word. Jett must have been the silvery silhouette character.

*If the men are going to have their boy time, I guess we should slip away and pay our dear friend a visit.* I was about to reply to her, but my train of thought was suddenly scattered.

"Stay inside." Ryker bent down and whispered in my ear, using one finger to trail along my cheek in a slow fashion. I felt my body coil tight at his touch, the electrifying pleasure affecting me greatly.

"Why do you bother if you know that I'll probably end up doing it anyway?" He sighed and pulled back.

"I don't know. Maybe I think that you'll be smart enough to listen." I bristled at his tone and separated myself from him completely.

"I'm smart enough to know when you're being insolent, so I'll just be on my merry way." I turned on my heel and strode off, a stupid part of me hoping that he would stop me. But he didn't. I chuckled dryly as I walked down the hall.

*"I'm going to get gray hairs from that man."*

*"It's a good thing we have silver hair then."*

*"You do have a good point,"* I said to her. She scoffed.

*"I always have a good point."*

*"Sometimes,"* I responded.

I walked into the empty kitchen and went out the back door. A few young pups were running around the yard, the afternoon sun hot and smothering but not seemingly affecting the bright balls of energy.

Kids were always fun to observe, as their energies were always so bright and full of life. Vibrant and beautiful.

*"You sound like a creepy pedophile."* I began walking towards the edge of the yard and stopped at the tree line.

*"Oh, sweet peanuts, I do, don't I?"* I shuddered. *"Let's just pretend I never said that."*

*"It's your guilty conscious, not mine."* I laughed out loud and smiled, staring off into the woods.

*"I guess so."* I let my thoughts wander for a moment, my mind on Ryker.

*"Let's go. Give him time to chill his paws before we confront him again,"* I said nothing but nodded at her words. With one last deep breath, I sprinted off into the woods and felt the excitement to see my old friend.

# Chapter 12

*Ryker Dare*

I shut the door and turned with my arms crossed, staring at the man sitting behind the desk.

"Your mate is something else," he grumbled. I cracked my neck and sighed quietly.

"She's a damn handful," I retorted, and Hale scoffed.

"You love it." I didn't say anything but watched as he got up and opened a dark wooden cabinet, pulling out a dark bottle of scotch. I went and sat down while he prepared two glasses and sat one full glass in front of me. I nodded to him in thanks and gripped the glass, tipping my head back and downing the whole thing. The alcohol burned down my throat and I relished in the feeling. Meanwhile, Hale nursed his slowly.

"So let's get to the real reason why you wanted to talk, Alpha Hale. I guess it has to do with my mate." he nodded and set his glass down gently, the dark liquid swishing slightly before calming.

"Yes. It seems that maybe Kei knows who is doing this or has an idea." I tapped absently on the empty glass before nodding.

"She does seem to know something. I'll question her about it when she gets back." My mood instantly took a turn when I recalled our earlier argument. Why the hell couldn't she just listen for once?

*"We just met her yesterday, and along with her attitude, we can't expect her to be a follower."* I clenched my teeth but had to silently agree.

"Alpha Dare." Hale looked almost hesitant to speak.

"You are free to speak, Alpha Hale. What is it?" He looked slightly uncomfortable until his expression changed to one of steel.

"There is a chance that Kei may be behind all of this."

My first instinct is to reach over and rip the man's head off for even thinking that my mate, *his* Luna, would be the one responsible for this. But instead, I stayed calm.

"What makes you think of this?" A look of surprise flitted across his features.

"I don't know," he admitted. "But it's a fact that we know absolutely nothing about her. For all we know, she's not actually blind." I was silent.

*"I hate to say this, but he does have a point,"* Axel almost sounded like he was in pain as he said this. I shut my eyes and sighed.

"Fine." I opened my eyes and looked at him with a hard look. "I'll keep an eye on her, however, you will not do anything against her. Even if she is the one behind this, it's clear to see she's stronger." He looked thoughtful as he nodded his head.

"You're right. I won't do anything being how we don't even know if she's involved or not." He suddenly chuckled darkly. "It's despicable what I am making you think of your mate."

"No, you're right. Even if she is my mate, I won't forgive her if she is behind this." I stood up and laid the empty crystal glass back onto his desk. "I'll take my leave. I have some other business to attend to." I turned and walked leisurely and opened the door. However, I stopped when he said, "Alpha Dare." I stood with my back towards him, tilting my head for him to continue.

"Be careful around her." I didn't reply and simply walked out, shutting the door behind me with a quiet *click*.

# Chapter 13

*Kei Valancia*

*"We're being followed,"* I commented with amusement.

*"Do you think I don't know that? He's part of Draven's pack,"*

*"Anyway, hurry up. I can feel his eyes on our furry ass."* She let out a wolf-snort before speeding up.

*"Don't worry, we're almost—"*

Rei never finished as we heard a loud yip and a huge furry body hit ours at full momentum. The weight instantly lifted off, and I jumped onto all fours. I bared my teeth in a snarl but stopped when I saw the familiar mint green aura. I shifted and stood, grinning.

"Draven, you Casanova, come give me a proper greeting." I heard him shift, his energy rippling momentarily before his black form turned into a tall man.

"You look ten times better than the last time I saw you, and that was five months ago. Why haven't you called? Sent me a letter?" Right after he finished his question, I was engulfed in a bear hug. I returned it with the same amount of intensity. The familiar scent of mint filled my nostrils, reminding me of all the times together.

"I missed you too you big lug." He pulled back at arm's length, and I could feel his stare on my face

"You get more beautiful each time you come visit. Now, come, Maria is going to be so excited to see you." We began walking through the woods, our arms linked together.

"How's everything going in the pack?" I asked him. He chuckled.

"If you're talking about rogues, don't worry. No attacks whatsoever." I smiled in relief.

"That's good. Now…" I stopped, and I felt him stop beside me, confusion evident around him. I lifted my hand and pulled it back, slapping him hard on the back of the head.

"What the hell?" He cursed, and he jumped away from me. I crossed my arms and stood there glaring at him.

"That's what you get for creating another psychotic groupie."

"What are you talking about?" He seemed to still be in pain, and I smirked.

"It so happens the pack that I'm in now had a woman that you had slept with. Lucky for me, she was insanely jealous and thought it would be great to try to kill me."

"Oh!" His energy and tone showed his sheepishness, a light beige. "Sorry about that." I scoffed.

"Oh, don't apologize to me. Apologize to the woman that you slept with. Goddess knows how much you had to beg to get her in your bed." I poked his arm teasingly, and he playfully shoved my arm.

"You're such a jerk you know that?" I laughed and threw an arm around his shoulders, pulling him down to my level.

"Fine, I guess I won't tell you the big news." I sighed dramatically and began walking, dragging him along with me. He groaned and walked beside me awkwardly.

"Kei," he whined. I shook my head in disappointment.

"No. I'm a jerk, remember? Then it's only natural that I act like one."

"Come on, Kei, just tell me." I tapped my index finger to my chin as if thinking.

"Well, all right since you're so adorable," I reached up and pinched his cheeks. He swatted my hands away but chuckled, straightening.

"You never change." His voice softened, and I shot him a wink.

"Of course, I haven't. Why would I?" He laughed and ruffled my hair. I let out an annoyed grunt and punched him in the side lightly.

"So, what's the big news?" I heard a thwacking sound as if he had picked up a stick and began hitting nearby bushes with it.

"Well, you won't believe who I met yesterday." He was silent in thought, letting my senses take in all of the information that was happening around me. The late afternoon wildlife was loud and wide awake. I could feel little pieces of the sun hit my skin while the cool shadows countered the heat. The normal auras of the plant life were a soft glow against the darkness, a few sparks of color from animals scurrying away. This was peace.

"Hmmm... Was it Larry?" I turned my head and raised an eyebrow incredulously.

"Larry?" I said his name with a scoff. "I haven't talked to that old coot in months, and I can bet my life he doesn't want to see me."

"All right. How about Abby?"

"I don't know an Abby." He paused.

"Oh, oh, yeah, you definitely wouldn't know Abby." I rolled my eyes at him.

"You're an idiot."

"But I'm a handsome idiot." I gave him a strange look.

"You just admitted to being an idiot."

"But a handsome one. Girls totally dig the stupid Prince Charming." I furrowed my brows.

"Uh, no, they don't."

"Sure, they do. Why else would they sleep with me?" He had a point.

"Touché, my friend, touché." We laughed, and I felt myself relax in a way that I hadn't for a while.

"Back to the main topic. Who did you meet?" I paused for suspense, and I knew that he hated it but stayed silent.

"It was Ryker Dare," that made him stop walking entirely.

"Oh, haha, very funny. Now, tell me who you really met."

"It was Ryker Dare. I swear with my life," he was silent.

"And why was he at that exact location that you were in?" I tried to decipher his tone but only heard the neutrality of it, along with his aura. Damn him, he knew how to mask his feelings, and now, I couldn't tell what he was thinking.

"He was coincidentally going to the same pack to offer his aid against the recent rogue attacks, and you won't even guess what happened next." I poked him. "Come on, guess." He sighed, but when he spoke, I heard the smile in his voice.

"I don't know. You tell me." I smiled big.

"He's my mate."

Complete and utter silence followed those three words. And then his color burst with the brightest electric green and dark lavender purple.

"Oh my Goddess, I'm so happy for you! Dammit, Kei, you leave me and then come back to tell me that you found your mate? You're a terrible friend." His tone of voice was ecstatic, the exact opposite of his words. I laughed happily as he turned and hugged me.

"I know. Here, I'll make it up to you." He gave me a doubtful look.

"How?" he said, his voice holding doubt. I smiled mischievously.

"I'll tell you how I beat the King if you'll forgive me," I told him. He laughed loudly.

"I knew you were such a badass," he commented, and I pouted.

"Of course, I am."

We continued to bicker until I noticed our surroundings change. I looked around, pushed out my powers, and noticed the black outlines of an open field, a large house nestled in between the cluster of trees.

"Why does it seem your house gets bigger and bigger each time I visit?" I mused. I felt the movement of his shoulders against mine as he shrugged.

"It's probably just your imagination," his humorous tone said otherwise. Rolling my eyes, I began making my way towards it. I noticed but didn't say anything as I felt four other wolves behind us, keeping watch. We walked in comfortable silence, enjoying the fresh air. About halfway, I saw a bright ball of energy burst out of the house and run towards us. I grinned widely and opened my arms just in time for a small body slam into mine.

"Kei!" A giggly voice squeaked with excitement.

"Hey, you little bumpkin," I could practically hear her pout.

"I'm not a bumpkin!" I laughed at the little girl in my arms, spinning her around. She laughed, her energy light and happy. The edges of her aura were tinted a light pink, representing of her innocence.

"I don't know, Maria. You smell like one," I wrinkled my nose in pretend disgust but smiled.

"Nu-uh! You're the one that stinks Kei," I smiled at her in amusement.

"Whatever you say, bumpkin." She poked my cheek, and I chuckled, setting the seven-year-old girl down back onto her feet.

"Rav, she's being mean." The air around Draven was tinged with a light azure of amusement.

"Now, girls, play nice." I glanced down at Maria and stuck my tongue out at her childishly. I can only imagine that she did the same to me.

"She started it." I bent down and poked her lightly on the arm.

"No, you started it!" I shook my head.

"Nope. It's all on you bumpkin." I smirked, and she grumbled under her breath.

"You both are acting like children," Draven said with an exasperated sigh. I straightened and looked at him with wide eyes.

"But I am a kid," Maria shouted.

"So am I!" I agreed, laughing.

"You both are idiots. Now, come on you two, the sun is going down, and dinner will be done soon." I noticed Maria's dark form being lifted up, her energy separated from Draven's as he picked her up. I hung back slightly as Draven bickered with his younger sister, a feeling of deep sadness filling my thoughts. I usually never thought deeply into my sight as I already have a different kind of sight to help me see. However, there are times that I would wonder what it would be like to see again. It's not something I usually dwelled on, but I can't help feeling that familiar grief creep back in from time to time.

"Kei, you coming?" Maria's voice brought me out of my negative reverie. Smiling slightly, I nodded.

"I'll always come for you guys."

With that said, I caught up with them and got lost in the familiar feeling of being home.

# Chapter 14

*Kei Valancia*

We entered the house, the air changing from hot and dry to cool and refreshing.

"Kei guess what?" Maria jumped out of Draven's arms and gripped my shirt, tugging so that I would lean down to her level.

"What?" I heard her giggle quietly beside my ear, the smell of lilacs filling my nose.

"I met a boy," she said still giggling, and my brows shot to my hairline.

"Oh? And what's this boy like?"

"I can't tell you in front of Rav, silly. He gets jealous." I heard Draven let out an annoyed groan.

"I do not get jealous. Stop saying that, sis." Maria and I both giggled, and I smiled brightly.

"Well, then, we'll just have to go somewhere more private, won't we?" I picked her up suddenly, and she let out a squeal. "Thankfully, I know just the right place." I turned and began heading out the door until Draven called, "Be careful you two." I waved a hand for a signal that I understood, and I went through the door that we had just come through. Setting her down, I gave her a stern look.

"Now, I'm going to shift, and you're going to ride on my back. But, make sure that you have a firm grip, okay?"

"I will! I promise." I chuckled and ruffle her soft hair, turning while rolling my shoulders.

"Step back." She did as she was told and I closed my eyes, feeling Rei become excited.

*"Let's get this show on the road,"* she yipped.

*"Please be careful,"* I said humorously, not really meaning it. We both loved Maria as if she were our own little sister and would die for her.

*"You know I will."* I didn't say anything back as I felt my body reshape into an animal that was the other side of me. I heard Maria let out a breath in awe.

"You're so pretty, Kei." I let out a wolfy chuckle and tucked in my legs underneath me to lower myself to her height. I tilted my head in encouragement for her to get on. She clapped her hands in delight before I heard her walk over, her small hands gripping a fistful of my fur and jumping a little to get on. She struggled a bit, as I was still quite tall even as I was in this position, but she managed to get on my back snugly. When I was sure she wasn't going to fall off, I stood up on all fours. She laughed brightly before kicking her heels into my sides.

"Let's ride." I shook my huge head before going into a lazy jog. "Faster!" I rolled my eyes but obeyed, going only slightly faster. I felt the cool shade as we entered the woods, my paws hitting the ground with muffled thuds against the bushy forest floor.

"Come on, Kei," Maria whined. "You're slower than Grandma Dhalia." Now, *that* was offensive. Everybody knows that Dhalia is the slowest werewolf, a.k.a. her grandma. And yet, she's comparing me to her? Talk about rude. Fine, if she wanted to go fast then that's what I will do. I stopped and turned my head to look at her.

*"Maria, wrap your arms around my neck and hold on tight. Whatever you do, don't let go,"* I said through mind link. Her arms wrapped around my neck in a tight grip while burrowing her face into my fur.

When I was sure she wouldn't fall, I faced forward and relaxed my muscles, adrenaline buzzing through my blood. Throwing my head back, I let out piercing howl before launching full speed between trees. Maria let out a screech of surprise that soon turned into loud laughter.

"Faster!" I rolled my eyes.

*"If I did that, you wouldn't be able to keep your grip."*

"Aww, please?" I heard her pout on my back.

*"Nope, princess, you're just going to have to deal with this speed,"* which was already a fast pace anyway.

I was darting between trees about seventy miles an hour, and if Maria were anything other than the alpha's daughter, she wouldn't have been able to hold on. I leaped over a fallen tree. The surprised squeal was lost in the wind breezing past.

Maria clutched tightly to me, pressing her small body to mine as I ran past a small herd of deer, their peaceful moods suddenly splattering with the coppery brown of fright. I ignored them and darted passed, feeling that our destination was close.

*"Hold on tight,"* I warned her before I burst out into a clearing, the trees disappeared, and I knew from memory that a large lake would be spread across ahead of me.

"Kei, don't you dare!" She managed to scream before I sprinted and jumped high, the warm sun blazing on my face and the weightless air beneath my feet. This feeling only lasted a second, however, when I was pulled back to earth and into the warm water. If Maria's grip was tight before, it was in a death grip now.

Her words were muffled as she spoke words underwater, bubbles floating up to the surface. I noticed the occasional flashes from the aquatic inhabitants before I started paddling up with Maria still on my back. Once we broke the surface, I felt a slap on the top of my head.

"Kei, that was not funny!" I chortled, the sound strange out of my wolf mouth.

*"Princess, it was hilarious."* I felt another slap on my head. Her words were an incoherent grumble as I began swimming back to the shore. Once we were on dry land, she jumped off and landed onto the ground with a muffled thump.

"You can shift now." I shook my head in response.

"All right, I'm going to need you to get on my back," I told her while bending down on one knee. She didn't spare another second as she hopped onto my back, and I grabbed hold of her legs wrapped around my midriff before I started walking closer to the water. I let my powers flow around me as I pieced the picture in my mind of our surroundings. Large boulders lay just a few feet to our right, the lake large, while the air began to cool as the sun set. From the corner of my eye, I saw the flicker of something in the woods but instantly recognized it as one of Draven's men before taking a running start and jumping up high, all the while Maria's small arms wrapped around my neck in a tight chokehold. Landing gently on the boulder, I pulled Maria's fingers off me and sucked in a breath.

"Maria, keep choking me like that, and you'll end up killing me," I joked, poking her lightly in the ribs. She squirmed in my arms before pulling away from me.

"That wasn't funny." She began pouting once again, and I laughed.

"Princess, I have to find some entertainment somewhere," I teased. She huffed, and I heard her plump down. I chuckled and sat down beside her, stretching my legs out and resting on my palms with my arms behind me. We were both silent for a few moments, just enjoying the silence and the sound of the water as small waves crested onto the shore. The late afternoon sun shone brightly still, and I welcomed the warmth with a smile.

"Do you like my brother?" I tilted my head towards her questioningly.

"Sure, I do," was my reply.

"Do you like 'like' him or just like?" Now, I turned fully to her.

"What's with all these all of the sudden? Weren't we going to discuss your little boyfriend?" I noticed her black form shrug, her emotions flashing quickly around her.

"I like you, so if you married my brother, I would be really happy!" She faced me, and I had to imagine that she was smiling brightly or she could have been giving me the dirtiest glare, but the happy dark lavender suggested otherwise. I smiled gently at her. I opened my mouth to reply but was interrupted by a ground-shaking roar. The funny thing was, it sounded familiar. Turning to the source of the noise, I froze at the black, glittery cloud spreading across the sky.

"Uh-oh," I muttered and stood up. I watched silently as the black form stalked its way towards us.

"Kei, who is that scary man?" Maria whimpered quietly and hid behind me. I guarded her with my body and clenched my jaw.

*"Why is he here?"* Anger radiated from the man, the taste of sour lemon filled my mouth with this feeling.

"Kei, you have some explaining to do." Ryker stopped about ten yards away from the rock that we were standing on, the red intensifying with each second. I crossed my arms defiantly.

"I don't have to explain anything," I spat, my own annoyance rebelling against him. Of course, that may have been the worst thing that I could have said given his feelings at the moment, but I was still a little bit miffed from earlier. His loud growl was full of anger and menace, a loud promise meaning that I would regret it later.

"I am your *alpha*. You either obey me or you will be punished." I scoffed and rolled my eyes.

"Oh, so now, you're going to play the alpha card, aren't you? Fine, *Alpha*," I spat out the word as if it was the most disgusting thing on earth, "I don't really care that you're my mate. If you continue to be ill-mannered and insufferable, then I wouldn't take the time to deal with you until you want to actually have a real conversation with me. So why don't you go back and chill a bit so that we can have a calm conversation?" His power surrounded us, trying to make me submit but I stood my ground and glared at him icily. Emotions flashed, ranging from awe to glowing rage.

"You infuriate me so much sometimes, you know that?" The glittery blackness reigned back in until it was now a tame flicker. "Fine, when we get back I want a full explanation of this, and I will not back down on this, either." His words held a finality to it that I knew if I objected, he would get angry again. But that's really not surprising anymore, though. Sighing, I nodded.

"All right, King, I guess you deserve this much at least." Turning my back on him, I bent down so that I was level with Maria. "I'm sorry. We're going to have to cut this trip short."

"It's fine." She leaned closer. "That man is mean." I threw my head back and laughed.

"Aww, sweetie, he's just mean because he doesn't get his daily dosage of sass. Now, let's go back," I told her gently. She agreed happily. I picked her up, and we dropped back down to the ground. I ignored the looming figure behind us and noticed other figures in the woods. Shaking my head, I set her down.

"King, wait for me back at the pack house. I need to drop off Maria." I was suddenly gripped by my shoulders and turned around, now facing his looming form.

"Every time you order me around like this, I get fed up beyond belief. Do you know how much I hate being ordered around?" He whispers the last part in my ear, causing goosebumps to appear on my skin. I raised my hand and cupped his cheek.

"But do you know how much I love getting you all worked up?" I smirked and turned away, taking a few steps away from him before shifting. I bent down to allow Maria to jump on. Once she was settled, I walked to the edge of the tree line before stopping and turning to give a long stare at Ryker. My emotions were mixed about this matter, but I knew I would have to explain it all if I wanted him to trust me.

Because the dark green of his mistrust said it all.

# Chapter 15

*Ryker Dare*

I followed the two from a distance, watching as Kei dodged the trees with ease and grace.

*"She called us ill-mannered. That's a first,"* Axel remarked dryly.

*"Can't really say I'm surprised,"* I retorted back. I felt the presence of four other wolves, all keeping their distance from us.

*"They all must be part of this pack."*

*"This is the Black Stone territory, the second biggest pack after ours. How would Kei know them?"* Axel sounded mystified yet impressed at the same time.

*"At this rate, anything to do with Kei won't surprise me any longer."*

Kei had stopped as we entered an open field, a large mansion in the distance.

*"This is the one place that I can truly call home."* Kei sounded almost distant as she slowed down to a walk. I caught up and strolled beside her.

*"How do you associate with this pack? From what I can recall, the Alpha and Luna never had another girl."* She shook her furry head.

*"I'm not their kid or anything. They just took me in when I trespassed onto their territory. Of course, I found it strange that they would want to keep a half-deranged pup,"* she said the last part bitterly, as if recalling something unpleasant.

I didn't say anything in return until Kei stopped suddenly. I stopped beside her and gazed at her. She nodded her head towards the girl, Maria, and they seemed to be having their own silent conversation. I waited patiently and watched as the girl jumped off of her back and ran the rest of the way back to the house, now noticing a young man standing in the doorway with a guarded expression.

Thick, coppery brown hair glinted brightly in the sun, his features similar to that of the little girl.

"Rav!" The girl jumped into his arms and the man's face transformed into a bright smile. He whispered something into her ear, and she nodded before hopping out of his grasp and disappearing inside the house.

His smile faded, however, when he looked back at me.

*"Stay here,"* Kei ordered. I growled lowly in response.

*"Only in your dreams, Lune."* She didn't say anything but shook her head again. I followed closely behind her as we made our way towards the house. She turned her head and shot me a look of annoyance before hitting me in the face with her tail.

*"I do have a bubble, you know? And right now, you are too deep in it."*

"*Fine,*" I muttered back to her and moved back just a little. Once we were a foot away, we stopped. The man and Kei stared at each other, a silent conversation in their eyes.

"I'm going to do give Alpha a quick call about you guys. You can just wait out here for a second while I get their approval." He turned and went into the house.

Kei surprised me by sitting next to me, nuzzling my side playfully.

"*Don't look so vexed. It makes you look like a grumpy old man.*" I huffed and gave her a look.

"*I don't look like an old man,*" I retorted. She let out a bark. "*Besides, how can you even tell what I look like unless you're not really blind?*" She rolled her eyes.

"*I am blind, and if I recall, you said something about being over two hundred years old. In my book, that's called old, pretty much ancient. Plus, you forget that I can see your aura.*" She head butted me gently, her laughter ringing in my head. I tried to give her a menacing glare but instead smiled wolfishly.

"*It's not my fault. I don't start aging until—*" Before I could explain, the door slammed open, and the man from earlier came out with a wide smile on his face.

"As I thought, they can't say no to the king. Now, why don't you two come in and we can have some dinner?"

"Sounds good to me," Kei answered, already shifted back. "What are you serving?"

"Coincidentally, your favorite." Kei brightened and ran up to him, throwing her arms around his neck and hugging him.

"I'm glad I decided to come here after all." She pulled away and turned around to face me with a grin, but her smile slipped away from her lips as she saw the air around my raging emotions. My whole posture was stiff, and I didn't doubt that my eyes were darker than the night sky at this moment. Not only that but I would bet Kei was seeing the strong emotions of jealousy and anger emanating off of me right now, whatever that looked like to her.

"Well, I'll go set up everything." The man looked at us uncomfortably before turning and disappearing into the house. I stared her down, trying to get not only my emotions but also a raging Axel to calm down.

*"I swear to Goddess, I will sink my teeth into his neck and let him bleed beneath our feet."* He snarled.

"You really shouldn't have done that, Kei." I managed to say through my clenched jaw. She grimaced and scratched the back of her head. "You should know by know how possessive I get of you. Yet you go and do something like that?"

"Ryker, you know that I don't like him like that." I snarled viciously at her, my patience towards her waning so thin it was almost nonexistent at this point. She didn't even flinch away as I stalked towards her, the rising moon shining down on her like a spotlight.

"How? Explain to me, Kei. How would I know what you're feeling towards that man is? I barely know you at all, and you just expect me to know?" She looked up at me sharply, her ruby eyes shining brilliantly with emotion.

"Yes, well, I can see your distrust in me quite clearly, and yet here I am, still trusting you with the people I consider family. So let me ask you this, Ryker." She stepped closer, the distance between us now only a centimeter as she stared me straight in the eyes. "What do you want from me?" It was heartbreaking, feeling the weight of her eyes as they stared into mine unblinking as she waited for my answer and honestly, I could not give her a good answer that would make the guilt that I was feeling go away.

"I am not trying to make you feel guilty, but instead, I want you to honestly think about it."

"I just want to know you," I said softly, the words hanging between us like a rope that she could take yet hung precariously by a thread. I reached up and cupped her cheek in my palm while leaning my forehead against hers, sighing quietly as I closed my eyes. "I understand that a day has barely passed that we even knew about each other's existence, but that still doesn't mean that I don't want to know every single detail about you." I opened my eyes to see hers shut instead, hiding the thoughts that I wanted to see so desperately

"It doesn't help how you fight my every word, going against everything that I ask—" she interrupted me with a scoff, and her lashes lifted to reveal the shining emeralds.

"Ask? Ryker, that word hasn't been in your vocabulary since you were a kid."

"My point, Kei, is that I would like for you to just open up more." I finished.

"Ryker—"

"Hey, you guys ever going to come in?" The man stuck his head out of the doorway.

"I'm sorry, Draven, but something came up. Do you mind if we just head out?" Kei asked apologetically. He nodded his head while giving her a concerned look.

"Is everything all right?" I didn't miss the way his eyes slid to look over at me.

"Yes, everything is fine. We just need to—"

"Actually, do you mind if we borrow a room for the night?" I interjected. He nodded again but slowly while his brows furrowed.

"Sure, Kei can pick a room. She knows where everything is." I nodded my thanks, and Kei grabbed my hand and pulled me inside the house, walking briskly through the rooms. It seemed we had entered what appeared to be some sort of laundry room before entering into the kitchen. An amazing smell filtered through my nose, but before I could properly register what it could have been, Kei barreled through another door that led to a dim hallway. She was a woman on a mission as I hardly noticed where we were going with the twists and turns of the house, finally barreling through a dark room. I closed the door behind me, leaving us in the dark.

"Is this what you see?" I muttered to myself, but she heard me anyway.

"Thankfully, not all of the time. I'm assuming that there isn't a light on in here."

"You would be correct, of course," I answered. Her hand slipped away from mine as she walked through the dark room with ease. In a moment, the room was filtered with light from a lamp by the bed.

"This is my old room," she said softly, and I instantly began studying the room. It was empty except for the queen-sized bed that she was currently standing by and a wooden vanity desk pushed up against the wall off to the left. Another door to the right had me guessing that it was a connected bathroom. Overall, the dark red walls were bare of anything, and the bedding was just a plain white comforter.

"It doesn't really show the fire that you have," I said. She laughed lightly and nodded.

"I imagine. I never wanted anything due to the fact that I couldn't see it, and so I thought, it was just a waste of space." She smiled so achingly sweet up at me before walking back over to me and reaching for my hand, entwining our fingers together. She proceeded to lead me over to the bed across the spacious room, our footsteps muffled by the plush carpet. She sat down on the edge and pulled me down with her. Once I had settled fully onto the bed, she crawled into my lap, and I automatically wrapped my arms around her and placed my chin on the top of her head. I felt and heard myself and Axel purr as our mate lay safe in our arms. The silence between us was comfortable and more relaxed than the atmosphere from earlier.

"I guess I should tell you what you're getting into. I mean, I can't blame you for being wary of me. I'm not in a pack nor am I a rogue. But I know who is behind this whole ordeal about the attacks," she said.

"I'll let you start wherever you want," I told her quietly. She didn't say anything in response for a long moment, probably trying to figure out her next words.

"I lost my sight at the age of six." She suddenly blurted out. My arms tightened slightly in surprise, her answer catching me off guard. Her finger traced patterns absentmindedly on my chest, and I felt myself relax once more.

"One year passed before my pack was attacked by a group of rogues. I don't know if I was the only survivor or not, but I didn't meet anybody else when I was escaping, so I could only assume that I was. Now, just imagine a little seven-year-old me wandering around the woods with no sight, terrified beyond belief, but I guess you could call it a gift in disguise because along with this crippling fear, a new sense came along." A small smiled tilted up her lips as she recalled a memory. "That's when I acquired this sight, so to speak. Yet the history of my bloodline is quite unique already, but I should actually tell you who my parents are."

"That sounds like a good plan." I smiled and shifted back, pulling her along as I settled my back against the headboard and kicked off my shoes off and pushed them off of the bed. Once we had become comfortable once more, her head on my chest and my hand in her hair, she began her story.

# Chapter 16

*Ryker Dare*

"I became blind as a side effect from a binding ritual." Kei began as I twirled her hair with my finger lazily. "It was the witches that did it, three sisters to be precise, and from what little knowledge I know about my childhood, they are close to the fae king. I am assuming they are still alive," she said with a shrug.

"Why exactly did you need your powers bound?" I asked, trying to piece it all together.

"I'm not exactly sure myself. My memories around that age are spotty at best, and what I do remember are only little snippets of the bigger picture. What I do know is, at my young age, I was beginning to develop into my potential a tad bit too fast."

"Just what kind of powers do you have?" I asked, my hand dropping away from her hair.

"That's the million-dollar question and one that I would love to know as well," she said with a sigh. "But over the years I've been asking around as I traveled—witches, vampires, every supernatural being you could possibly think of I asked, except for the fae ironically, and what I managed to conclude in the end was that I was beginning to show signs of possessing some rare Gifts."

"That's just another mystery to add to the list about the fae," I remarked. She chuckled lightly before nodding.

"Here, I'll try to clear up some of the confusion for you. As you know, the fae can possess up to six Gifts with varying uses while the sixth gift is the rarest out of all of them." She sat up to face me, holding up her index finger. "The first of these strange powers is the most common, and that is the ability to manipulate one of the earth's elements: wind, water, fire, earth. These are pretty common not only in the fae but as well as the wizards and witches."

"The second Gift is what I have. The power to see energy or, as I put it, auras. That allows me to see emotions, but I've heard rumors that some can even taste other people's feelings. The third is also seen pretty frequently, and that is the ability to actually speak to nature." I raised an eyebrow at this.

"As in, talk to trees and things?"

"I would assume so. I think that includes animals as well," she said thoughtfully. "I wonder what plants think about, anyways."

"Didn't you say you could see their energy?"

"Yes, but I can't tell what they are thinking. Personally, I find it strange that plants can talk at all, so this one seems more like a rumor than a truth to me."

"You say this while we are living in a world where scary werewolves and bloodthirsty vampires aren't supposed to exist," I said.

"Good point. Now, the next one is where the powers start to become rarer. The fourth would be the power to heal. I researched a lot about this one and what I learned was that there are two different types of healing; physical and mental. There is a downside to this, however. Not only could one heal but they also have the power to destroy and make the damage done to a person ten times worse, quite a dangerous double edged sword, I would say."

"No kidding," I said wryly.

"Don't worry; the next one isn't as bad. Actually, it's pretty awesome I think." She laughed before explaining, "Gift number five allows you to stop time. Is your mind blown yet?"

"Kei, my mind has been blown since we've met."

"Well, isn't it completely blown away now?" I chuckled at her teasing smile and finally nodded.

"Yes, my mind is so far gone that not even the Goddess could get it back." She let out a low whistle from my explanation.

"Dang, I didn't know I was that good."

"What's the last one, you teasing woman?" She laughed and looked at me with twinkling green eyes, the sight momentarily making my heart stutter in my chest.

"Do you love ghost stories, King?" I shrugged.

"I can't say I've heard a good one to give me chills." She leaned closer, a secretive smile on her face.

"The next one is going to knock your socks off then. The sixth and final Gift allows you to see the dead." My brows furrowed.

"Why is that?" She shrugged.

"No one knows. But here's the kicker to this one. A fae has to die and come back to life for them to receive such power. A story I've heard is that there was one fae who held such power, but there is not much known about what had happened. Only one fae in history was ever documented, though, and therefore, a lot of debate has been going on as to whether it's really a Gift. I think it's just a bonus if you come back to life and see the dead."

"If you died, why would you want to see the dead when you came back to life?" I raised an eyebrow at her.

"You can't tell me it wouldn't be cool to have dead people as your friends. They could give you all the dirty little secrets hiding behind every wall," she expressed with excitement. I shook my head at her.

"I don't find the pleasure of knowing every little secret going on. If I did, I might go crazy."

"Really? I would be entertained beyond belief. It would be way better than whatever TV shows people watch nowadays since I can't even watch it. Though, I do get curious about some shows. From what I heard of Jersey Shore, it leaves me to wonder what goes on in the human world. Goddess knows I am so far behind in most technology pleasures of this generation." She became silent to let me digest all the information that she just told me.

*"She definitely shed some light about this mysterious race,"* Axel commented.

*"Yes, she did. But she is also just as much in the dark as we."* As I stared at Kei, who oddly started to braid her hair, a thought occurred to me.

"Kei."

"Hmmm?" she responded.

"Why didn't you ever go back to the fae?" Her hands froze before starting slowly again.

"I tried, but as we all know, the faes are experts at hiding."

"So you couldn't find a way where they were located?"

"No, and I'm not too worried about it at this moment. I have more pressing matters now, but once my grandfather sends for me, then, I will consider on going."

"Wait, your grandfather?" She finished her braid before tossing it over her shoulder without tying it and nodded.

"This is where I explain who my parents are, which may give reasons as to why I'm so rebellious towards you."

"Oh, I want to hear this," I told her. She chuckled and turned, settling in front of me while grabbing my hand and entwining our fingers.

"Does the name Declan Valancia ring a bell?" I tensed in surprise, and she nodded. "That was my father."

"If I remember correctly, he was the alpha for the Silver Rose pack," I said lowly.

"He was," she replied softly. "I remember how guilty he felt when I lost my sight, not only him but my mother as well."

"He was a good man. I remember once he came to my territory to discuss some pack issues, and he would talk nonstop about his beautiful little girl." I chuckled as I remembered the light-hearted man and how he would gush about his young daughter.

*"Goddess, don't you realize how creepy we sound? We are talking to the woman who was the little girl of the man who would go on and on about how adorable she was."*

*"It is quite comical I think."*

"I can only assume that the little girl he was talking about is me," Kei said.

"Yes, and he loved you dearly. They both did." Her hand tightened around mine.

"I know. And they showed me every day." I heard her swallow before sighing. Trying to ease the pains of the past, I kissed her cheek gently.

"We can take a break if you want," I told her gently. She shook her head.

"No, it's all right. Besides, me being an alpha's daughter allows me to be just as bossy and possessive as you," she said playfully.

"That's alright. I'm curious to see your jealous side," I teased her and she scoffed.

"Oh, you'll probably see it here soon. And when you do, you better get some popcorn 'cause it will be quite the show." I laughed out loud, loving how she could admit it so easily that she would be jealous.

"Not only my father; my mother was pretty strong willed as well. Low and behold, she was the princess to the fae race." My eyes widened, and I leaned to the side so I could see the side of her face, a small grin adorning her lips as she tilted her head to face me.

"So what you were saying earlier is, your grandfather is the king?"

"Yes, but I haven't heard about him in years, and I don't know if he sent people to come find me once the news about my mother reached him. Of course, I do not hold anything against him. I pretty much disappeared off of the radar for a long time." She suddenly became quiet, and I waited. "I don't know where I get my eyes from. What I can remember is that my father had blue eyes while my mother had hazel. However, my silver hair did come from her side."

"You seem to come from a very powerful family," I said in amusement.

"This is probably why my powers are a little more potent than the average supernatural person."

"You don't say," I replied dryly, staring at Kei in a slightly new light. If she were involved with this whole rogue mess, which I was beginning to doubt, she would definitely be capable.

"I know. Crazy, huh? So, fast forward five years and I was twelve years old, five years after escaping the rogue attack on my family."

"Wait, if your parents were so powerful, who were the rogues that were able to kill them so easily?" Her expression suddenly became clouded.

"Werewolves weren't the only ones involved. You do know a vampire's blood can be quite deadly against a fae if entered into the bloodstream." I gritted my teeth as I was suddenly filled with rage, my power crackling around the room.

"You mean to tell me that the blood bags were involved?" I managed through gritted teeth. She nodded.

"Yes, my father was shot with a bullet infused with Black Roza right through the heart while my mother was stabbed with a sword engorged with vampire blood. Even if my mother was the princess of the fae kind, she wouldn't be able to survive very long without some help of some kind. What made her death sealed was that she was bitten.

"Even vampires venom is poisonous to us. Everything about their kind means the end of ours, it seems. That's how they got the name of the Silver Reapers from the fae kind," she said bitterly, her other hand fisting beside us. "Yet, I can't make myself hate them because I was saved by two of them." I jerked in response to this, my mind blank with shock.

"Two vampires saved you?" She nodded.

"Yes. They were a kind couple, but circumstances made it where we had to split ways and haven't heard from them since. Which brings me to the part that I dread the most about telling you. I was twelve, and I was going from pack to pack, picking up all kinds of different information for survival. I was lucky enough for five years to be shown kindness, but that was mainly because I was only a child still. However, that luck ran out when I was kidnapped by another pack of rogues, and let's just say, they didn't care if I was a kid or not. I was a young girl, and they were all men. You can only imagine what happened next." I felt my blood freeze in my veins, the cold fury seeping through my bones.

"What?" I said the word slowly, trying to reign in my anger as much as I could.

"I was… sexually assaulted in other words." Her voice came out as a quiet whisper now, yet she kept going. "That wasn't the worst part, either. I became pregnant, and I tried to hide this fact even though it was created by the monsters that held me captive, I still loved him. It was my baby, and even at such a young age, I felt my motherly instincts kick in. However, they found out." I felt one of her tears land on my hand, and I pulled her back closer to my chest, the emotions in me raging like a blazing fire.

"They didn't want to deal with a pregnant little girl, so they chose the easy way, and that was to get rid of it. That was the worst day of my life, and I would rather die a million times than experience that pain ever again." She shuddered against me as she recalled the horrors of her past. "I still feel their touch. The men that kept me captive for two years always found new ways to torture me. At one point, I wondered what it would be like to die, to finally have relief from the Hell that I had lived. I was almost at my breaking point until I was saved. Or so I had hoped." She let out a choked laugh.

"Turns out, I was simply thrown into a darker nightmare. The man that I thought was my savior was the exact opposite. Granted, he taught me most of what I know today about my fighting skills, but then, he kept me as a pet of some sort. For some reason, he was always so fascinated with me, and I could never figure out why. Of course, I don't know if that was a blessing or a curse as his weird fascination saved me from my previous predicament, but now, I think it's both."

"Why is that so?" My emotions were raging inside my body and mind like a storm, but I still wanted to know more about her and her dark past. She looked up at me, her lashes dark and long.

"Because I was able to escape, travel everywhere and, finally, meeting you." My mind calmed, and I stared down at her as she stared up at me with such vulnerability that I knew with absolute clarity that she had no involvement whatsoever with today's present problems. Gripping her chin gently with my thumb and index finger, I lifted her face up and laid my forehead against hers.

"We are so lucky, Axel and I, to have you as our mate." My words were barely louder than a whisper, and her eyes showed a determined glint.

"Mark me," she said strongly, her voice holding no hesitation. I cradled her in my arms gently, holding her as if she were made of glass.

"Kei, you just told me a part of yourself that wasn't really easy to say. I think we need some time to—"

"Please don't tell me to wait," she said with a groan. "I mean, I appreciate how you're worried about me don't get me wrong, but let's face it, I am a woman with some emotional issues. You can trust me when I say I am completely clear-headed in this decision." I smiled down at her softly.

"You're really amazing." I was happy to see her familiar smirk make an appearance.

"King, that's our line." She raised herself up onto her knees and leaned forward, rubbing her nose against mine and smiled. I wrapped an arm around her waist, pulling her closely while I reached up with my other and pushed her hair away from her neck. I placed small butterfly-like kisses down her neck and stopped at the juncture where her neck met her shoulder. She sighed against me, pushing her body even closer to mine. I could feel all her soft curves against my hard planes as her slender hands reached up and tangled in my hair. Pleasure and anticipation made me dizzy as I felt my canines lengthen.

Kissing the spot one more time, I bit into her skin before pulling back and tilting her face up. I memorized the way her red eyes glowed and her small smile playing on her lips.

"Well, what're you waiting for?" I chuckled and bent my head down, meeting her lips gently with my own. The mating process is a lot slower and sweet than one would expect. You cannot run into it head first with the fires of passion nipping at your heels. No, these moments are what make the whole thing more sacred to our kind. It brought the mates closer together, not physically but emotionally.

"I gotta say. That was the sweetest thing I've ever tasted." She licked her lips and grinned at me.

"You haven't been tasting what's been on my tongue, *Lune,* or what's going to be." She raised an eyebrow while her smile widened.

"Was that a dirty innuendo that just came out of your mouth?"

"Hmmm, was it?" I murmured. "I simply meant that I would do this." I leaned forward to lick her cheek. She laughed and slapped my arm playfully.

"You know, I would have found that gross if I wasn't part dog."

"Good thing for me, then," I said, grinning. She chuckled and began kissing my neck the same fashion that I had earlier, the electricity between us heating the air in the room until it almost felt like a sauna.

"Did I ever tell you what you smell like?" she murmured.

"Not bad I hope," I joked.

"No. You smell so divine. It's almost like I get a sweet tooth whenever I catch a whiff." I frowned a little.

"Do I smell like a dessert?"

"You smell like dark chocolate. I love chocolate." She pulled back to face me, and her expression was so serious I had to hold in my laugh.

"You better hurry up and mark me, or else, some other she-wolf will think that I am free as a bird." She looked at me, unamused.

"Guess I should speed it up, then."

"Go ahead and make me yours," I said quietly, just as she bit into the same place that I had with her. I closed my eyes and felt the pleasure build up inside, not only that, but I could even see our connection become a solid thing between us. A golden string, thick and strong formed between us, and her mind was now open to me as was mine to her. I saw her memories flicker quickly, too fast for me to process, but I did catch thoughts that she was having at this moment.

*"Was this too quick? He better not run away or else I will down his furry butt until he has nowhere else to hide."* I chuckled her thought filtered into mine and smiled.

*"Lune, you don't have to worry about us leaving. Not even the Goddess herself could separate us now."*

*"Good, 'cause if you ever decide to leave just know that even Hades or Hell or whatever place would be a better place than what I would have in store for you."*

"I don't doubt it," I said out loud, watching as she pulled away. She licked at the excess blood and smiled at me, giving me a quick peck on the lips.

"Now, let's go to bed. I can only imagine how late it is, and we have to go back to Brad's pack in the morning." She yawned and got off the bed, slipping her jeans off but keeping her tank top on. I pulled my t-shirt up and over my head, leaving me in just my sweats.

When I had settled beside her, she scooted as close as she could to me and wrapped a leg over my own. I chuckled quietly and wrapped my arm around her waist.

"Have sweet dreams, *Lune*," I said into her hair, kissing her forehead.

"You too," she said with a chuckle, yawning once more as her eyes drooped shut. I smiled softly and stared at her for one more moment, once again reveling in her beauty.

*"We're so damn lucky."* Axel seemed to be entranced by her as much as I was.

*"I know."*

Without another word, I closed my eyes with her sleeping face the last image on my mind before I fell into a dreamless sleep.

# Chapter 17

*Kei Valancia*

I felt a warmth surround me like a comforting blanket, burrowing even deeper.

"Kei." A deep voice grunted at me, barely filtering through my mind in a haze as I ignored it. Instead, I wrapped my arms around a narrow waist, snuggling even closer to my own furnace. "For the love of Goddess, your knee is digging—" I raised my hand and smacked it against his mouth, trying to shut him up.

"Shh. It's rude to be so noisy in the morning," I mumbled terribly, but it was still coherent.

"Kei," he said again with exaggeration. Growling in slight frustration, I sat up and propped myself on my elbows, hovering over his body and looking down at him with a frown.

"Is this better?" I asked with a raised eyebrow. He made a noise that sounded like a groan and a grunt.

"No." I sighed and plopped onto his stomach, which felt like I was landing on a boulder.

"You need to get some fat. I like my men squishy," I said, poking his abdomen. I felt his chest rumble while his hand brushed my hair.

"Sorry to disappoint." He chuckled softly. I grinned and sat up, straddling his waist in the process. I stretched my arms above my head, arching my back and groaned as my bones popped in various places. I felt Ryker became rigid and I cocked my head to the side as I stared down at him.

"Why are you so tense?" I asked, laying a hand on his bare chest and feeling the hard muscle flex underneath my fingertips. Absentmindedly, I began tracing patterns on his skin.

"The sight of you looking gorgeous in sparse clothing will do things to man," he replied thickly. "Especially in your lacy underwear."

"I don't have lacy underwear," I said with a scoff. I felt a finger trail up my bare thigh and hook into my alleged lacy undergarment.

"*Lune*, this is the epitome of lacy." I pouted and huffed, still straddling him.

"Yeah, well, they're ultra comfy, and I love cute underwear even if I can't see them."

"Then how can you tell if they're cute?" he asked rather quizzical. I flicked him on the chest.

"I ask the store clerk what they look like," I said. "Of course, I gotta try them on so they can judge how good they look on me." I winked at him and laughed at his groan.

"Kei, why do you love to torture me?" He sounded rather strained, and I leaned down close to his ear.

"What else do you expect me to do with my time?"

"I could think of some things," he said suggestively. I rolled my eyes and covered his face with my hand.

"Get your mind out of the gutter, King. It's way too early to be thinking like that."

"Says the little vixen who loves to tease me. I think anytime is the best time," he laughed. I reached up and tugged a tuft of his hair.

"Figures that you'll think that," I teased. I continued to play with his hair, the silky locks of his so soft on my fingertips. "I love your hair." He chuckled before sitting up and kissing me on the tip of my nose.

"I love everything about you," he murmured. I smiled sweetly up at him.

"That was so corny but so adorable. You're just too cute!" I wrapped my arms around his neck and pulled him to my chest, a goofy smile on my face. I laughed as his words were muffled as his face was in my boobs. When he finally managed to pull away, his breaths came in ragged gulps.

"Goddess Kei, are you trying to kill me?" I laughed and sat up. He arranged himself so that he was able to pull me into his chest, tucking my head underneath his chin.

"How did you figure it out?" I joked and smiled at him teasingly. His laugh rumbled out of his chest like smooth chocolate.

"I knew it," he teased back. A laugh bubbled out of me, and a strange feeling came over me.

*"We're happy,"* Rei said, and I agreed with her. The feeling of wholeness that I now felt from our bond was something that I never would have imagined feeling.

"What are you thinking?" Ryker's lips brushed against my temple, sending shivers up my spine.

"You... life... Everything."

"Wow, that's deep." I smacked him on the chest lightly as he laughed.

"All right, smart aleck. What time is it?" He hummed and became quiet for a moment.

"It's ten right now."

My eyes widened, and I bolted out of bed.

"We are so late," I cursed softly as I blindly flailed about until my hand brushed up to what seemed like a dresser. Exploring the flat surface, my hand came into contact with soft material— clothes.

"Is this yours or mine?" I asked, turning around to face Ryker with the clothing in my hands. I heard the bed creak as he shifted his weight to get off, his strides silent as he walked over to me.

"Yours. I didn't allow anyone to come in while you were asleep." This made me pause, and I stared in his direction with my hands on my hips.

"You can trust these people, King. I promise you." I walked over to him and caressed his cheek gently. "Now, I'm gonna need you to step out for a moment. A girl needs a little privacy sometimes."

"*Lune,* we're mates. And besides, I'm going to see it all sooner or later." I put a hand on his chest to stop his advances.

"Nope. Don't you know in Algebra, you can't get to the X if you don't have the Y? Or is that the other way around?" I second-guessed myself.

"Are you really going to compare our relationship to an algebraic equation? And I don't think that's how it works." He sounded incredulous, and I smirked.

"The point is, you need one to help find the other because relationships are like equations. You need to figure out all of the factors before solving the main problem. Equations come in steps, as does relationships. And just like algebra, relationships are just as confusing and maybe even more." He sighed deeply when I was done with the mini lecture.

"Of course, she uses algebra. It's only the most difficult thing to understand, and so it's only natural that she uses it," he muttered under his breath before turning around, his usual glittery blackness calm as he kept muttering incoherently. I poked his back.

"Algebra is not difficult, quite simple really if you think about it."

"Like hell is it simple; its numbers with the alphabet added. Why in Goddess's name do we need it?" I shrugged off the shirt I was already wearing and began putting on the new clothes.

"It's actually very useful," I said. He scoffed in return.

"Yeah? What do you use it for?" I pulled my hair from out of the shirt, the material soft against my skin.

"I use it to make me sound really smart and watch with open amusement as people struggle to try to understand what I had just said. It's really entertaining to watch all of the colors swirl around them erratically as they become so confused," I told him. He didn't say anything in response, and I had pulled on what seemed to be jean shorts, very *short* jean shorts.

"What are these?" I looked down at my body and in return only saw black. I poked my bare thigh and frowned slightly.

*"They're kinda comfy,"* Rei mused.

*"They are. But there is so little material that I'm curious if you can actually call it pants."* I heard the shuffle of feet as Ryker turned, but I looked up in curiosity as I felt him tense beside me. I noticed with a raised eyebrow as the familiar angry red deepened his aura and the hilarious color of violet.

"What's wrong?" I tried to hide the humor in my voice, but I knew that he heard it, anyway. Why is he mad and turned on at the same time?

*"Must be the shorts,"* Rei concluded. I agreed with her.

"I'm going to kill him," Ryker finally said through clenched teeth.

"Who?"

"That damn Taven man." I choked on a laugh.

"Do you mean Draven?" His tall black outline waved a hand in a dismissive manner.

"I don't care what his name is. He purposely gave you those… those *shorts*." He spat the word "shorts" as if it left a rancid taste in his mouth. I sidled up beside him and tilted my head up at him with an amused smile.

"He probably knew that it would rile you up, and it is." He growled and wrapped an arm around my waist possessively, pulling me to his side.

"Of course, I'm going to get angry. You're half naked." He sounded exasperated.

"Hmmm. Maybe but they're so comfy. Besides, Draven is like an older brother, and he probably only did this to see how you would react and let me say, you're passing with wonderful colors."

"This isn't some test, Kei. You make it sound like you've done this before." His words became brittle, and I could practically feel his accusing eyes bore into my face. I sighed and rolled my eyes. There go those accusations again.

"Really? You're still so unsure? You need to get your head on straight, King." I pulled away and frowned at him. I noticed with slight awe as I saw sparkling gold begin to creep around the edges of the glittering black.

"You're right; I do need to stop these childish acts." I tilted my head and looked at him. His voice was the same yet not. It still sounded like the deep baritone, but it had a different feeling underlying the words.

"I'm guessing you're Axel?"

"The one and only, *Lune*." I chuckled as he took a step forward, his hands gripping the dresser behind me and trapping me with his steely body.

"Why do I get the impression that you're a playboy?" I could feel Rei stir in my mind.

*"Make him cry,"* I said to her before I let her have full control.

# Chapter 18

*Axel*

I watched with fixation as the gold ring in her eyes brightened, revealing that the drivers had changed.

"You are an idiot that needs to learn to have more trust," her voice slid around me in smooth waves, her eyes half hooded as she looked up at me.

"I won't deny it," was my reply as I leaned down until our noses brushed against each other.

"We told you our story, yet you continue to be disbelieving? What more is it that you want?" Her eyes flashed brightly with anger, and I found it absolutely sexy.

*"Don't you dare say what I know you're going to say,"* Ryker warned, yet I couldn't make myself listen. I leaned ever closer and watched with hunger as her body shivered from my warm breath on her ear.

"I want all of you," I murmured, reaching up and brushing her cheek with my knuckles softly. She didn't say anything but stood with a slightly stiff posture, her breathing coming out slightly ragged.

"Don't you remember the equation?" she asked rather thickly. I bent my head down and nibbled her neck.

"Screw the equation. I would prefer to just skip to $z$."

"But $z$ isn't even in it," she replied thickly.

"It's in mine," I said before trapping her lips with my own. She moaned loudly as I pushed her against the dresser, my hands firmly on her hips. I felt her magical fingers come up and grip handfuls of my hair, pulling me down closer to her.

I felt her soft curves underneath my fingertips, and it felt like I was in Heaven with her hair brushing my face, the silky strands smelling of lilac. She pulled back, her eyes bright and cheeks flushed.

"Never forget the equation," she teased and pinched me lightly in the side. I jolted at the sharp pain, and she slid away, her laugh echoing around us.

"Rei, stop moving away." I made a move to grab her, but she simply slid out of my reach. She stopped in front of the door, her eyes twinkling with mischief and a smirk on her lips.

"You do know I have a job to do, right?" she said, her hand resting on the door handle.

"Babe, I do love your outfit. However, I cannot allow giving the joy to another man to see you as you are now."

My eyes raked up and down her form, taking in the tight fitting tank top and ripped Daisy Dukes, showing off her long legs. I licked my lips hungrily, and I took a step forward.

"Yep, definitely not happening," I said huskily.

"Hmmm, we'll see." Before I could take another step, she had opened the door and darted through the opening with swift movements.

*"And there she goes,"* Ryker sighed.

"Don't be such a downer. The game has only begun after all." I smiled wickedly and followed with slower steps, still bare-chested but now clothed with sweats that Ryker had put on earlier.

*"Good luck 'cause you're going to need it."*

*"Thanks,"* I replied, using our connection to find our little mate. I felt the bond travel throughout the house, and I felt amazement that she had traveled a good amount of distance in that little sliver of time.

Becoming even more motivated, I began to follow her trail. I walked with long, purposeful steps through the halls, passing many other people who stared and bowed. Amazement and a hint of fear from the men, heated and longing glances from the woman. I ignored everything, of course, and focused on winning our little game. I had turned down an empty corridor, pictures hanging on the walls of smiling pups and families from the pack.

I may have a strong dislike for their son, but I had a deep respect for the present day Alpha and Luna. They had a strong sense of righteousness and treated everyone with equal kindness. I had called ahead of time to come onto their land, and we had chatted for a few minutes with Alpha Ray and his wife off somewhere else for pack matters.

I felt the bond go behind a closed set of double doors, the dark mahogany, and a beautiful contrast to the lighter decor. Intricate designs carved the wood, a sea of wooden swirls gave the sense of something important hid behind the doors.

*"Come on in, King. I have something to show you,"* Rei's voice floated through my mind like a gentle breeze yet hid the underlying tone of a ravaging storm. I didn't say anything as I reached out and gripped the shiny brass knob, turning with a smooth twist while pushing the heavy wooden door at the same time. I let the door swing slowly open, revealing the room hidden within.

I felt myself freeze in surprise as I stared into a room full of every kind of weapon you could imagine. It was a long rectangular room, looking like it was twenty feet long and fifteen feet wide. From samurai swords to the most advanced gun in today's society hung on the walls; the metal gleaming dangerously under the light. Standing in the middle of the room was Rei flicking a deadly looking knife up in the air and catching it by the end of the blade.

"Pick a weapon," she said, extending her arm out in a sweeping gesture. I walked over to a wall full of rather sharp looking swords and gripped one by the hilt gingerly, keeping my eyes on her.

"What is this for?" I asked, taking a couple of practice swing with the sword, the blade gleaming almost menacingly.

"We are going to have a good old fashioned duel, my King." I rolled my eyes and lowered the weapon.

"Why must everything end up with a fight with you?" She shrugged.

"Because it's fun, and you made me wake up late, therefore making me unable to get back in time to train the pups." A dangerous light gleamed in her eyes. I sighed, but a smirk edged my lips up.

"Fine but please, not the face," I said seriously. She chuckled and turned, motioning me to follow her.

"Come on, then, I need to stretch my muscles." I followed her silently as she walked over to a door hidden in the shadows of the corner of the room, a large wooden cabinet standing beside it seemingly ominous.

We walked into a spacious room, black mats spread across the floor and a floor to ceiling mirror covered the walls. Our reflections walked over to the middle of the room, a couple feet of empty space between us.

"To be honest, King, I really wanted to take you down and make you ours right when we found out that we were mates," she said casually, twirling the blade with easy grace.

"Why didn't you?" I asked with just as much ease.

"I knew that it would have been a terrible idea." I stared at her.

"I don't see how. You are mine, and I am yours if you had made a move to mark us, we wouldn't have had made a move to stop you." She pursed her lips and flicked the knife into the air, the blade just a blur of silver before coming back down, and her nimble fingers gripped the sharp edge with ease.

"The thing is, King, it would have been too easy. Just think if we had confessed our love and utter devotion right there, and our lives had ended with a happy ending at that moment, wouldn't it have been boring? It really doesn't make a good love story." I twirled the long sword, getting used to the lightweight feel.

"No, it wouldn't have. It would be terrible to disappoint our future pups with a boring story on how we met." She stopped her twirling and faced me, her head tilted.

"Already thinking about the future, I see," she murmured.

"Of course, I am. What's stopping you?" She looked at me in disbelief.

"Really, you're going to ask that question? First off, we need to fix your little trust issues, and two, I have a damned sociopathic werewolf hunting my ass. So, my future right now isn't looking so bright." She finished her rant, but I had stopped listening after 'sociopathic werewolf.' I felt my temper flare, and my eyes narrowed.

"You never said anything about being hunted." Something in my voice made her freeze.

"Ah, well, um, you see, I wasn't supposed to tell you…" She trailed off, and I noticed that she had actually blushed. I would have taken more notice of it if I hadn't found out that she was in danger.

*"Why the hell didn't she tell us?"* Ryker sounded pretty ticked, and I was almost there. I didn't reply to him but, instead, stalked over to Rei, her head down and her hands fidgeting. Once I was right in front of her, I lifted tilted her chin up with my index finger so I could look into her eyes, noticing that the golden glow was gone.

"You're going to explain the whole situation to me, and I want no bullcrap this time." She looked as if she were going to argue but stopped herself. Closing her eyes, she let out a deep sigh.

"This is why I can't throw damn surprises." I heard her mutter before shaking her head. Backing up, she turned, reared back her arm and threw the knife. It flew with such velocity across the room that only a few silver flashes were really seen before it stuck into a target dummy. The impact of the knife was so hard that it caused the target to crash to the ground. "All right, fine, I'll tell you everything you want to know about my crazy abductor. But this was not what I had planned at all today," she said the last part grumpily and stalked over to a couch located at the far left of the room, pushed up against the wall along with a small table and a mini-fridge.

I didn't take any more notice of the cozy corner; instead, followed her lead and sat beside her, stiff as a board. Crossing her arms across her chest, she reluctantly began to tell a part of her past that seemed darker than I had ever imagined.

# Chapter 19

*Kei Valancia*

*"This is the last time I'll let you have control for a while,"* I griped grouchily at Rei.

*"Didn't I say I was sorry? Besides, he has a right to know."* I just sighed one more time before starting story time once again.

"The man's name is Leon Grayson, a rather ruthless man. I remember the night when he had 'rescued' me." Sarcasm leaked from my words, and I smiled without showing any teeth. "The bastard waited until dark to ambush one of the patrollers on duty and killed both wolves without much of a fight. He infiltrated the rogues' hideout without much trouble and found me cowering in a corner after slaughtering the whole pack.

"You should have been there to witness it. They were all so scared I swear they peed their pants." I chuckled without emotion.

"And then when I noticed I wasn't getting butchered, I fell to my knees and cried. Leon didn't do anything but just stand there until I finally quit. After I was done, I was taught a lesson." I heard my voice become more distant, getting caught up in the memories.

"Leon hated to see weakness, much less tears, and I found out just how much he hated it." I leaned my head back and stared blankly into the darkness. "He was so angry, saying how I should already be used to such things. But he had the wrong idea. I wasn't scared; I was hopeful. The burning ember in my heart that had nearly gone out suddenly flared to life, telling me that I was going to be free. But no; instead, I was sucked into another hellish world, and that's when those flames became extinguished almost immediately. My wishful thinking died in an instant.

"And you should have seen it," I murmured. "The way his energy seemed to infect those around him. It bubbled grotesquely, the color a sickly yellow. It was like his own energy was sick." I covered half of my face with my right palm, a grimace adorning my features.

"You can't even imagine what it felt like to have his hands touch me. It felt as if my very own being was becoming ill from breathing the same air as him." I couldn't help but growl lowly. "It just makes me so furious that I can't see his face so I could rip it off." I stood abruptly and began pacing.

"I did corner him once. Got this close to killing him," I pinched my thumb and index finger close together, leaving them just a centimeter apart. "But then his lackeys came. Another man, a wizard that worked for him, came and nearly killed me. "I ran a hand through my hair roughly, ignoring the sharp tugs on my scalp.

"Then after that, I began to truly notice how much Leon favored me. As the wizard was about to finish me off, Leon attacked the man, killing him in seconds. I didn't see it, thank Goddess for being blind for once, but I did hear it. And it was…" I trailed off, remembering the snarls mixed in with the fleshy tears of flesh and the cracking of bones. I shivered.

"Anyway, that's when it started to dawn on me that I was something that he found sick interest in, and for years, I was almost treated like a little pet. And I hated it." I could feel my eyes become full of unshed tears, trying to push their way out but I didn't let them. "But then I was rescued a third time, this one more positive than the others." I smiled faintly at nothing.

"It was a man and a woman, both vampires. They were just passing through but heard my screams one day. I was being punished for breaking a dish," I explained vaguely before continuing. "So they came to investigate out of curiosity and saw Leon... doing things." I decided to leave out the details being as how Ryker was already furious enough and any more he might explode.

"I remember the man—"

"What was he doing?" Ryker interrupted, his voice low and steely. I had my back to him, and I could practically feel his anger prick on my skin.

"I don't think that it is relevant at the moment," I replied, nervousness starting to bubble inside of me. I didn't hear him at all as he suddenly appeared in front of me, his hands reaching out and gripping my shoulders.

"It's relevant to me." It sounded as if he was trying to hold in his snarl and to which caused his voice to be strained. Red filled my vision, along with a dark gray showing his sadness for me. I reeled back and blinked several times, the feeling of wanting to cry even stronger.

"I don't want to talk about it right now, please." I hated how I sounded so weak, so broken, but I couldn't help it. I smiled without any feeling. "Isn't it pathetic how it still affects me even after all of these years? Sometimes, I wonder if I'll always be stuck, never be able to move forward without his ghost following somewhere behind me." The time had come for my sadness, anger, and hopelessness to finally break through. Tears poured down my face in streams, and I wrapped my arms around myself to keep from falling apart completely. A loud sob broke through my lips, and I bowed my head so he wouldn't see how unsightly I was. That was until I was pulled into a hard body and wrapped up in an addicting embrace. I froze momentarily from shock before I registered what was happening.

"Don't worry. Everything is going to be fine because I'll hunt his ghost and rip his head off so that he'll never haunt you again," he murmured, patting my head in a soothing manner. "I'll make it my life's mission to hunt down every single bastard who laid a hand on you." I chuckled while still crying, wrapping my arms around his waist and pulling him closer. I burrowed my face closer to his chest and let myself cry for what seemed like years.

Ryker simply held me, at one point, picking me up and carrying me over to the couch. He cradled me in his lap like a child. But for once, I didn't care. I just let him. I cried silently into his shirt, gripping onto his shoulders tightly with emotion.

It might have been hours, but it surely was only just a few minutes before the tears stopped flowing, and I just laid there, emotionally spent. Ryker was still running his fingers through my hair, murmuring comforting words. Once he noticed that I wasn't crying, he stopped. I pulled back and looked up at him. I heard his sharp intake of breath at the sight of my vulnerability.

"I bet I look like crap on a stick, huh?" I tried to smile but managed only a small upturn of the lips. He was silent as I felt his fingers trail down my cheeks where the tears left their trails.

"You're even more beautiful," he said and hugged me, cupping the back of my head in his large hand. I was shocked once more. I expected some contact of the lips of some sort but not this sweet as sugar hug. I felt like crying again but, this time, not from sadness but just from being treated so sweetly by my mate. I lifted my arms and hugged him back, playing with his hair at the nape of his neck.

The silence between us was comforting as we relished in one another's company, feeling comfortable. Until I heard a noise. I stiffened and pulled back to turn my head. Not a moment later, Ryker stiffened also as he heard it.

"Oh, lovebirds, where are you?" I heard the familiar voice of Draven as he walked into the room, his presence light and cheery. I noticed his form stop once he spotted us. "Sweet goddess, you weren't about to have sex on my couch were you?" I don't know what compelled me to, but I just threw my head back and laughed. I laughed until I had cramps on my sides and I nearly fell off the couch if Ryker wasn't there to hold on.

"Alpha, I'm sorry to say, but I think I broke your mate with my humor." I heard Draven say.

"If you did, I'd break you," was his reply, and he sounded serious too. Once my laughter became into spastic giggles, I looked towards him.

"Don't worry, you didn't break me."

"Good because I was starting to get worried there." He sounded almost relieved. I chuckled once more and tried to make a move to get up but was stopped by the iron bars of Ryker's arms.

"Was there anything you needed?" I questioned, recalling how he seemed to be looking for us.

"Oh, yeah, Alpha Hale called asking when you guys would be back."

"Right now," I replied almost instantly. I managed to untangle myself and stand up.

"So quickly? But you haven't gotten to see Mom and Dad yet, and I know they would be thrilled to see you. They'll be back from pack business in just a little bit." I smiled warmly at the mention of his parents.

"Don't worry, I'll come back again," I assured him. I walked over and gave him a bone-crushing but quick hug before pulling away. I noticed how Ryker didn't say anything but lace our fingers together once I was back at his side.

"Well, all right. Maria is busy with her tutor at the moment, but I'll tell her that you had to leave on a very important mission." I rolled my eyes but smiled thankfully at him.

"Thank you. I'll come back to visit as soon as I can but in the meantime, behave." He laughed, and I could hear the grin in his voice as we began walking away.

"You know I can't keep the ladies at bay," he joked, and I laughed.

"Yeah, the *old* ladies," I retorted back before the door shut on his loud laughter. Once again, we were left in silence as Ryker gently tugged me along through the hallways.

He didn't say a word as he led me outside into the early afternoon air. We stood in the middle of the yard, and I tilted my face up towards the sun, letting myself soak up the warm rays.

"You know," he started. "I love it when you laugh, but I don't get to hear it often." I smiled and opened my eyes to look up at him.

"Maybe because your humor is as funny as a rock," I teased. He chuckled, and I felt him pick up a lock of my hair and tickle my face with it.

"I would be offended if it wasn't true." I laughed out loud once more, and I saw the happiness radiate from him, the dark lavender beautiful with his black.

"I'm glad you're aware," I said while poking his side. He wrapped an arm around my shoulders while my arm snaked around his slender waist, and we walked towards the edge of the woods. I could see the colors of all of the wildlife stretch beyond my vision, the sparks of life comforting me from the black abyss.

"I've decided that when we get back, I am going do what I should have done when I first saw you," he stated.

"And what would that be?" I asked, amused. He didn't say anything for a moment.

"I am going to take you out on a date." He paused. "Unless you would prefer not to."

"King, I can guarantee you that I'll go anywhere with you at this point." He pulled me closer in response.

"Oh? Well, how about we go to the bedroom then." His voice became a deep husky sound, and I almost melted right then and there.

"How many times will I say it? The equation," I stated, surprised to hear that my voice sounded clear while my insides felt like goo. He groaned but kissed my head.

"Algebra can go to Hell," he grumbled, and we began getting ready to shift. I smirked over at him.

"Algebra *is* Hell," I said before shifting and taking off.

# Chapter 20

*Ryker Dare*

*"Can a person cheat in algebra?"*

*"You could if it wasn't in relationship form,"* I grumbled back to Axel.

"Now, everyone, I want you all to focus on defense. Remember, the better the defense, the better you can do on offense. Begin!" I watched with hidden amazement as everybody watched Kei with absolute adoration, completely enamored by her.

Two weeks had now passed since I had run into her in the woods, and these two weeks were heaven on earth. She had stayed firm about me getting my own room, but after long hours of doing extra work with the pack and trying to locate the rogue's hideout, I would come back to my own room and find her sleeping in my bed with the light on, waiting for me to come back. On the very few nights that I was able to relax, Kei and I would usually sit on the couch and watch a movie with her snuggled in my arms. Her laugh danced in my ears as we joked. Her humorous mood, however, was nowhere to be seen at this moment.

She stood tall with her hands on her hips and an expression of cool calculation while her eyes scanned the sea of bodies fighting against each other. It was times like these that I forget that our little mate can't see.

I sighed quietly before turning back to my own group of trainees. They were older, all of them around mid-twenties, and I noticed with slight pride to see them doing well.

"Everyone, take a break." They all stopped and turned their heads to look at me, bowing slightly before chattering with each other as they made their way towards a cluster of trees to get out of the sun. I glanced one last time towards Kei before turning to go back into the house. I heard the sounds of giggling voices and childlike squeals come from somewhere inside the house, the sounds emitting from the opposite direction that I was heading. I didn't knock as I entered the room. Alpha Hale sat rigid in his chair, his eyes guarded while staring at the man who was the exact opposite. With his relaxed posture and easy going smile, you would have thought the two were old friends. Yet, appearances were deceiving.

"Well, if it isn't the Alpha King. Come to save the day?" The man sounded smug for whatever reason.

"It won't be your day that I'm saving, Thomas." My whole mood hardened as I stared at the man. Thomas Lowe simply smiled.

"Don't be like that; I thought we were all friends?" Brad and I shared a look.

"King and I have only just met, but we both already have one thing in common: our dislike of you." I raised an eyebrow at the alpha, surprised at his brutal honesty. Thomas chuckled and leaned back relaxed into the chair.

"Ouch, you wound me. Truly, you do. Fine, I don't have any particular like for any of you either, so you can imagine I'm not here for niceties." His expression turned serious. "Instead, let's talk about the roach problem we all seem to have." I leaned against the wall beside the doorway, crossing my arms and looking at him coolly.

"I'm not surprised that they have also reached your part of the woods. You seem to attract other bastards like a magnet," I remarked. He sent me a sarcastic smile.

"Well, you've seemed to have gotten a sense of humor from the last time I've seen you in about fifty years. Don't tell me, you found your mate." My expression remained passive.

"No, I haven't." I would rather face off a whole army by myself rather than tell him. This man and I have butted heads countless times over the years, and we both each have a mutual dislike for one another. This caused us both to avoid each other like the plague unless it was absolutely necessary.

"I feel sorry for the poor woman who is yours. Who would want to deal with your uptight ass all the time?" He snickered to himself and my glower only intensified as did my dislike. Probably feeling my increasing murderous intent, Alpha Hale cleared his throat and began to speak.

"Alpha Lowe, I would watch what you say. King Dare has not been in the greatest of moods come of late," Hale said lowly. Thomas eyed the both of us with critical attention before shrugging, and his trademark smirk slipped back on.

"Fine, keep your secrets. I just wanted to know how we'll keep the rogues off my land." The hidden anger underneath his words seemed genuine, as did the gleam in his eyes. I studied the sudden tension in his shoulders and knew that something had happened.

"How many did they kill?" I knew that he would get what I would mean.

"Twenty," he growled out. "Those damned rogues killed twenty of my pack members—twelve men and eight women all in a span of two weeks. I don't give two flying shits if they go after me, but you don't mess with *my* pack." He abruptly stood up and slammed both palms on Hale's desk, the loud smack resonating throughout the room. Hale and I shared a look, the feeling of surprise flickering on both of our faces.

"Alpha Lowe, what exactly did you come here for?" Alpha Hale gave him a long look while Thomas lifted his head and stared at him.

"I came here to try to get help to find those bastards. I've tried tracking them down on my own, but unlike Dare over here, my connections are not as widespread as his." I looked at him with raised eyebrows.

"Never knew I would hear those words leave your mouth. This rogue problem is obviously starting to get out of hand,"

"Obviously." All of our heads snapped back to see Kei standing in the doorway, a sense of deja vu came over me. "Didn't any of your mama's say that it was rude to stare?" She smirked and leaned against the doorway.

"How can you tell that we're staring?" Hale asked.

"I didn't, but now, I do." Hale and I chuckled at her antics.

"Who's this?" I tensed as Thomas looked at her with curious interest. Kei looked him up or down, or whatever she did being how I don't know what she actually "sees."

"I should be asking the same question." She shot me a glance. "Your friend over here smells very strong." To demonstrate, she leaned forward towards his direction and sniffed. A growl rumbled out of my chest, and I took a step forward.

"Woah there, tiger, no need to be uneasy. I promise it's just a platonic sniff, nothing more to it." She put her index finger on her chin in thought while looking at us. "While we are discussing these rogues, why don't we all sit and share ideas to where they could be, yeah?"

She didn't wait for a reply but, instead, walked into the room, shutting the door behind her as she did. As she brushed up against me, she reached out and gripped my hand, tugging me behind her to the couch. I sighed but didn't resist as we both settled ourselves, the other two men in the room watching us.

"You do have a mate." Thomas's tone was accusing, and I shot him a sharp glance. I opened my mouth to object, but was cut off by a sharp pain in my leg.

"Oh, darling." Kei's voice was honeyed in my ear. "Why does this man think that you don't have a mate? Come on, tell me, I'm just dying to know." I looked down at her to see her eyes swirling in red, flashing from controlled anger.

*"I do not have time to explain,"* I said through mind link. She only smiled sweetly in response.

"Don't worry, babe, you'll have time. And when that time comes, you sure better explain it good. Now"—she pulled away with a bright smile—"let's get on with this little meeting. I have to begin training once more in about an hour." She scooted away, but I wrapped an arm around her waist and pulled her back to me. She shot me an irritated glance before rolling her eyes. I noticed how Thomas stared at us with an amused expression.

"What's your name, hot stuff?" I growled even louder at him, but I was cut off by Kei's laugh.

"King, did I hear him right? Tell me my ears didn't just witness a terrible thing right now." She laughed once more. "Who says 'hot stuff' anymore? I thought that died off along with baggy jeans. Thank the goddess I was unable to see that for that generation would have ruined me." She shivered before staring at Thomas with a more serious gaze.

"Let's get this straight, Potato Man. I will only be referred as Kei to you and nothing else."

"Fine, but my name is not Potato Man, either." She waved her hand.

"You reek of guilt and vengeance, which equals that to a potato." We all stared at her. She sighed. "I have come to find out that guilt is a

rather light brown, and it reminds me of a potato I guess you can say."
We still stared at her.

"Kei, we still have no idea what you're talking about," I finally
told her. Sighing, she leaned against my shoulder.

"His aura, it's tinted light brown like a potato. Plus, he smells
strongly of damp earth. I don't find it particularly pleasant, but it's better
than some." She shrugged.

"Uh, thank you?" This was the first time since arriving that
Thomas actually looked slightly ruffled.

"Don't take it the wrong way, Potato Man. It's only natural that
you feel guilty and mad at the rogues who killed your pack members.
Trust me, you're not the first potato dweller that I have met," she said
and seemed to buzz with energy. "So, does anybody have any idea where
the rogues could be?" Her question was answered with silence. She hung
her head with a deep sigh.

"Thought so. Thankfully, I may have an idea to who is behind
this." This caught everyone's attention.

"Who?" Thomas took a step towards us, and I growled at him.

"Mind your step," I warned. He didn't seem to hear but, instead,
focused all his attention on Kei.

"Tell me. If you even have the slightest hint of who it could be,
then I want you to spit it out now."

"Or what?" I groaned internally as she had that familiar,
challenging glint in her eyes.

"Don't worry, sweet pea. I have my ways."

*"Let me beat his face in,"* Axel snarled loudly inside my head. I
had to grit my teeth from the pressure, knowing that if Thomas kept this
up, I wouldn't be able to hold him back any longer.

"Too bad you're not going to be able to try them. If you even
dare to do anything to her, I'll be the one to be worried about instead of
the rogues." He simply scoffed.

"How do you put up with this? I bet I can show you a better time."

His smile was the thing that made me finally snap, and my world went red with Axel's rage.

# Chapter 21

*Kei Valancia*

Was it totally horrible that I found Ryker's rage so enjoyable? Yes, yes it was. But you know, the mate bond is such a big B, but you have to live with it.

I sat in amazement as his power engulfed the whole room, the dark glittery form writhing around his body.

I relaxed deeper into the couch and watched silently as Ryker's black form disappeared a moment before reappearing behind the other outline of the Potato Man.

*"He was totally holding back on our fight,"* Rei pouted. I chuckled quietly.

*"Then I guess we'll have a rematch soon,"* I said. I watched as the Potato Man was lifted in the air and thrown across the room, over my head and crashing into the wall. Ryker hadn't let up, however, as he appeared beside him in a flash.

The walls shook as Ryker lifted him up and slammed him against it, his arm outstretched while his hand seemed to be clamped around his throat. I heard Potato Man's choked gasps, and his hands scrambled to unwrap Ryker's fingers. I knew it would be impossible to do so.

*"Kei, do something!"* Brad's voice said through mind link. I turned my head to give him a pouting look.

"Aww, but it's so fun. Come on, you have to admit that he was asking for it."

"Even so, if Ryker kills him, Thomas's pack will be even more vulnerable from losing its alpha." I couldn't argue so I sighed and got up slowly.

"I hate it when you're right." Sighing again, I strode over to where the two men quarreled. The man was now on the ground while Ryker stood over him, his black power now pushing down onto Potato Man, I guess who is named Thomas. Before I interrupted, however, I studied the way Ryker's power grew, filling the whole room with its intensity.

"Kei." I must have been standing there a bit too long as Brad warned me again.

"All right, all right, I'm going," I walked over and stood beside Ryker without touching him. "Come on, babe, we all know you're livid, and you want to kill the man, but let's try and let your anger out in a more productive way." He ignored me. *Uh, excuse me?* "King, come on. Put the man down." I said again, trying to be soothing.

"Kei, stay out of it," he growled back at me.

No, no, no, no. Did he just growl at us?

*"Yes. And we're going to deal with that later, but right now, let's just ignore it."*

"I know. But dang it, he's lucky he's my mate," I muttered before finally laying a hand on his shoulder. Just as I did, Potato Man had to open his fat mouth once again.

"Why don't you listen to your little mate, King?" I facepalmed. *He was really asking to die, wasn't he?* Ryker made a move to do something, but I wrapped my arms around his torso.

"Woah, there hot shot. Let's just let the Potato Man go and talk like civilized people. Sound good?" I patted his chest while I hugged his back. His muscles were coiled tight underneath my hands, and I could sense his anger waning.

"Don't worry, King—" I leaned over Ryker's side while unwrapping my arms and threw a punch at Potato Man's face. My fist made contact, and that shut him up. Ryker still had a grip on his throat but not as tight as he was able to breathe more easily.

"Look, Potato Man, I would really suggest that you shut your mouth." I reached up and gripped Ryker's hand that was around his throat, gently unwrapping his fingers.

I managed to get Potato Man out of his death grip before he fell to the ground, his back sliding down the wall. I interlaced our hands, and I pulled Ryker away.

"Well, that was close. Maybe you'll learn your lesson to shut up next time." Thomas coughed loudly before I heard his sharp intake of breath. Ryker stood beside me quietly, and I shot him a sideways glance. Even though he seemed calmed down, I could still sense the animosity underneath. His power was also writhing around like an angry snake.

"You—" I was cut off by an intense wave of heat going through my body. I choked on my next words and gripped onto Ryker's arm like a lifeline. I honestly didn't know what was worse; breaking twenty bones or getting blasted by what seemed like a flame thrower. Why did the Heat have to be so painful? Sure, I got it. We are part wolf and not, needing to mate and all, but isn't the monthly curse enough? *I guess not.* I could see Ryker's worry suddenly bloom around him.

*"Don't say anything. Follow me."* My voice sounded weak even through the mind link, but I managed to drag him towards the door without stumbling.

"Brad, King and I have some business to attend to. We'll deal with Potato Man when we come back."

I didn't give him a chance to reply as I pulled the door open with unnecessary force and yanking Ryker behind me. He still hadn't said anything, but I could feel his growing concern. As the door shut behind him, my knees collapsed from underneath me, the pain almost unbearable. It ripped through me like knives, tearing and burning everything inside. I hardly noticed Ryker wrap his arms around me to keep me from hitting the ground, my senses all blurry.

"Take... Me... Room..." My words were broken by my heavy gasps and pants. Seeming to understand, he immediately picked me up, hooking one arm underneath my knees while wrapping the other around my back to cradle me to his chest.

I didn't notice how we suddenly appeared into my room, the black outlines of the furniture and walls blending together into an inky mess of black. Another shot of heat filled my body, and I reached up and ripped my shirt off. I felt myself being lowered onto the bed, clutching to Ryker's shirt tightly. As he made a move to slide next to me, I slapped him weakly on the arm.

"What was that for?" he questioned, sliding his hand over my clammy skin. Almost instantly, cool relief filled the places where he touched. I sighed in relief before relaxing slightly.

"After... all... of these... is done, I require a... rematch." I was still out of breath from the pain, and it still lingered just beneath the surface. I closed my eyes, and my hand searched around until I finally found his.

"Why do you say that?" He sounded amused, and I squeezed his hand lightly.

"Because you didn't fight with your full powers."

"What's with you and your need to fight me? Can you just be satisfied with your win?"

"No."

He sighed. We lay there for a few moments in silence before I started saying, "The reason one is that I practically abused you since you didn't even really fight back. You do know that it's okay to hit me for real when we're practice fighting."

"But you're a woman." I opened my eyes and stared at nothing. Literally.

"I respect your morals for not hitting a woman. Actually, I think that's amazing, but you have to know that I am stronger than what you give me credit for. The fact that I am a woman overshadows the fact that I am part werewolf and fae and, might I add, born from very strong bloodlines, yet you treat me like I am made of glass. That's not bad, but there is going to be a time where I am going to be battling right beside you if you like it or not. So when I am in a practice fight, I'm going to throw real punches as if the person I'm up against was the enemy and I expect that other person to do the same."

When I was finished with my little rant, Ryker stayed silent for a long time. His hand stroked my stomach comfortingly. I opened my mouth to say something but quietly groaned instead as another wave of heat crashed over me. The Heat is something happens naturally in many animals, such as wolves, dogs, cats, and so on. With werewolves, it's the same concept when the female begins to go into Heat, and she is ready to complete the mating process with her partner, her body going through phases to speed it up. One of those steps would be a hormonal war going on throughout the body, which is one of the main reasons why I am sweating out of every pore that covered every inch of my skin while Ryker's touch provided a short reprieve of the inferno that is my body.

To put it simply, it's just another thing that woman have to deal. *Hurray, girl power.*

I felt the bed creak as Ryker got up, his hand leaving my stomach. I lay still, clenching my jaw as the pain rushed back full force before Ryker slid back beside me.

"I'm sorry," he whispered against my hair, pulling me close to his now bare chest. The skin-on-skin contact helped greatly to ease the pain. Now, it was a dull ache, and my skin was slick with sweat.

"It's not your fault," I replied weakly. "Sometimes, being a woman sucks." He chuckled, and the vibrations were transmitted to my cheek which was plastered to his chest.

"Being a man has its downfalls too."

"Oh? And what would those be?" I had closed my eyes and ignored the stabbing heat as it became more prominent.

"For one, we have to beat other men with sticks to keep them away from our woman," he said in a serious tone.

"It's especially a chore with me," I teased weakly, not really meaning it.

"Yes, it is." He sounded serious. Chuckling, I drew formless patterns on his chest with my finger.

"I guess I should apologize then."

"*Lune*, I enjoy it." I gave him a weird look.

"Why?" I felt his hand absentmindedly play with my hair.

"I let off steam that way," he answered.

"You do know that you don't literally beat them off with a stick." I felt the movement of his shrug.

"Let's not worry about the details." I laughed and felt my eyes droop. He rubbed my back in soothing circles, keeping the pain at bay.

"Stay with me," I mumbled as sleep began dragging me down.

"Always."

# Chapter 22

*Ryker Dare*

I watched as Kei breathed evenly in her sleep, her face relaxed and so much younger than normal. Brushing a stray hair out of her face, she nudged closer to me. Smiling softly, I lay beside her and made sure she was fully tucked under the covers before making myself comfortable.

*"She looks like an angel,"* Axel murmured.

"With an attitude of a demon," I remarked dryly. Before I could react, Kei raised her hand and covered my face with her palm.

"I know I have a soul blacker than tar and all but at least talk about me when I'm not in earshot," she muttered before rolling over and falling back to sleep. I stared at the back of her head for a long moment, not quite sure what just had happened.

*"I thought she was asleep."*

*"She is."*

"I'm not quite there yet," Kei said, her back still turned towards us. "You and Axel are louder than two teenage girls gossiping about…" She trailed off, and it was replaced by her quiet breathing. Chuckling quietly, I wrapped an arm around her waist and pulled her back to my chest. Smiling slightly, I soon followed her into the darkness.

* * *

I woke with a start as I heard a small knock at the door. I sat up slowly and stared down at Kei's sleeping form before carefully slipping out of bed. I looked out the window to see the night sky twinkling with the stars. Padding over to the door, I swung it open to see my beta, Clark, standing in the hallway looking disheveled. Instantly, I got a bad feeling in my gut.

"Give me a minute." I shut the door and began getting dressed quietly. When I had finished slipping my shirt on, I walked over to the bed. I leaned down and brushed a stray hair out of Kei's face. She wrinkled her nose slightly before it smoothened out. As if habit, I bent down and kissed her cheek softly before pulling back and stepping away. I heard her let out a quiet sigh as I shut the door behind me. Facing Clark, I began walking down the hall.

"Tell me what has happened." Clark's hair was out of its usual neatness and was sticking straight into the air as if he had run his fingers through it multiple times. His clothes were ruffled and looked as if he just thrown them on without a care.

"Alpha Hale has caught wind of another rogue attack that is supposed to happen tonight." I glanced sharply over at him.

"What time is it now?"

"It's 3 AM right now, alpha. He got the message about 2:40." Before I could ask any more questions, we had arrived at his office, and I swung the door open without knocking.

Alpha Hale and another man were talking but stilled once I entered the room. They, however, relaxed once they knew it was me.

"Alpha Dare, we have things to discuss."

"So I've heard." Clark and I walked in, shutting the door behind us. "Who is this man?" I scrutinized the man calmly, noting that he looked familiar.

"This is Jett. He's my beta." He bowed his head in respect. I finally remembered where I had seen him, recalling that he was the one who took the woman that attacked Kei in the infirmary. He was a broad, muscular man with long light brown hair up in a ponytail. His eyes were a light hazel and had a critical look at them.

"Alpha Dare, it's an honor to meet you." He held out his hand to shake to which I took it.

"Likewise," was my reply and pulled away. Turning to Alpha Hale, I turned serious.

"When did you get the news of this attack?"

"One of the missing bodies was found just at the edge of the woods just a little over an hour ago. Upon inspection, a note was found on his person."

"Do you have it?" He didn't say anything but pulled out a piece of paper out of his pocket of his suit pants and handed it to me. Unfolding it, the neat handwriting surprised me only slightly before I began reading the single sentence.

*"You better be ready at dawn, Alpha Hale."* That was all it said, and I looked up as I finished reading.

"I'm assuming another rogue attack will take place," Hale said, his tone hard. Folding the note back carefully. My thoughts swirled around. Whoever this person was, it seemed they were the masterminds behind all of these attacks, but the question was why?

Handing the note back, I sat down. Everybody followed suit, knowing that it was a silent permission to do the same.

"Whatever it means, we should expect the worse. I don't get the impression that these are ordinary rogues at work here." Alpha Hale nodded in agreement.

"Whoever wrote this letter wanted to warn us about whatever is to come, but I still have no clue what to expect," he said with a shake of his head.

"It's probably well-known now that I am currently here as well. That means that they either have a plan to take both you and me or they are extremely powerful."

"They probably know that my pack isn't the strongest and see this as an opportunity to take over," he added. I shook my head at his reasoning.

"Maybe, but he would have waited to attack when I was gone. Having me here would prove to be disadvantageous for him. Yet, he sends this now with me still here." I sighed and pinched the bridge of my nose. "Let's not dwell on the 'why' for now. We need to prepare for the attack, Clark."

"Yes, Alpha," was his immediate response.

"Get my men ready. Tell them of the attack at dawn and to be prepared."

"Yes, Alpha," he said again before standing and bowing, leaving the room silently.

"Jett, go make sure that everybody is in place," Hale ordered. He nodded and left the room.

"Are the others already being evacuated?"

"Yes, and while you were here, I sent for my sister and her mate to get Kei." I raised an eyebrow.

"You have a sister?" He chuckled.

"Yes, I do. Her name is Sophia, and her mate is Elijah Hughes. I'm happy to see that a man can put up with her craziness." He chuckled to himself, but I saw the love for his sister shine in his eyes.

"I would like to meet her sometime," I said.

"Maybe after this is all over." He sighed heavily, and I stood up

I looked at the clock on the wall to see it was 3:27. The sun didn't rise until 5:40.

"I must go—" I didn't get to finish however as the door was slammed open. A woman stood in the doorway with a grave expression while a man stood behind her with the same look.

"Sophia," Alpha Hale stood up in surprise. "I thought you went to get Kei?"

"She's not there," I froze and stared at her.

"What?"

*"Don't panic. She probably wandered somewhere like she usually does."*

*"And that's supposed to make me feel better? How?"*

"I'm sorry, but I think she was... kidnapped." Sophia looked at me with an uneasy expression, but I didn't have time to dwell on it. Without warning, I disappeared and reappeared in her room, my eyes searching frantically for her.

*"Kei? Can you hear me? Kei!"*

Nothing, only silence, the gold string that connected us was still there but dim as if she was still asleep. I followed the string to her location but it only ended up in blackness, and I opened my eyes to the empty room. I felt panic, and uncontrollable rage began to envelop me, storming over to the bed with the covers all messed up as if she had tried to fight. Letting out a roar filled with anger and pain that shook the air itself, I punched a hole in the wall.

"That bastard! He took her." I felt my canines elongate as it finally dawned on me and my power thrash around the room. I stared at the spot where I last saw her, her face relaxed and looking like an angel. Yet now she was gone, and I had no idea where she was. Clenching my hands, I felt my claws grow and pierce my skin, but I couldn't make myself care.

"Alpha King." I didn't turn to look at Hale.

"There won't be an attack at dawn, Hale. They already have what they wanted. It was all a damn distraction, and I fell for it so easily." My eyes scanned the bed as if Kei would magically appear. Just as my gaze rested on a pillow did I finally see a piece of paper lying on it. Reaching out, I grabbed it and almost tore it in the process of unfolding it.

*Alpha Dare, if I may be blunt, you are surprisingly easy to deceive given how long you have lived. I would have thought that you would have caught on even after reading the short message that I had left for you. But I guess I can't complain. I have what I wanted. Your stupidity has let me get what I have been chasing for years. Don't worry; Kei is finally with me once more where she was meant to be. I'll break her once more, and she'll never think of you ever again.*

Red was such a horrible color, the color of anger and everything bad. Tearing the paper, I roared. I suddenly shifted and ran right out of the window, the glass shattering around me like sharp raindrops.

All of the men stared up at me in surprise and fear as I landed on the ground with ease, shooting off like a bullet into the woods. I searched for her scent, but it was futile. She was gone, and I knew that whoever had her was the one that had created her demons. Stopping abruptly, I threw my head back and howled. You could hear my sorrow and anger ring through the air.

Yet, I knew that I would do whatever it takes to find her. I would burn the whole world just for her if it meant getting her back. Whoever had her better be ready for the hell that I was bringing.

No one messed with our mate.

# Chapter 23

*Kei Valancia*

Being kidnapped was probably the most cliché thing to happen. Being kidnapped while *sleeping* is just so predictable. But it happened, and I will forever feel the shame of it.

"Come in here, you rat faced psycho! I think we need to have a little chat." Nothing, no response, whatsoever. Sighing, I slid down the concrete wall.

When I had woken up, I couldn't get a visual of the room at all. Not even a little spark of power would come. So I had to explore everything by hand, finding out that I was in a box-like concrete room with no windows. I had felt ridges that indicated a steel door but found no door knob. I also couldn't tell if there was a light on, and it didn't really matter anyway. However, there was the mattress that I was currently lying on, and that was about it. Nothing else occupied the room except for me and my humiliation of being taken.

*"Don't forget we're still in heat also."*

I groaned and thumped my head against the wall. "Don't remind me. I really don't want to think about being burned from the inside at the moment," I replied out loud.

*"It's going to happen whether we want it to or not."*

"I know, I know. But it's like pushing junk under the bed and then forgetting it's there until something starts stinking and then you actually have to deal with it."

*"So in other words, you're going to push it under the bed until it starts burning."*

"Bingo! It's no use worrying about it now if it's not bothering anyone." I heard her laugh.

*"Whatever you say."*

"Besides, we have another problem that we need to be worrying about. For example, our crazy captor." Her sigh resonated through my head.

*"There's nothing we can do without our powers."*

"You make it sound like we can't fight without them. We've trained how to fight for years for when the time like this came."

*"You're right. I'm sorry."*

"No need to apologize. It does seem kind of bleak." I chuckled to myself. "But don't worry; we have enough skill to kick some butt." This is how it went for hours, or maybe it was minutes. My sense of time was just horrible. Rei and I chatted about everything and nothing, trying to keep our minds off of what we really wanted to think about. I was lying flat on my back, staring up at the ceiling or the blackness that was supposed to be the ceiling, anyway.

"I'm so bored." I huffed.

*"Then maybe you shouldn't be kidnapped."*

"It's not like I was asking to be! Going into heat sucks out a lot of strength, and you know that. It's only natural that I take a little nap." I heard her scoff.

*"You were out like a light."*

"Fine," I mumbled. "I was tired and not even the sound of the world ending would have woken me up."

*"Yeah, I could tell. I was the one trying to fight them off."*

"Okay, yeah I'm lame." I sighed and shut my eyes, not like it made any difference. I made my mind absolutely blank when I felt the invasive tendrils poke into my mind.

"What are you hiding, darling?" A man's voice broke the emptiness of my thoughts.

"Nothing that concerns you; that's for sure," I replied coolly. His chuckle sent chills through me.

"You seem to have grown beautifully, physically and emotionally. The way you keep up that icy persona to protect what you're really thinking is just delightful, dear."

"You seem to still be a creepy, psychopathic werewolf who needs to find a new hobby, preferably one that involves jumping off of a cliff." His laugh boomed around me, this one in reality and in my mind. I stayed still as I heard the sound of a door creak open.

"My, your beauty strikes me every time darling."

"I'm glad I'm blind so I don't have to witness the horrors of your face," I replied dully. His chuckle was my answer.

"Let's not be so hostile. I mean, it's been so long since we've been in each other's arms." I stood up without warning.

"If you dare touch me, I'll rip your limbs off and feed them to the dogs." I snarled and backed away from him. Whatever he had surrounded the room depleted everything in me. I only caught a spark of what would be his aura.

"Now, I don't think you're in the position to speak like that to me." I didn't see it coming at all as I was gripped by the throat and slammed into the wall. The force cracked the wall, the sound a loud cracking noise.

I didn't bother to fight back. Why would I do that if it only gave him pleasure?

"Oh my, you've gotten quite rebellious since I've last seen you. Why's that?" he said the last part almost to himself.

"Oh, I don't know. Wait! Maybe it's because I was away from you. It worked miracles, really." The punch hit me from nowhere, and I knew that I was slightly screwed.

*"You think?"*

*"While I'm getting my butt whooped, try to see if you can come up with a plan, yeah?"*

Just as I had said this to her, I pulled back my head and head-butted him hard. He groaned as his grip loosened, and I took this chance. Slipping out of his grasp, I crouched and kicked his feet from underneath him. I was already at the door before he even hit the ground. Turns out, I remembered it didn't have a doorknob and being blind, I couldn't see if there would be anything else that would make the door open from the inside.

"Great, my first obstacle is a door with no doorknob. Why does life suck sometimes?" I kicked it angrily before turning back to face the biggest douche on the planet.

"Well, that was a surprise." He chuckled to himself, and he must have stood up because I heard the sound of him brushing off of his clothes. "You've gotten quite strong. But like every wild beast, I will tame you." I couldn't help but scoff.

"What is with you and every other male that wants to tame me? Goddess, I don't want to be tame. I want to be me, and not you nor any other man will change that. I will only be tamed by the one that is mine and no one else. So I would just pack your bags and get out of line." He was silent for a long moment, doing what, I have no idea.

"You actually think you have a mate? Where did you get such a ridiculous thought?"

"Well, it's certainly not you, Leon." I was taken by surprise by his snarl and hardly noticed that I was shoved against the wall again.

"You are mine. I raised you to be this way. Therefore, you have an obligation to me."

"Obligation? Making me into a murdering machine and torturing me into submission is not only enough, but now, I have an obligation to you?" I hadn't felt such rage in years. Only the man that held me captive could make me this angry.

I reached up and gripped his wrist tightly that was pinning me to the wall. I squeezed it so hard I felt the bones pop beneath my fingers.

"You have no freaking right to say that. I spent years living in hell because of you and not even the pope, president, and the goddess could make me have any feeling towards you other than hate. So take that bit of info and shove it up your psycho ass." I tossed his arm away from me while pushing his body with my other elbow. I felt him stumble away while saying nothing. I stood there glaring in his general direction, but he could have moved somewhere else in the room, and I wouldn't have noticed.

When I sniffed the air a couple of times, however, I could tell that he was only a few feet away from me. I stood tense, waiting for him to lash out like he used to do, but he never did. He obviously expected me to feel this way as he chuckled.

"You're not the only one to change, love." I was relieved to hear his footsteps retreat back to the direction of the door. "However, don't expect your *King* to come rescue you. He can't find what he's looking for if it doesn't exist." With those words, he left with the slamming of the door. I hardly heard it, though, as his words echoed through my mind. His message rang loud and clear. If Ryker can't feel our connection, he's going to think that I'm dead.

*"Can I start being pessimistic now?"* I leaned against the wall and slid down to the floor, the feeling of the familiar despair come back to me.

*"You can be more negative than an old man."*

# Chapter 24

*Kei Valancia*

*Black.* Black was the only thing I could see. You never truly value something until you've lost it. These thoughts struck a distant memory in me, and I was pulled back into my past self — the one who was lost and scared, the one who wandered the forest looking for something, anything to help. But even seven-year-old me knew that help wouldn't come. That sense of hopelessness struck me once again, but anger quickly followed.

I was acting like a child, sitting here wallowing in self-pity. Hell, some kids wouldn't be doing what I was doing at this moment. Sure, Ryker probably had no clue where I am and had no idea that I'm even alive. But I was, and I knew that he would look for me anyway. Just because he's a stubborn two-hundred-and-something-year-old coot and also because he is my mate. Plus, I love him, and if it were he that was kidnapped, of course, I would bust my butt searching for him, so hopefully my feelings would somehow reach him. I highly doubt it, but a girl could dream, right? Sighing, I thumped my head against the mattress. I wondered how long I'd been gone.

It's a curious thing, time that is. It's a force that is as powerful as the goddess herself, maybe even more frightening. It's the enemy that I could never defeat. The years that I've been captive, Time was the biggest butt of all. It moved slowly, sluggishly as if I were moving in mud. However, the moments spent with Ryker flew by in a blur, and I felt regret for acting the way I did. To be honest, I knew I wasn't the best person to hang out with, but that didn't stop me from fixing my attitude. Does this make me a bad person? *Probably.* This was motivation enough to leave this place alive so I could put on my big girl pants and start acting like an adult.

*"Now, you want to be good."* Rei scoffed.

"Yeah, well, being here gives me a lot to think about since it's so boring." I flipped over and buried my face into the mattress but instantly regretted as the smell of mold and something like pee filled my nostrils. I jumped off of the bed and landed on my butt on the cold floor.

"You would think that I would be immune to such smells, but that was just gross." I made a noise of disgust in the back of my throat. "It's terrible. I've become a big sissy."

*"There's nothing wrong with being one."*

"No, but I don't have time to be one." Standing, I brushed my clothes off, finally noticing that I was just dressed in a large shirt with the hem falling to my upper thighs, glad that I was dressed in underwear also. "I'm really losing it, Rei." I groaned and paced the floor.

*"Calm down. Take a deep breath and relax."* I stopped mid pace and closed my eyes. I followed her instructions, took a deep breath, and let it out slowly.

*"You calm?"* I smiled.

"I'm calm. Thanks," Walking around again with less vigor, I splayed my hand against the wall and dragged it along as I walked. The bumpy surface cold and it made me feel lonesome. Shaking my head, I continued on, but about forty minutes of feeling every crevice and small mysterious holes, I could not find anything that would help me in escaping.

"All right! We are royally screwed." I had just thrown my hands in the air in exasperation when the door squeaked open. Twirling around, I bent down in a slight crouch. I smelled the familiar scent of smoke and disease. Leon had paid another visit.

"I see you're quite restless," he mused. I smiled dryly.

"Your observation would be correct. Now, what do you want?" I heard him click his tongue. Suddenly, I felt his presence right behind me.

"Aren't you, at least, a little curious as to why I'm holding you in here?" His breath brushed against my ear, and I had to hold in a horrified shudder.

"I can't say that I really care," I responded deadpanned. His arm wrapped around my neck and squeezed, cutting off my oxygen. Yet, I didn't react at all.

"Oh, you should because in a month. You're going to become one of the most powerful wolves on the planet. Not even the Alpha King will be able to do anything." He sounded gleeful as he whispered in my ear, and I wanted to turn around and punch him so hard in the face that not even he would be able to recognize it.

"And do you know the reason, my love?" He loosened his arm slightly so that I could answer. Inhaling quietly, I answered him.

"I don't have an inkling of an idea what you're talking about."

"Well, my dear, isn't it your birthday next month?"

"So what of it?" He giggled, and it made me want to vomit. It was just too creepy.

"You get the best birthday gift ever! Your powers." I stiffened further in his grasp.

"I already have my powers, you crazy oaf." A punch to my ribs was a warning to shut up.

"No, darling, you're real powers. What you have now is just a tidbit to what you actually possess." He pushed me away from his chest abruptly before turning me around to face him. He was so close that I could feel his hot, damp breath on my face. "Imagine it like this, the powers you have now is like a single raindrop. But the cloud that produced that single raindrop is getting bigger from holding in all the rest of the raindrops just so that there isn't a downpour. However on your twenty-first birthday, that cloud is going to get too full, and it won't be able to hold back the flood that is destined to happen.

"So you see, Kei? The powers you have now are only a single raindrop. Soon the cloud is going to burst, and there's nothing you can do."

He held me closer, his nose now brushing against my own. I didn't move, talk, or hardly even breathe for a full minute. The only sound was the even breaths of Leon who seemed to be waiting for my answer. Finally, I let out a small sigh.

"First off, no, I don't see. What don't you get about me being blind? And secondly, you really are a crazy son-of-a-gun, aren't you?" I pulled back my fist and punched him as hard as I could in the face. Taken by surprise, he let go of me, must have flown across the room and slammed into the wall as a loud crash echoed inside the small room. Shaking my hand, I strode over to where the sound came from and kicked out with my foot until I felt a leg. I pulled back expecting a hit but was shocked to find that nothing happened. Almost timidly, I poked him again with my toe before freezing for his reaction. Still nothing.

*"Maybe you knocked him out?"* Rei questioned.

*"I don't know. He hasn't attacked yet, so maybe I did. If so, our luck hasn't run out yet."* Scooting around his body, I felt my way around and guided myself with the wall. Reaching out blindly, my hand came

into contact with something soft. As if bitten, I pulled back and held my hand to my chest.

"*Don't tell me that was his hair. Crazy bad guys do not get soft hair.*"

"*This one does. Now, feel above him, I think that's where the door was located.*" Reaching my hand out, I once again touched what seemed to be his hair which was soft, and it felt wrong that this evil person should get soft hair. Moving upward, however, my fingers came into contact with a cold surface with ridges that felt like the door.

"*Okay, so we figured out that this was the door. It still seems to be intact, and therefore, any hope of us actually getting out of here went below zero again.*" A groan made me pull back and take a few steps back as Leon began to stir.

"*Hurry, punch him in the face again.*"

"*I would, but I don't know where his face is!*"

"*Then just swing your fists, woman!*"

Without a second thought, I pulled back my fist and let it go, but sadly, it never made contact. At that exact moment, I felt his hand enclose around my fist, stopping my attack. Not a moment later, I found myself flying across the room and slamming against the wall, my head snapping back.

*I should get a medal for most times getting slammed into a flat surface,* I thought to myself. I felt my own conscious begin to wane, and if I could see, my vision would be black around the edges. Faintly, I heard footsteps coming towards me, but I no longer had the energy to move. They stopped beside me, and a voice spoke right beside my right ear.

"You will get your powers, and you will do what I say. So, you better enjoy your stay because it's going to be a long month." I didn't reply; more accurately, I couldn't. I hardly even heard his retreating footsteps and the slamming of the door behind him.

Slumping against the wall, I held in my tears and welcomed the blackness that made me numb.

# Chapter 25

*Ryker Dare*

Two days had passed, two grueling days without the contact of our mate, and I would rather feel my heart being torn out than endure any more of this pain. Axel was angry, not only with me but also with himself for not figuring it out sooner. I didn't give him any words of comfort. How could I when I knew it was all a lie?

"Alpha, I'm sorry, but we couldn't find any leads." I didn't do anything but instead slammed my fist through the wall. Clark only looked at me with worry.

"Alpha Dare, please try to stay calm. If we don't have any clear heads, we aren't going to have a good time finding her." I turned on my heel and glared at Alpha Hale.

"Don't you think I don't know that? I can't feel her anymore and have no clue to where that bastard took her." Sucking in a deep breath, I exhaled slowly.

"Who are we looking for exactly?" Clark asked.

"A man named Leon Grayson." I growled his name, and I wanted to use every torture technique that I knew, slowly and painfully. As Hale tensed it caught my attention. "Does the name sound familiar to you?" He stared at me but shook his head.

"I haven't heard that name in years."

"You know him?" I stalked over to his desk and placed both palms on the surface, my presence a demanding one.

"Yeah, I knew him, never stopped working and was the most eccentric man I've ever known, but back then, he was harmless. Until now, it seems. Why do you think it was him that took Kei?"

"He took her and held her captive for three years until she was rescued." I ground out, feeling the familiar anger as I remembered what Kei told me. I watched as his face blanched. "And it seems he wants her back."

"Yes but for what?" he questioned.

"The reason doesn't matter. What matters is that we find him and get Kei back as soon as possible." I've just realized something, and I had to hide my surprise as Axel spoke.

*"What is it?"*

*"Kei is still in heat."* My temper flared, as did my ever growing worry. I straightened and turned on my heel towards the door. As I yanked it open, I heard the creak of the doorknob groan under my hand as I held it tightly.

"Alpha Hale, contact the other surrounding packs and set up a phone conference in about an hour. Clark, come with me." I didn't give him time to answer and walked briskly down the dim hall. I heard the door shut and hurried strides catch up to me.

"Clark, round up all of the men. Get them ready for another search, but I will be taking three men. I'm heading back to the pack house."

"What is it that you will be doing?" I stopped and stared him straight in the eyes.

"I'm getting a damn army."

* * *

I stood along with three of my men at the edge of the tree line.

"Let's go," were the words that spurred them and myself into action. Shifting with a roar, my massive paws pounded the earth as I shot off into the woods.

I made sure to slow down enough for them to keep up, but I was still ahead about twenty yards. Just as I felt that we had left the territory, another scent made me skid to a halt, and I let out a piercing growl. I heard my men stop a few feet behind me and copy my actions. Before us stood a tall man dressed in a black tailored suit. He smiled as he caught sight of us, his canines gleaming in the sunlight. It was an odd sight, seeing a man dressed in a suit standing in the woods, but underneath his air of nonchalance held danger.

"Hello, King." I narrowed my eyes. Shifting, I stood to face him.

"What are you doing here?" He simply kept smiling. I growled lowly as he reached into his pocket and began pulling something out.

"Don't worry, Alpha, it's only a phone." He pulled out a plain black flip phone. I eyed him carefully as he opened it and began punching in numbers.

"Hello?" He listened to the person on the other end. Smirking, he extended it out to me. "It's for you, Alpha." He didn't wait for me to answer but, instead, tossed the phone to me. I caught it and slowly put it next to my ear, watching the man the whole time.

"Who is this?" I heard a sharp intake of breath on the line. "Answer me," I commanded.

"Bossy as ever I see." I froze as the voice registered.

"Kei?" It was silent for one nerve-wracking moment.

"Yo, how's it going on your end King? I'm glad to hear you're still alive." I heard her chuckle, but it sounded force even through the phone. I didn't share her humor, however, and her chuckles died down. "You know, my jokes would be funnier if you laughed at them."

"Sorry if I don't find this situation funny," I remarked dryly. She huffed.

"The situation doesn't have to be funny for the joke not to be. I'm trying to lighten the mood here," she muttered. I smiled slightly before getting serious again.

"I see that the chat is going well?" The man brushed the invisible dirt off of his pressed pants.

"Where's Kei?" I demanded, Axel becoming agitated. Kei herself was surprisingly silent on the other end, her breathing barely audible.

"Why don't you ask her yourself? Go on, Kei. I know you can hear me."

"That ever-loving psychotic piece of crap knows that I don't know." She hissed over the line.

"You can't expect a blind person to just know where they are." The man sighed.

"Can you put the phone on speaker, King?" she requested. I didn't answer but followed her request. "I swear if you hurt one hair on King's head, I will personally rip your limbs off one by one until you're just a useless, bloody stump, Leon."

Blood roared in my ears, and my eyes zeroed onto the man before me. This was the Leon Grayson, and every fiber of my being wanted to shift and rip him to shreds. Unperturbed by my growing murderous intent and Kei's threats, he chuckled.

"Oh, my love, you should be more worried about yourself. Everybody, begin."

*"Get him,"* I commanded through mind link, and the three men roared in answer. As they ran past me to the grinning Leon, I made a move to shift but stopped as a scream ricocheted through the phone.

"Get your filthy hands off of me!" There was a clattering sound as if she had dropped the phone and vigorous shuffling followed after. "King! Don't underestimate Leon and try not to—" She grunted, and my grip nearly shattered the phone. "—worry about me. He's not going to do anything to me but"— more grunting and a cry of pain—"he'll kill you to get to me. And one last thing, I'm sorry." This time, a sharp scream full of agony belonged to Kei herself.

"Kei!" A muffled thump was heard close to the receiver. The silence was slowly killing me, and I forgot everything around me. I heard my men shout through the mind link, saying that Leon had vanished, but I couldn't make myself care at the moment.

"I'm sorry…" Her voice was barely audible, and it broke my heart to hear her like this.

"Kei, you have nothing to apologize for." I felt my emotions stretching thin.

"I just… wanted to tell… you that." There was another sharp cry before the line went dead. I stared at the screen blankly before uncontrollable fury took over everything. Crushing the phone into smithereens, small plastic shards digging into my skin which caused blood to drip between my fingers.

"Alpha, we lost him," Jarrod said, a look of resignation on his face. I turned my gaze on him, and he took a step back, his eyes widening.

"We are continuing our way back to the pack house. Go." He bowed his head quickly and left without another word. I could smell their fear, but I didn't care. No one had seen anything yet, and Leon Grayson better gets ready. I'm about to show him just what happens when you piss off the Alpha King. I threw the trashed phone on the ground and shifted. Sprinting through the woods, I sent a promise to Kei.

*"I'm coming, Lune. Whatever it takes, I'm going to bring you home."* Just as I had thought this, an excruciating pain burst through my chest and my neck where my mark was located. Howling, I staggered to a stop.

*"Kei!"* Axel's pain filled howl echoed through my skull, and I instantly knew what was going on.

Someone was erasing our mark.

# Chapter 26

*Kei Valancia*

I gasped and shot up, unseeing. Gripping my chest, my heart pounded like a thunderstorm, and I tried to calm down. It has almost been a month since I was captured, a month away from Ryker. And it hurts, everything in me does. My heart throbs every day; Rei hardly even speaks to me anymore, and Leon still comes to pay a visit. Hugging my knees to my chest, I curled in on myself.

"You know if life gave me lemons, I would squeeze the juice into Leon's eyes so they would burn, and I would take that time to stab him with the dullest, dirtiest knife in the world," I muttered. Of course, muttering gruesome images of Leon's death was now a frequent thing, and it seemed to be the only thing that kept me sane. I lifted my hand and scratched the spot where he bit trying to get Ryker's mark off. I remember clearly as if it had happened yesterday when his canines sank into the soft flesh of my neck. The pain that stiffened my muscles was the worst that I had ever experienced. To be honest, I would rather go into Heat for a year then feel that pain again.

"Goddess, I swear if I don't get my happy ending at the end of this sick, twisted yellow brick road, then I'm going on a rampage. I'm serious." I sat up slowly and looked pointedly up. All alone in the dark could really screw with your brain you know. I'd never really got to experience being "blind" in the sense where it's all black, but now that I've been living with it for a month, it's a real eye-opener. I snorted to myself.

"I see you still have your sense of humor." I jumped, startled to hear Rei's voice. I sat crossed legged and dug my finger into the mattress.

"If I don't have that, then what will be left of me?" I replied back with emptiness.

"I didn't say that it was a bad thing. I'm just surprised you still have the energy to crack jokes." I smiled brokenly.

"Yeah, well, sitting in this hellish room for almost a month makes a person go stir crazy you know."

"I suppose so."

I sighed heavily before standing up. I was careful not to bump the tray of food which consisted of dry chicken and broth with water. Not bad, it could be worse. Pacing, I ran a hand through my oily hair. I was surprised to find out that Leon would actually let me take a shower, but he stopped letting me a week ago. Now, I'm gross and feel like a slimy fish.

Why am I worrying about being stinky? "Only because it diverts my worries from my biggest one: Ryker."

I knew his mark was still there, and I knew that our bond was still intact. I couldn't link minds with him or feel whatever he was feeling, but I knew he was alive. That's all that mattered to me at this point. Actually, the bond seemed rather strong today. Usually, I barely noticed it, but today, it felt as if the connection was stronger and I felt myself drift to the door.

"Something is off," Rei said, guarded.

"Something is." I pressed my ear against the door, trying to hear anything but came up empty. Huffing, I took a few steps back, and just as I did, the door screeched on its hinges, and I was barely able to move further in the room in time as it let out a loud snap. It was silent for a second before it seemed to land on the floor just foot away from me. I stood in the middle of the room, and my mind went blank.

"What am I supposed to do in this situation?"

"Run?" Rei offered. I felt my noodly limbs and felt that if anything, I might as well try. Taking a step forward, I prepared myself to make a mad dash, but instead, I was tackled into a hard body. I stiffened in surprise and made a move to thrash around but was stopped by a rumbling voice.

"Kei." His voice cracked on my name and tears instantly flooded my eyes. His familiar warmth flushed into me, and the connection between us crackled with energy.

"Ryker? I swear if you're a mirage, I'm going to punch you." His chest rumbled with his laugh.

"I promise I'm not. I'll even prove it." He didn't give me time to react as he bent down and kissed me. That was what did it for me, the feeling of his soft lips on mine insistent yet gentle. Reaching up and wrapping my arms around his neck, I let the tears fall down my cheeks as I returned it with just as much passion. When we finally pulled away, we were both breathless.

"You're so freaking amazing. You know that, right?" I murmured. His hand trailed down my face softly.

"Only for you." I smiled and then realized about my hygiene. Pulling back, I raised my hands in a defensive manner.

"Now, that's settled. It's best to stay away for a bit. I'm rather potent to the nostrils at this moment." I could practically see him roll his eyes at me.

"Do you think I really give a rat's ass that you stink? I haven't seen you in a month. I think your body aroma is the least of our problems." I pursed my lips and nodded.

"I guess you're right. By the way, how did you find me?" I didn't fight him as he wrapped an arm around my waist and began pulling me along.

"There was a note sent to me. It didn't have any signature to it, and no one saw who dropped it off. It spoke of an old run down building with a cellar, and there I would find my mate." He laughed dryly. "So, you can imagine how I sent everybody on a wild goose chase searching for a building fitting this description."

"Well, whoever tipped you off, I'm glad. Now, that I think about it, where's Leon?" I didn't need my powers to feel his mood darken.

"He wasn't here when we came. No one was actually." I stiffened and quickened my pace.

"That does not sound good at all," he agreed. With the help of Ryker, he guided me through a dank space, his words about a cellar coming to mind. It seemed like ages when we ascend the steps. I had counted five steps before I felt him move, and a door creak opened above us.

"Come." He held my hand, and I followed, feeling suddenly dizzy. Funny since I can't even see. As we reached what seemed like the top, I stumbled. Ryker managed to catch me before I completely fell, wrapping one arm underneath my legs while he used the other to cradle me close to his chest.

"Kei, are you all right?" I felt my best friend called pain make an appearance. She plunged her dagger through my being, ripping my insides to shreds. I let out a muffled groan as it felt like pain itself flowed through my limbs. "Kei!" I hardly noticed that I was thrashing against him and he cursed.

"Kei! Baby, tell me what's wrong?" I distinctly heard other footsteps pound closer to us, but I ignored it all. Gripping onto his shirt, I pulled myself closer to his face painfully.

"It's starting." I managed to say, my conscious waning.

"What is?" I felt my grip loosening, and my hand dangled in the air.

"My birthday... My powers are supposed to come or some crap like that." I clutched my chest as it felt like my heart was about to burst. "Yet... I don't... Pain..." My words came in a stuttering mess, making me almost incoherent.

"Don't worry; we're going to get you help. Everybody, let's go!" he barked out, and I felt him hold me tighter as he began to run.

"Don't worry... I'll be..." I never finished, as I couldn't seem to form the words to finish the sentence. The last thing I heard was the desperate cry Ryker calling my name.

# Chapter 27

*Ryker Dare*

I sat beside the bed with my head hung low. With Kei's limp hand in mine, I brushed my lips across her palm. A day had passed since we rescued Kei from the abandoned house, a day since I've last seen her awake.

"Please wake up," I whispered, stroking her hair. Her dark lashes brushed her cheeks, and her lips were tilted down in a small frown. Her usual creamy skin was paler than usual, and I felt my control over my emotions crack each time that I looked at her.

"Alpha." I didn't look away from her sleeping face as Clark entered the room. "There's a man here, says that you would know who he was."

"I don't care. Tell him I'm busy."

"Yeah because staring at Kei's face like a creep is very time-consuming." I jerked my head and saw the Draven man standing in the doorway. He smirked, but I noticed the dark bags underneath his eyes.

"What the hell are you doing here?" Instead of sounding annoyed, my voice came out tired. Clark took this as a sign to leave and left the two of us alone with my unconscious mate.

"What do you think I'm doing? I'm here to see her." His eyes drifted over to Kei. I growled quietly automatically before sending him a glare. Draven saw this and rolled his eyes. Strolling over, he sat on her opposite side. He reached over to grab her hand, but once he saw my withering glare, he seemed to decide against it.

"You know, even if you don't believe me Kei is like a sister to me. Though, you should have seen the time when we very first met." He chuckled to himself. "If you think she's bad now, she was horrible when she first began living with us. I remember it clearly when I introduced myself. She only stared at me blankly, and she sneered at me. It was rather a frightening sight actually."

"Why are you telling me this?" He shrugged.

"Maybe because you're her mate? I don't know. But during your last visit, I noticed how much happier she looked, and that's all I really want for her." As he said the next part, he stared right at me. "So, if you do anything that hurts Kei, Alpha King or not, I'm going to hunt you down and kill you."

I didn't say anything but stare at him. I knew he was telling the truth by the way he clenched his hands and the determined look in his eye. His body language was tense, and if he was lying, then he deserved an Oscar. I smirked.

"I'll hold you to it then," and that was all I said for the rest of his visit. We sat together in silence, looking at Kei or getting lost in our own thoughts.

*"She seemed so tame and innocent when we first met her,"* Axel mused.

*"We were completely wrong to think that."*

*"Yeah, we were."* It was quiet for a moment. *"Wait, did you see her hand twitch?"* I didn't, but I directed my gaze towards her still fingers. We waited, and I squeezed her hand gently. I held my breath, and it seemed like days until I felt her, a gentle squeeze back. I straightened and leaned closer, forgetting that Draven was even here.

"Kei? Can you hear me?" This time, what I saw next excited me even more. Her eyes were fluttering erratically like a scared butterfly. "Come on, baby, come back."

Finally, after another tense filled moment, her eyes finally opened fully. Slowly, she lifted her gaze to me, and for one hopeful moment, I think that she actually saw me.

"Ryker?" I wanted to cry in relief, but I didn't. Instead, I brushed a lock of her hair behind her ear.

"It's me, baby." I noticed that her grip in my hand tightened, and she smiled. However, it soon faded. "What's wrong?"

"I can't see." Draven and I looked at each other.

"What do you mean?"

"I can't see anything at all, no auras or anything like that. Rei seems pretty quiet too." She began to sound worried. "She's not answering me at all." Concern was beginning to lodge in my gut.

"Maybe she's still asleep?" This came from Draven. Kei tilted her face in his direction.

"Draven?" He smiled softly at her.

"Of course, you didn't think that I wouldn't come visit you, right?" She smiled brightly at him, and I had to cage in my jealousy pretty damn quickly, or else, I would do something that I would regret later.

"Well, I'm glad that you made it." She became silent with her thoughts for a moment, and I took this chance to marvel at her. Her eyes were still bright and changed from red to green, their brilliance breathtaking. I noticed that her skin seemed to be more flushed and less pale.

"How long have I been asleep?" she asked, getting me out of my daze.

"A day." She pursed her lips.

"My birthday is tomorrow."

"Happy birthday?" Draven said it as a question. She shook her head.

"No, not like that. Leon made it sound like I would get all of my powers on my birthday, but I don't know. It sounds farfetched especially right now when I can't use any of my usual power." I had to grit my teeth from the surge of anger at the mention of Leon Grayson.

"Let's say you do. There's nothing that he can do because let's face it, you could kick his ass." Kei chuckled at Draven's statement.

"I guess so. However, I would like to find him." Her whole persona became dark, her eyes glittering dangerously. I became worried.

"Kei, what exactly happened to you?" Her expression became pained.

"A lot of things but I don't think this is the right time to say." Her eyes were downcast, and I knew whatever happened to her, it wasn't good. I clenched my jaw and stayed silent. I looked up, however, as Draven stood up abruptly.

"I'm sorry to leave so suddenly, but my parents need me back." Kei shot him a worried glance.

"What's wrong?" Draven heaved a sigh and ran a hand through his hair.

"There seems that there was another rogue attack."

"Is it still going on?" she asked. He nodded grimly before saying, "Yes."

"Take some of my men. They should help get rid of the majority." Draven stared at me for a long moment, his expression blank but then he laughed dryly.

"I don't know how I feel about you yet but thanks." I didn't say anything as he turned to leave, stopping in the doorway. "I'll see you later, Kei, Alpha." And he was gone.

*"Clark."*

*"Yes, Alpha."*

*"Accompany Draven to his pack. There seemed to be another rogue attack, and I want you to help. Take some men with you."* I closed the mind link but looked down as Kei groaned.

"Tell me what's wrong."

"Pain… everywhere." She sucked in a deep breath. "It sucks." She managed a shaky smile. I felt so helpless. The pack doctor was gone taking care of other pack members, and no one else here was certified to help her.

"I'm sleepy," she mumbled. I gripped her hand tighter.

"Baby, don't go to sleep," I begged, and I never beg.

"Don't worry… will wake… up soon…" She dozed off to a deep sleep once again. The sense of defeat was overwhelming, but I knew I would wait forever.

She was my forever.

# Chapter 28

*Kei Valancia*

Every bone in my body ached. *If this is what an old person feels like, then I am deeply sorry for what you have to go through because it sucks horribly.* But no, this wasn't the only freaking problem. All of my powers gone? It's no longer here, freaking missing and everything under the sun, it's no longer here. I could only imagine what everyone else thinks about my powers being gone. *Oh, you can live without them. You kinda deserve it, anyway.*

Yeah? Well, I probably do deserve to get my powers get taken because honestly, I know I'm not the best person to hang around. Just ask Draven. To be honest, I don't really have one ounce of care for them. All I care about was Rei. She's the one I'm worried about. Screw me, what about Rei? She's not as crazy as I am. All of these worries and pains, I thought sleep was a sweet gift where I get to be in oblivion. Obviously, not me. If I could, I would sigh until I could sigh no longer. Here's another thing, what will happen to Ryker?

*"You worry too much, you know?"*

*"Rei?"* She chuckled.

*"The one and only,"* she teased.

*"Where the hell have you been?"*

*"Ah, you know, around,"* she answered cryptically.

*"How can you be 'around'?"* She laughed.

*"Here, I'll show you."* It was a weird feeling. It felt as if I was being pulled, but I only saw black. It was almost as if she was pulling me by the wrist, as I felt a warmth where my hands were usually but couldn't see.

*"Where are we going?"*

*"You're going to meet a new friend of some sorts."*

*"A friend?"*

*"Of sorts."* I didn't ask any more questions. Instead, I got lost in the feeling of being tugged yet not feeling like I was moving.

*"This is weird,"* I commented.

*"Tell me about it. I was freaking out the first time when this happened."*

*"And when was this?"*

*"I was pretty sure last month. I don't know. My sense of time is sort of out of whack."*

We didn't say anything after that.

The feeling of being pulled lasted for what seemed like forever in a decade, and it might have been. Rei was right about the time here. It wasn't really accurate to the real world. Soon, the feeling ceased, and it felt as if I was standing still once more.

*"Umm. Where are we?"*

*"Give me a second,"* she said before concentrating on doing whatever she was doing.

In the meantime, I went back to thinking. Mostly about Ryker. I tried to imagine what his face would look like but I couldn't seem to get a right picture. Of course, I haven't seen another person's face in years so trying to construct a human face from scratch was almost impossible.

*"Here we go,"* Rei finally said, sounding satisfied. Before I could ask what the heck was going on, a white form was beginning to appear in the darkness.

*"Uh, Rei, what's happening exactly?"*

*"Shh! Just watch,"* she chided, and I would have rolled my eyes if I could. I stayed silent as the white blobby thing started to take shape in the silhouette of a woman. She began to shine brighter, and I instinctively made a move to cover my eyes and was surprised to see that my hands did indeed cover my eyes. When I noticed that the light was no longer there, I lowered my hands slowly. There standing in front of me was a woman. And I could see her face. I could see everything, her clothes, her long golden brown hair. I could even see her pearly white teeth gleam in the glow that she emanated. I pointed at her with my mouth gaping open.

"I can see you!" She smiled in amusement.

"It seems that you can." I was literally on the brink of freaking out and going crazy with excitement. Not even thinking, I ran over to her for a closer look. Her eyes widened, but she didn't step back. Poking her arm, I saw the way my finger indented the soft skin just above her elbow. I mean, I freaking saw it. And I wasn't making a crappy joke, either. I could physically see her tan skin, and her wearing a regular pair of blue jeans and a white tank top. I literally jumped up and down and squealed. I freaking squealed.

"I can see for the first time! It feels like the first time. It feels like the very first time!" Soon, I'm singing "Feels like the First Time" by Foreigner and prancing around the mystery woman with a goofy smile on my face. Don't ask me why I was singing it. The song itself is about a man who obviously happens to do the baby-making process with a woman who makes it feel like it was the first time, or that's how I interpret it, had nothing to do with my eyesight. But I'm happy, and the song got stuck in my head after I listened to Pitch Perfect. Yeah, you can't judge me. A hand on my head stopped me mid-prance and lyric. I looked at the source to see the woman in near hysterics from laughing.

"This was definitely not the meeting I was expecting at all." I straightened and stared at her with a curious look, still awed that I could actually see.

"Well, you know. I've been blind for some years now, and it's amazing to actually see you in the flesh." I poked her arm again but looked up at her. "May I ask who you are?" She laughed once more before answering my question.

"My name is Estelle Luna. And you've had a rough journey so far, haven't you, Kei Valancia?" I nodded and studied her. Why did her name sound so familiar? After staring at her for a good solid minute, it finally clicked.

"You're the first werewolf ever that created the other werewolves, right? The goddess?" She smiled.

"You would be correct though you're the first to ever do that in my presence." She didn't sound mad but instead seemed to find all of it extremely hilarious. I shrugged in return.

"I've never seen any pictures of you, so I didn't really recognize you until you told me your name." "I expected that much, yet the singing threw me off guard," she said with a smirk. I chuckled and smiled sheepishly.

"Sorry, I just got excited." She waved her hand at me.

"No need to apologize. Your reaction seemed appropriate."

"So, I don't think you're really here for a friendly visit, right? There's obviously something going on if you're that desperate enough to talk to me." She rolled her eyes, and it was weird to see the goddess of the wolves do that.

"You make it sound like you're a terrible choice for the job."

"Aren't I? I'm definitely no saint." She came to my side and laid a hand on my shoulder.

"You don't have to be a saint for the thing I'm asking you to do." I groaned as I started to realize something.

"I don't have to save the world or anything, right? Because I've heard stories of the heroine and she defeats the evil guy. Then everybody has a happy ever after," I paused. "Never mind. That sounds delightful. I guess Leon is the bad guy?" I looked at her with a hopeful expression, and I crossed my fingers. Seeing this, she chuckled once more.

"Yes, the bad guy is Leon." I let out a yell and threw my fist in the air before stopping. Lowering my arms, I frowned.

"The thing is I don't have my powers. And I know I should have more faith in my mate, but I still worry about him fighting Leon. Does that make me a terrible mate for not believing in him?" She saw the vulnerability in my eyes and smiled softly.

"No, it doesn't. You have some faith in him, right?" I nodded. "Then that's what matters. It's only natural to harbor some type of worry for a mate when they go off to battle, not even the mighty Alpha King is indestructible, and therefore, your worry is well placed."

"Yet, I want to be treated his equal, and I was a hypocrite for asking something when I wasn't willing to give, either." I sighed heavily.

"You know your mistakes now. What you choose to do in the future is all up to you. But first, let's see if you can get rid of the past." I looked at her.

"I don't necessarily want to get rid of the past. It's what made me who I am today however cliché that sounds but it's true. All I want is to make it stay in the past so it won't come into the present to ruin the future. Therefore, I will do whatever it takes to kick Leon's ass into the next world." I grinned up at her wickedly, and her eyes twinkled.

"Even if you don't have your powers?"

"Yes, even if I don't have my powers. If I'm going to try to start to be a good mate, then trusting and relying on Ryker is the first step. Of course, that doesn't mean I'm still going to sit on the sidelines. He needs someone to cover his back." I smiled at her. She studied me with a blank look before I saw a burst of pride shine in her eyes, realizing that for the first time I couldn't see her emotions. A moment of sadness passed, but I knew that I would just have to get over it because my old powers weren't coming back.

"Your parents would be so proud of you. They are proud of you." She surprised me by bending down and kissing my forehead. Just as she pulled away, my vision began to get fuzzy.

"Dude, kiss a man, and you'll drug him to death," I mumbled, and she laughed. She caught me just as I stumbled forward.

"Good luck, and may the Goddess watch over you," she teased.

*Oh, that sly woman* was the last thought I had before being swallowed into the abyss.

# Chapter 29

*Ryker Date*

I slammed my hand down on the desk. My eyes were tired from looking at files all day, and a pounding headache pulsed through my skull. Now, in my own pack house with Kei in my bed, I had finally left after putting five guards in front of the door and five outside in the yard in front of the window. And now, I had to deal with the one man that I considered to be the biggest thorn in my side

"Thomas, I don't have time for this." I gritted, my annoyance level reaching its peak. He glared back at me with equal aggravation.

"You don't have time for the rogue attacks?" He snarled, and I bared my teeth, letting my power fill the room like cotton.

"I don't have time for your complaints. I'm working on the attacks, but having you complaining in my ear every five minutes isn't going to make the process faster." We both stood, glaring at each other with both our powers flaring around us. Finally, after not letting up, he finally backed down. Sighing, he ran both of his hands in his hair while yanking at it painfully.

"Just what is going on?" I shut my eyes and breathed deeply through my nose. "That's something I can't answer right now. Just go back to your pack and be on guard. That's all you can do at this point." As I opened my eyes, I saw him studying me quizzically.

"And what are you going to do?" I looked to my right and out of the window into the dark night.

"I'm going to wait."

* * *

Walking down the dim corridor, I noticed five of my men standing at attention. When I passed them, they all bowed their heads in respect.

"Go, get some rest. I'll call you if something goes wrong."

"Yes, Alpha," they said in unison, and I nodded before entering the room and shutting the door behind me. I stood still, studying the sleeping form in the king sized bed. I could hear her soft breathing from all the way across the room, and my heart clenched.

Finally taking a step closer, I watched as the moon shining through the window reflected on her hair, making it twinkle like liquid mercury. My gaze darted over to the clock on the bedside table to see that it was 11:40 PM, twenty minutes until it would be Kei's birthday.

Closing the distance, I slipped my shoes off along with the stuffy suit jacket and tie. Flinging the clothing on the couch that was placed in front of the empty fireplace, I sighed and walked over to a cabinet, opened it and pulled out a brandy. Pulling the cork out with a pop, I looked over to see Kei still soundly asleep. Taking a swig from straight out of the bottle, I walked over to the bed and sat on her side.

The bed dipped from my weight, and I stared at her sleeping face. Now, she looked peaceful, unlike when she was at Hale's. Holding the bottle in one hand, I traced the contours of her face with the other.

"What exactly are you dreaming about?" I muttered to the empty room. She didn't respond. Turning away, I squeezed my eyes shut and rested my elbows on my knees, the brandy hanging precariously between my fingers. "What is going on?" I sounded broken even to my own ears. Who knew that a young she-wolf could bring the alpha king to his knees in over a month?

"Why must it be like this?" I asked once again to no one. "Why does Kei have to suffer? Hasn't she suffered enough?" Now, I was rambling angrily, and if anyone had walked in, they would have thought that I would have finally lost it, which I did. Standing, I gripped the glass bottle so hard I heard the glass crack in my hand. "Dammit! Why?" I turned and fell to my knees, facing the bed. At this time, the glass bottle couldn't handle the pressure any longer and finally broke, pieces of glass sticking in my hand while the booze ran down my arm. I had become numb enough that the fiery burning didn't register one bit. Instead, I swept the glass away and held her hand with my uninjured one, caressing it with my thumb.

"Kei, don't you see what you're doing to me? You're making me unravel gradually, slowly. And then, when I finally get you back, you go unconscious, leaving me alone again. Kei, don't you understand that I've been alone for over two hundred years with no mate to come home to?

"After all of these years, I had lost hope, but you know that I'm still a virgin," I remarked dryly. "Deep down, I still hoped that I would find my soulmate, my other half. And I did. I found you." I felt a strange heaviness in my eyes, filling with a substance that I've never known.

"Kei, baby, my world finally found its axis after you came into my life. And now that you're not here with me, awake and smiling beautifully, my world has lost its spin, and I'm standing still once more." With my bleeding hand dangling by my side, I bent my head and clutched to her limp hand in mine as if it was a lifeline. That's when I felt it, the salty wetness of tears rolling down my cheeks one by one like dutiful soldiers carrying out their orders.

"Kei. Wake up, baby, please," I pleaded gruffly, not caring one ounce about crying. I felt everything inside crumble slowly. The world that I had made for myself wasn't enough for only me anymore. Kei had made her place, and now, I needed her. With my head still bent, I cried silently still holding her hand. I was so consumed with my own emotions I didn't notice the fluttering of her eyelashes or the way her hand twitched and then finally grasping my own. What I did notice, however, was the way her hand lightly flitted through my hair, combing it through her fingers. I looked up slowly to see a sight that I would never forget for the rest of my years of living.

Kei Valancia was sitting up with her long hair around her face. Her eyes a soft green glowed from the moonlight and then bleeding through to red. A sweet smile beautified her features even further, and I felt the air in my lungs catch. I watched as her eyes looked at my cheeks, and an unknown emotion flickered on her face before it disappeared. Her hand in my hair trailed down to cup my right cheek, wiping my tears with the pad of her thumb.

"I'm sorry," she whispered, and that was what broke me completely. Standing, I loomed over her, and she looked at me with that same soft expression. Getting on the bed on one knee, I reached back and cupped the back of her head, pulling her in. She didn't resist as I closed the distance between our lips, her familiar taste coating my tongue. Sweet and salty with my tears, this kiss showed all of my raw emotions for her—how much I cared and all the sorrow, and how much I loved her.

Pulling away, I leaned my head against hers and closed my eyes. I felt her eyes on my face and finally dawned on me that she couldn't see my face. But then my eyes popped open to her staring at me. How did she know that I was crying?

*"Maybe she saw our sadness,"* Axel offered.

*"Maybe. But she couldn't have been able to tell where to wipe the tears."* Her smile, this time, was wide and bright, and then I knew.

"You are more gorgeous than I could have ever imagined. But my imagination sucks, anyway. You should see how I draw my stick figures," she said in a teasing tone. I was frozen, hovering above her with disbelief.

"You can see?"

She grinned. "Pretty cool, huh? Now, I get to see your sexy abs. Do you by any chance have any tattoos?" Without warning, I wrapped both arms around her and pulled her close to my chest. I nuzzled her hair and inhaled deeply.

"Kei, Goddess, you don't know how much I've missed you," I said, feeling her hug me back just as tightly.

"I missed you too. Oh and Ryker?"

"Hmmm?"

"I love you." Pulling back, I stared at her. Her eyes were clear and true, the love that I saw enveloped me, and I knew that whatever happens next, she was going to be there by my side no matter what. And I would do the same for her. Leaning down, I brought our faces so close that our noses touched. I smiled gently and cupped her cheek in my hand, making sure to keep my injured one off of her. Kissing her lightly on the lips, I inhaled her scent another time. Staring deep into her eyes, I said the words that have been stuck on my tongue since the moment I met her.

"I love you, Kei Valancia. You're my world, my forever and my queen. Whatever happens next, baby, I'll always be by your side. But just know, it's going to be one hell of a ride."

# Chapter 30

*Kei Valancia*

I stared openly at his face. I mean, it's freaking perfect. His strong jawline was dark with stubble, his cheekbones high with his long, dark lashes shadowing against them. And his eyes... Damn, his eyes were an intense black that glittered, just like his power, and they entranced me. His tall, lean form was bent towards me with his kissable lips tilted up in a soft smile.

I brushed back a lock of his midnight black hair, the ends brushing the nape of his neck. I noticed everything about him was dark, sexy and mysterious. But I knew how soft he was inside, and I loved him more for it. While I was devouring him with my gaze, I smelled and saw the blood dripping from his hand and onto the floor.

"What in the world happened?" I panicked and gripped his hurt hand, plucking out the pieces of glass embedded in his skin gently.

"Nothing out of the ordinary," he commented flippantly. I glanced up sharply at him and saw humor dance in his gaze. I felt my heart melt, but I stayed firm.

"Come on." Maneuvering around his body, I slipped out of the covers and stood. The colder air nipped at my bare legs like an excited puppy, and I looked down at myself. My first thought was, *Man I'm white.* And then, *This shirt is huge.*

Ignoring my half-naked state, I tugged on his wrist gently leading him to what seemed like the bathroom. The room was black, and I relapsed at that moment. Call me stupid. But I felt safe. The blackness was all I've ever known. Granted, I had the Gift of being able to see auras, but the dark was still there.

"Here," Ryker said, reaching past me and flipping the switch. I squinted my eyes as the bright light filtered through the room.

"Ow," I said simply before pulling him further into the room. "All right, sit," I commanded, gesturing towards the huge as hell Jacuzzi tub. He complied and sat down obediently, holding his hand with care. I turned my back, and I was met with a large mirror with a girl reflected back. I was momentarily stunned and poked my cheek to make sure it was actually me. The girl copied my action.

Silver hair hung low around my face, the long strands swaying by movements. My face flushed a light pink with my lips parted. What caught me off guard were my eyes. They changed from a red to green. Oh, my goddess, not going to lie but that's pretty cool.

"You're so beautiful," Ryker murmured, catching his gaze in the mirror. I looked away with a blush and began opening random cabinets. But then I stopped when I figured out that I had no clue what I was looking for.

"Uh, what does a first aid kit look like?" I asked while turning my head to look at him, a sense of mortification coming over me. Sure, I know I was blind and all, but I still feel slightly embarrassed for asking the question.

"It's a plastic box shape. It will have a sticker on it with a red cross. It should be in that drawer." He pointed at the drawer just to my right, and I smiled before looking in it. It was indeed in there, and I got the light plastic blue box out, the red cross vivid.

Bringing it over, I kneeled down beside him and set the kit down. Opening it, I found various ointments and bandages. I was hit with the sense of helplessness. Shaking my head, I started with a cotton ball and standing again. Opening the cabinet that I was in previously, I saw the bottle of alcohol. Grabbing it, I poured some onto the cotton and walked back over to him. Setting down the bottle, I had to ignore his gaze watching my every move and instead focused on doing the task at hand.

Grasping his hand in mine gently, I made sure to look for any more pieces of glass before beginning the cleaning process. Dabbing at his wounds gently, I noticed all of the small cuts on his palm. We were silent as I cleaned and dressed his wounds, concentrating on picking the right medicine. I had to admit, there was a slight concern that I would address the wrong thing, and his hand would fall off or something just as disastrous. But luckily, Rei was there to help me. Or not.

*"Pick that one. Wait, never mind it's the other one. No, the other one!"*

*"I'm just going to ask Ryker."* Almost shyly, I turned to face Ryker.

"Uh, King? Which one is it?"

"It's this one." He reached over and picked up a small tube, Neosporin written in bold letters. Taking it gratefully, I began to apply it to his cuts. When I was finished bandaging his whole hand, I leaned back on my heels and felt a small sense of accomplishment.

"There." I took it and kissed his palm gently. This sign of affection must have surprised him as I heard him suck a deep breath. Heck, it surprised me.

"Kei." I looked up, and just as I did, soft lips met mine. Instantly, I responded and pushed on my haunches to get closer to him. With his other arm, he wrapped it around my waist and pulled me onto his lap. My knee bumped into the kit, knocking it across the floor, but it didn't matter.

What mattered was the man before me, kissing the living daylights out of me and the one who confessed his love. And might I say, he looked hot doing it. Any man who had shedded tears for the woman he loves is perfect in my book. I wrapped my legs around his waist, and he tightened his grip on me to keep me steady. I cupped his face in between my hands and felt so lucky. I pulled away first, breathless. With his eyes hooded, he looked at me as if I was the most precious thing in the world.

"You are," he said, answering my thoughts. He must have seen my mystified expression because he chuckled and pulled me closer. "Mate bond, it lets me get a peek inside your mind every now and then." I didn't want it to happen, but I felt my mood darken slightly. Noticing this, his eyes became cautious.

"What's wrong?" I sighed and wrapped my arms around his neck, hugging him. He returned the hug after a moment and squeezed me tight. I buried my nose into his neck, and this time, it was my turn to inhale his mouth watering scent. I found it strange that he smelt of dark chocolate, but it made him even more appealing. It smelled of home.

"Kei?" His words pulled me back to the present, and then, I noticed that I was crying. He tried to pull back to look at me, but I only clung onto him tighter.

"I don't want you to look deep into my mind yet," I croaked, my voice thick with tears. "You don't deserve to see the horrors just yet. I know I told myself I would become a better mate and let you in, but it's hard." I pulled away and stared at him unabashed with rivers flowing down my cheeks.

"I'm sorry. I'll try harder. I promise." He simply reached up and wiped the tears away with aching sweetness. This made the tears flow more.

"Baby, you don't have to try hard to be you. But there is something that I need to see, Kei. I need to experience the pain that you felt while being captive with that bastard." Anger glittered in his eyes, and I leaned my forehead against him, a decision leaving my lips.

"All right." He stared deep into my eyes, looking for the truth. Once he found what he was looking for, he stood up, his arms like steel bands. He carried me back into the room, shutting the light off and putting me down on the edge of the bed. Kneeling in front of me, his face was now level with mine, and I became awestruck by his beauty once again.

His white collar shirt was unbuttoned down his chest, showing the hard muscle underneath. Oh, and his abs; damn his abs for being so sculpture perfect.

*"I know we are having a serious moment but can we ask him to take his shirt off? I would really love the view."* I could practically see Rei's mouth wide open with drool spilling out of her mouth. That visual made me bark out a laugh. Ryker raised an eyebrow.

"What's going on inside that pretty head?" I smiled at him.

"Nothing. But you know, it would be better if you took your shirt off." His smile brightened his whole face, and my lungs stopped working.

"If that's what the Queen wants, then that's what the Queen shall get." He simply ripped the rest of the cloth off and threw it over his shoulder, his muscles flexing beautifully by the action. It was my turn to drool. His skin was a flawless tan, his lithe frame was corded in muscle, and it was fantastic.

Being the alpha king, you would expect him to be big and broad, intimidating. Ryker, though, wasn't huge but, instead, slender yet still full of muscle. He definitely wasn't considered scrawny, and he was still tall and just as sexy.

"Like what you see?" He smirked. Grinning, I ran a hand down his chest.

"Yeah, I am. Now, come here." I had him come onto the bed with me, settling down where I had him lie his head on my lap with my back against the headboard. I combed my hands through his hair absentmindedly and let out a shaky breath. I pictured a door in my mind, with chains locked around it.

*"Can you see it?"*

*"Yes."*

*"Are you ready?"*

*"The question is, are you ready?"* I smiled gently at his words.

*"Yes."* And the chains fell away, the door swinging open. And that's when I showed the darkest part of my life to Ryker, baring my heart and soul, and setting me free.

# Chapter 31

*Ryker Dare*

The door opened, and I stepped inside Kei's mind, the furthest that I've ever gone since we've created the mate bond. I was sucked in, and everything turned black.

I couldn't see anything, just only black. That's when I realized I was in Kei's memories and that I saw everything in her eyes, "seeing" being a relative term.

"Rei, where are we?" I was surprised to hear a voice talk abruptly, sounding high and had the tone of a child.

"I don't know, but wherever we are, it's not good." This time, this voice echoed around me, belonging to Rei who was speaking in Kei's mind.

"Yeah." Suddenly, there was a sound of a door opening off to the right. As I heard footsteps walk in, colors sparked in front of her eyes.

*What in the world?* I thought. The lights blended together, and I couldn't make it out. Neither could Kei it seemed.

*I can't understand his feelings,* Kei thought.

"Come here." I felt a hand grip my, more specifically, Kei's arm.

"Let go!" Kei hissed, getting a smack across the face in return. I had forgotten that this was a memory, and I snarled.

"How dare you hit your queen?" I growled and cursed, but nothing happened. Nothing would happen.

"I wouldn't do that if I were you, little girl." A hand suddenly appeared on her stomach, and Kei kicked. Her foot made contact with something that resulted in a fleshy smack. A howl of pain reverberated through the room.

"You bi—"

"Stop right now," a deeper voice commanded, power filling the room. It became silent for a moment until footsteps drew near. They stopped right in front of us, and a hand gripped her arm before yanking her up.

"Who told you that you could touch her?" There was a long pause, different colors swirling in the darkness.

"No one did, sir."

"Then what are you doing putting your hands on her?" He was met with silence. The voice sighed as if disappointed. "What a shame?" A fleshy rip that was then followed by an earsplitting scream. A warm liquid splashed on Kei's face, the substance dripping down her cheek. The heavy smell of metal permeated the air, and the trail of what she concluded was blood left a coldness in her heart, seeping into her bones. She slowly lifted a hand and touched her cheek, pulling it away with her hand now sticky with it.

"Why did you kill him?" A thud sounded just right beside her and Kei sat frozen.

"Why, you ask?" There were colors of a horrible yellow and green as if that person was sick. A rough, calloused hand cupped her cheek, and Kei held in a flinch. "Simply because he had the audacity to touch what was mine." A new sense of boldness took over Kei, and I felt proud yet knew deep down that whatever she was going to say next was not going to be the best option.

"I am nobody's." She spat. "And I will not bend to your will." As if it was an instant reaction, something yanked her hair, pulling her across the floor. Kei let out a cry and clawed at the hands blindly.

"We'll see about that," the man growled out and dragged Kei across the concrete floor. The skin in her bare legs was getting cut, and the feeling of blood oozing down her skin made me hate the man more. Kei finally stopped fighting, and instead hung limply. The man didn't seem to care for her state and kept on dragging her. After going making the billionth turn around a corner, he stopped. He let her hair go, and Kei was luckily quick enough to catch herself before letting her head hit the ground. She looked up and glared at the man. Or I thought so as I didn't have any sense of direction in the blackness and the occasional flashes.

"Stand up," he ordered. You can only imagine how Axel was doing, cursing and snarling. Even if this was a memory, we did not take well to be ordered around kindly as you can imagine. Kei sucked in a breath and stood up with shaky legs. There was one terrifying moment where her legs lost all feeling, but then she locked her knees and gritted her teeth.

"Now, do try not to die. I want to have some fun with you, and you interest me." Before Kei could utter a sound, she was pushed from behind and into what seemed like another room. She tried to keep her balance but still felt too weak and ended up in a heap. A door was slammed behind her, and she inhaled, the smell of sweat and metallic blood filled her nostrils.

"Hey, look. We have a new toy," a child's voice sneered, sounding like a boy.

"Ain't she pretty too? It makes me sick." This time, a nasally high-pitched girl's voice joined in.

"Let's see how far we can push her until she breaks," the same voice said, sounding gleeful. Kei stayed still, but her thoughts were a blur. Several footsteps padded over to us, yet Kei still stayed in the same bent position, her hair tickling her face.

*"There are five in total. Can't tell what ages they are but I'm going to guess they must be a couple years younger."* Kei began thinking.

*"Don't take them lightly. They've seemed to be experienced in whatever sick twisted game this is."* Rei sounded disgusted, and I couldn't blame her.

*"Don't worry, this isn't my first rodeo."* A smile appeared on Kei's lips as the feet finally stopped in front of her, the air becoming still. When the first fist made contact with the back of her head, everything in me snapped to pieces, and I had to do everything in my power to reign it in. Yet, I felt that control waning as each punch pounded my mate.

That's how everything in me froze as she laughed. It wasn't maniacal or crazy. It was just her blissful laugh. This reaction caused everyone else to freeze also as there wasn't another blow to her body. Kei slowly stood, still chuckling. She had her eyes closed so not even the flickering colors could be seen.

*"I'm so tired, Rei,"* she spoke weakly with fatigue and my already fully healed heart cracked once more.

*"I know, Kei. So am I."*

*"But you know, I still have the will to fight. Am I stupid for fighting?"* Rei was silent for a moment.

*"No, Kei. That just means you're strong."* Tears filled her eyes, but they didn't fall.

*"That's a relief,"* she said before everything in her world sparked with color.

\* \* \*

I was pushed out of the doors and back into my own mind. My eyes popped open, and I straightened. Kei was breathing heavily while leaning back against the headboard. She smiled weakly at me.

"I think both of us need a break to calm our emotions." She tugged at my hair playfully. "You, especially, when you go all Hulk like that, it's hard to keep you in." I had caught her hand before she pulled away.

"Was it too much?" I asked softly. She smiled and tugged my hand for me to get closer. I did. But before I could hold her in my arms, she pecked my cheek and slipped underneath me. I blinked and turned my upper body to see Kei skipping her way towards the bathroom.

"Sorry, babe, but I really need a shower." She blew me a kiss and shut the door behind her, leaving me dumbfounded in the way that she only can. Finally, I tipped my head back and laughed. I laughed for the joy to have my mate, for the love that filled me, and for the simple feeling of being happy.

My existence finally meant something. And that something was Kei Valancia.

# Chapter 32

*Kei Valancia*

The warm shower washing away my grossness was heaven.

*"Goddess, we stank so bad I'm not sure how Ryker put up with us,"* Rei said with disgust.

*"Maybe he secretly likes our stink,"* I said jokingly.

*"We should go dumpster diving then. Gotta keep our man on his toes, or else, he'll find a stinkier woman."*

*"I don't think that's going to happen."*

*"How do you know? Ryker is a man you can never be sure what he will be thinking,"* Rei concluded.

*"Why are you so weird?"*

*"Why aren't you weirder?"*

*"That's the thing. I'm usually the weird one, and you're the semi-normal one in this relationship. What's going on?"*

*"I want to change places."* She pouted. I sighed again but longer and thumped my head against the marble, and I mean marble wall. And I could freaking see the black rock sparkle.

It… was… so… cool. There was suddenly a loud bang, and for some weird reason, I got into a karate pose. My arms were in front of me as if that would help in my present vulnerable state.

"Kei? Are you all right?" I dropped my arms and tried to cover everything below my neck.

"Yep. Everything's A-Okay except that I'm naked and you are in the same room as me." He walked over just in front of the opaque glass, his blurred figure dark against the light. The water pounded on my back, and I kept my eyes on his every move. I saw his blurry arm lift, and his hand grabbed the edge of the glass sliding door.

"I swear, if you open that door, I will karate chop you," I threatened. It seemed to have worked, though, as he did freeze.

"You're so adorable when you threaten me," was all he said before yanking the door open. I squealed and jumped back.

"What in the actual heck? Ryker, I'm too white. If you stare at me for too long, I'll burn your retinas." He didn't say anything but stare. I felt my whole body flush as his gaze crept slowly down and back up again, taking in every detail.

"You didn't say that when we first met," he said, his voice hoarse.

"That was before I saw I was whiter than paper." He took a step inside the shower, his jeans getting soaked, and water droplets ran down his golden chest.

"Do you think I would really care if you were the colors of the rainbow?" I quirked an eyebrow.

"I will admit. That sounds cool." He took another step, getting closer to every move.

"The point is, Kei, it doesn't matter what color you are. I will love you as if the world depends on it."

He had taken small steps towards me until his chest was pushed against mine, and my breath hitched in my throat. He looked down at me with hooded eyes, his hair sticking to his forehead. I reached up and pushed it away to get a clearer view of his twinkling eyes. He wrapped one arm around my waist, pulled me closer until there was no space between us, and used the other to trail his hand up my bare spine. His fingers lightly traced the path, and the feeling sent shivers up my spine.

He bent down and whispered in my ear, "Cold?"

"Yes, yes, I am." And I was. The water had gone into arctic mode all of the sudden and me butt naked was not going to provide much warmth. Goosebumps dotted my skin, and I shivered again. Yet, I gripped the hair at his nape and pulled him down for a kiss. Because why not? I might be cold, but kissing Ryker heated me until I felt too hot. I hardly noticed when Ryker searched until he found what he was looking for, turning the water off. He cupped his hands around my face and used his body to push me against the wall.

"I should probably dry off." I managed in between kisses.

"Is that really such a great idea?" he muttered. A red flush had splattered across my skin, and I nodded.

"I hate to break the moment, but I have to just add something." He pulled back and raised an eyebrow at me.

"Oh? And what would that be?" he asked. With a serious expression, I stared at him straight in the eyes.

"You still haven't found the $x$ in the equation." At the mention of the equation, he rolled his eyes and groaned exasperatedly. He turned and walked out of the shower. I let out a breath that I was holding and felt myself begin to calm down.

*"Get rid of that stupid equation,"* Rei harped at me.

"Don't wanna," I smirked just as Ryker appeared once more but, this time, with a plush towel, now dressed in a loose navy blue t-shirt and a dry pair of jeans.

"Come on before you catch a cold."

"Yes, sir." I would have saluted, but I thought I better get dressed before I did anything else. Walking gingerly over to him, I made sure as to not slip on the wet tiles as he reached around me and wrapped me in the warm towel.

"Do you think I could borrow some of your clothes?" I asked him. He nodded, and with his arm still wrapped around my shoulders, we walked back into his room. First, he directed me to the bed and pushed my shoulders down so that I sat on the ridiculously soft mattress, and he walked back into the bathroom.

I was just sitting there playing with a piece of loose thread on the towel when all of a sudden a memory flashed through my mind.

\* \* \*

*I was walking through the forest when I was about ten years old and three years after I had gotten Rei. I was traveling on to the next pack to learn ways on how to protect myself and the ones that I loved.*

*"Rei?"*

*"Hmmm?"*

*"I know it's stupid, and we might not even find our mate but…"*

*"But what?" I took a deep breath.*

*"I want to wait."*

*"Wait, for what exactly?"*

*"I want to wait to be fully mated with my true soulmate until we get married." Rei was silent for a moment.*

*"Kei, werewolves don't get married as regular humans do."*

*"I know, but some do. I've heard stories about the brides wearing the most beautiful gowns with her best friends standing beside her," I paused. "And then when the bride walks down the aisle the groom is standing, waiting for his love with a look of awe.*

*"I know it's a childish dream, but it's something that I've given a lot of thought."* Rei was silent for a long time, and I didn't add any more. I knew it was stupid to wait to get married when you're destined to live with your other half, anyways, but it's the thought. Humans are dominating most of the planet now and I always a strange fascination towards them. Yet when I think about it, I don't think I've ever met one in person. I sighed and held on tighter to the backpack straps. The usual colors gave me some comfort, and I relaxed into a rhythm.

*"It's not a childish dream,"* Rei suddenly spoke. *Our mate is the one and only for us. Having a wedding wouldn't hurt to have, and it may be fun.* I smiled brightly.

*"Thanks, Rei,"* she laughed.

*"Anytime, Kei."*

* * *

I blinked and found Ryker bent over me with a panicked expression. He relaxed a little as he saw that I was conscious again.

"Ryker?"

"Baby, how many times are you going to make me worry?" I sat up, noticed that I was now dry, and dressed in a large shirt, smelling of him. Ryker was lying beside me, holding me in his arms. I caressed his cheek.

"I'm sorry," in response he nuzzled into my neck

"Stop saying sorry. It's not your fault," he said against my skin. I looked at him softly before I lifted the covers up and around us. He was now dressed in plain black sweats, giving me a wonderful view of his body. I shook my head to get my mind out of the gutter before I laid my cheek against his chest, listening to his heart beat rhythmically against my ear. This action made me realize how tired I was. You would think for getting as much sleep as I have that I would be up and around like a hyper little kid. But no, my body is still too tired to do anything.

"I'll tell you in the morning. Right now, I think we need some sleep."

"Babe, it is morning."

"What time is it?"

"It's 3 AM." I felt my eyes droop.

"That's okay. I'll wake up early enough to show you some more of my memories before you have to go work..." I began to drift off while his hand played with my hair.

"Oh and Kei?"

"Hmmm?"

"Happy birthday."

# Chapter 33

*Ryker Dare*

I woke up with half the bed empty. I jerked up immediately, all sleep gone.

*"Kei?"* I said her name both out loud and through the mind link, instantly searching.

*"Yeah?"* I relaxed once I felt her down in the kitchen.

*"How did you find your way to the kitchen?"* I said, amused.

*"Well, King, after you interrupted my shower last night, I woke up smelling like the sewer. Like seriously, my mouth was the grossest thing ever. And then around that time, I realized I was ravenous. So after getting myself clean and presentable, I gave one more look at your adorable face and then went on my merry way in my birthday suit since it's, you know, my birthday."* I was out of bed and into the kitchen before she even finished the last word. Her eyes widened momentarily, but then, they twinkled with humor.

"Wow, tell a man you're naked, and they'll come real quick." My eyes raked up and down her form, relaxing when I saw she was wearing my shirt. It was big on her, and it ended mid-thigh along with one of her shoulders bare as the shirt dropped off. Sighing, I walked over to where she was sitting at the bar and hugged her.

"How I've missed your funny side?" She chuckled against me and hugged me back.

"Really? Even I sometimes think it's annoying." I pulled back to look at her with a raised eyebrow.

"And yet, you still do it?" She shrugged

"Call it a defense mechanism of some sort or a habit. I've been doing it for years now after I found out wallowing in self-pity wasn't the best option." I traced her jawline and kissed her lightly.

"It can be charming," I offered. She smiled at me while standing up.

"Maybe," was all she said before grabbing my hand. "Come on, I still have lots to show you." Just as we were almost out the door, she shouted, "Wait!" She dashed around me and into the kitchen. I watched as she grabbed an empty plate lying on the counter and walked over to put it in the sink. She washed it quickly before coming back over to me.

"I would feel bad for someone else to clean up my messes," she explained. This time, it was I who grabbed her hand, but I lifted it up to my lips and kissed it. She looked at me in shock, but then, it changed to warmth.

"What was that for?"

"Because our Queen is so amazing," I said seriously, pulling her close. She bit her lip.

"I feel like I still have some growing to do," she admitted. I stroked her hair and threw and an arm around her shoulders.

"Don't worry, love, we have an eternity to grow together."

* * *

"I have a question," Kei said abruptly, disturbing the quiet.

"Hmmm?" She had her head on my chest, and we were lying on the bed

"Why aren't you up and doing, you know, work?"

"I took the day off," I replied casually. She lifted her head to look at me.

"You can do that?" I shrugged.

"Of course. But I only have half of the day to do whatever I please. Afterwards, I'm going to have to go figure out who's behind the rogue attacks."

"Also, I have another question. Why do you call me loony?" I rolled my eyes but smiled.

"It's *Lune*. It's moon in French."

"French?"

"Yes. My parents had a soft spot for the city of Paris." I smiled softly as I recalled them.

"What were they like?" she asked.

"They were like most parents, loving, and spoiled me rotten, except for my father. He was the one to give me discipline whenever I acted up, but I knew he did it to help me become better as an alpha. Yet he was just as hard-headed as I am while my mother was the opposite. She was kind and sweet, but whenever she was mad, that was the time to run." I laughed quietly as I remembered my oddball of parents.

"What happened to them?" she looked up at me, her eyes gentle. I gave her a small smile before I began to tell her my past.

"A conflict between two packs were beginning to get out of control, and at that time, it was similar to that of a war. It had been going on years prior, and finally, my parents had had enough of it. They had a plan to infiltrate both packs and force them to get along, but that didn't go well as you can imagine." I smiled sardonically at her. "It was reported that when they arrived, a fight was already ensuing amongst them. My parents then tried to intervene, but in the end, their lives were taken in the chaos as a large wildfire had started amongst the mayhem. By the end of it all, only around fifty had escaped, and both of those packs disappeared."

"Wait, does that mean that you became the alpha king?" her eyes held sadness as she listened to my story, and I nodded.

"Yes, but you have to understand, my parents had been alive for quite a few hundred years when they passed." She held up her hand to stop me.

"Wait, did you just say a few hundred years?" I stared at her in amusement.

"I did. But by that time, they were beginning to age, anyway. It was a matter of time before they passed," I explained.

"How come you don't age?" I smirked and hugged her close.

"I think that conversation is for another day. We don't need to think that far ahead yet." She looked at me suspiciously for a long minute.

"Fine, I'll let it pass for now." She looked over and saw the time on the clock sitting in the bedside table.

"It's eleven now. I guess I better be quick about this so you can get to being the imposing and awe-inspiring King that I know and love." The word "love" made me smile, and I kissed her slowly.

"What exactly did you have in mind?" She sat up, so I mimicked her actions. She sat in my lap and pulled our faces closer until our foreheads were lightly pressed against each other.

"This." And the same door from last night appeared in my mind. But this time, there were no chains. This time, with no hesitancy, they swung open to reveal the darkness within. In real life, I stared deeply into her eyes. "Go on. But do try to keep your temper under control. I can only handle so much now."

"Now? What's wrong," she shook her head.

"I'll explain later. Now, hurry, we're burning daylight." I chuckled but closed my eyes, filtering into her mind. I stood before the door and watched the swirling darkness before me.

"Go on. It won't bite." Kei appeared by my side with a smirk.

"Knowing you, I have no idea." She laughed and grabbed my hand. Our fingers tangled together, and we took our step into the doorway.

# Chapter 34

*Ryker Dare*

Kei hung her head, her right side of her face sticky with something that must have been blood.

"I'm sorry," she whispered brokenly. She fell to her knees and felt tears burn her eyes. "I am so, so sorry. I didn't want to do it." She choked back a sob, and her small body shook. A door suddenly opened behind her, but she made no move to turn.

"You killed all of them." It was the man from earlier and this time he sounded pleased. "You are quite powerful. I was right in choosing you."

All of the sudden, there were footsteps, and he was right beside her. Kei continued looking blankly ahead, a dull, lifeless gray filling her vision along with the decaying scent of death.

"You are so beautiful now. The vivid red of blood suits you very well." The feeling of his lips brushing against her ear made fury bubble inside me, but I had to bury it deep inside so I wouldn't cause Kei any more trouble.

The past Kei made no reaction towards him and instead stood. The man chuckled and must have also stood as she felt a body standing behind her.

"This is going to be your new life from now on. I'll teach you all you need to know," A hand gripped hers and began pulling her along. She stayed silent the whole time as she was pulled out of the metallic smell of blood and rotting death.

"You're going to love it here," he said in a sing-song voice. "I have so many amazing plans for you. You'll begin training in two days after you've gotten some rest and food. You can also take this time to clean up. I can help you if—"

"No." It was abrupt and direct, cutting the man off effectively. He stopped, and his demeanor changed.

"Did you just tell me no?" His tone held something of a careful deadliness, making Kei wary for her next words.

"I mean, no sir. I appreciate your offer, but I like to be able to care for myself." He was silent for one long, tense moment, his hand squeezing hers a little more tightly.

"All right," he finally said and began walking once more. He did not utter another word as he led Kei to whatever he was taking her, the greenish-yellow flickering around in the blackness being the only thing to see. After another five minutes, he stopped. "This is your room. It's too bad that you can't see it, it looks rather nice I think." He was now back to being chipper, and he led her inside the room. "A nice Queen-sized bed for the princess." He let go of her hand, but she just stood still.

"Go on. It won't bite," he encouraged. She still made no move but after a moment slowly lifted her hand. She began searching ahead of her until her hand touched something soft and silky. "That's it. Doesn't it feel nice?" She nodded slowly.

"There's also a couch on the right side of your bed about four feet away. Let's go sit and have a little chat." He took her hand once again, leading her to the couch. When they got there, she sat down. The man did the same, the cushion dipping from his weight. Kei could feel his arms wrap around her shoulders gently, seemingly trying to be soothing yet sent chills down her spine.

"Now, how old are you?"

"Fourteen," she said dully.

"Well, you're a very beautiful girl. Now, what kind of name would a pretty girl like you have?" She suddenly stiffened as his hand landed on her thigh.

"I don't want to tell you," she said stiffly. His hand on her leg squeezed.

"I think you owe me a little for saving you from the big bad rogues, don't you think? If it weren't for me, you would still be in that hellhole. Now, tell me your name." This time, it came out more demanding, yet Kei shook her head.

"No." Kei was suddenly thrown across the room and slammed into the wall with powerful force. Kei let out a cry and landed on the ground with a dull thump.

"There's that word again, no. You see, I am a man that despises that word. I always get what I want, and what I want is you." Kei didn't hear footsteps, but she was lifted into the air and pushed against the wall. Nothing held her there but invisible hands.

"It seems you need to be broken until I can use you properly," he mused. "Don't worry; I'll keep a tight leash on you for now on." These words struck a chord in me, the memory of me saying something similar to Kei resurfacing.

"I don't need a leash," Kei gritted out, feisty even this young. The man sighed in disappointment.

"Only a wild dog would say the exact same thing. Fine, if you want to be treated like a rabid dog, then I will." She suddenly fell but before she could stand, a hand gripped the back of her neck as if by the scruff like a dog. He applied pressure almost too tight to where she couldn't breathe, dragging her by the neck out of the room and somewhere else. Kei scratched and choked, squirming in his grasp.

"This is what you get for being disobedient, little one. And I will not put up with it." It seemed like forever until we had reached the destination or what I thought was the destination.

"Don't let anyone come here to give her food or water until I say so,"

"Yes, Alpha," a gruff voice answered, and a door creaked open. The smell of dank earth and the cold air hit her face. Without another word, he dragged Kei through the doorway. He began walking down steps, dragging Kei painfully with him.

"I don't care who you are, but I will not answer to you." Kei croaked, her lungs burning slightly from the lack of oxygen. The man didn't say anything but kept on going. Her legs were now slick with her own blood dripping down from the cuts, the stone steps cutting into her soft flesh like butter. The earlier wounds were now opening back up again, making the burning pain more intense.

After an eternity, we had finally arrived at the bottom.

"Which one should I pick?" he mused to himself, walking some more. He stopped and stood still. "This one looks perfect. All right, my pretty little flower, this is going to be your new room until you begin to behave." He opened something that let out a piercing screech before tossing Kei in. She landed on her side, the cold concrete scraping her arms. The door slammed shut behind her with the sound of a key turning in the lock.

"There, now, you have some time to think about your actions." Kei slowly sat up and looked in his direction.

"I probably won't," she said. The man made noise in irritation.

"Your attitude just keeps getting worse with each passing moment. You know, you can be charming if you tried."

"I don't want to be charming, not for you," Kei surprised me by snarling viciously. This obviously surprised the man also as a sharp inhale could be heard.

"You really are beautiful," he said before his footsteps began to retreat. They had stopped before they had become too distant. "Just remember, my pretty little flower, Leon Grayson is going to be the one to break you. And when I do, I expect great things."

* * *

Kei pulled me out of her past. I was dazed for a second, trying to get my bearings before looking at her. Her face was white, and a look of panic began to filter into her features.

"What's wrong?" I gripped her shoulders in my hands, pulling her closer. The next words made my world turn hazy with hatred.

"Leon is here."

# Chapter 35

*Kei Valancia*

"Stay here," Ryker commanded. I let out a breath and fought my old habits of trying to rebel.

"Okay." He stopped and stared at me.

"You're not going to argue?" I shrugged and held my knees close to my chest.

"I would be more of a nuisance than a help. I'm too weak still, and I know when to back down sometimes." I smiled a little. He came over and kissed me on the forehead.

"Don't worry. I'll get that bastard for you." He gave me one last look as if seeing my face for the last time before turning and leaving. I sat quietly, the sounds of snarling now piercing the air.

*"Did you miss me?"* I clenched my hands into tight fists. I got out of the bed and looked out the window facing the backyard. About fifty wolves stood snarling at the lone man in front of the tree line, his tuft of brown hair neat and slicked back. He wore a dark red suit that looked freshly ironed, and he kept his hands behind his back. Even from

this distance, I saw him look up at me and smile. I, of course, flipped him off in response. He seemed to be amused by my behavior, and his smile widened, his canines gleaming. I shivered at the sight and spotted Ryker's form come through the sea of wolves.

He took slow, deliberate strides, and I prayed to the goddess that she kept him safe. When he was standing just a couple yards, he finally stopped. I saw Leon's mouth move as he spoke, but they were too far away to hear. The two men talked for what seemed like a decade, Ryker seemingly keeping his cool. However, I couldn't see his facial features as he was turned away from me.

*"We need to go down there,"* Rei suddenly said.

*"We do?"*

*"Yes. Now, hurry, Ryker is in danger."* Even with a small army of wolves, I knew that she was right. You could not trust the devil himself even if you had the best warriors by your side. I looked down at my attire and shook my head. *No time to worry about my wardrobe choices.* I opened the window and looked below.

I was on the third floor, and the grass looked ominous for the first time. But I will admit, it was a beautiful bright green. Maybe the lushness of it will help break my fall. Probably not. Taking a deep breath, I crouched in the window sill and looked up to see the two talking, Ryker now looking more agitated. My eyes scanned the woods, and I swore I saw the sun glint off of something. It was just a nanosecond, but I swore I saw it.

*So much for staying put,* I thought before I jumped. The wind whipped my hair, and the ground began to rush up at me like a fist. *This is going to hurt.*

Just as I landed, I bent my knees to absorb the impact, and I rolled. I kept my head tucked in and ended up on my back. I stared at the sky for one dazed moment, thinking that it was such a beautiful blue before snapping out of it. *Right, I'll have time to look at it later.*

Standing, it seemed like I had caught the attention of the nearby wolves, and I held my finger in front my lips in a quiet motion. They still gave me curious looks but went back to listening to the two men. Honestly, it's a miracle that they didn't hear me almost fall to my death.

*"Kei, what are you doing?"* Never mind; I peeked over the crowd of wolves to see him still facing Leon.

"How the hell did you take her powers?" I froze. Ladies and gentlemen, I'm screwed, and I didn't know how Leon knew, but he does. I really did wish that he burned in the deepest, darkest part of Hell where the flames were the hottest. Leon chuckled.

"I didn't take her powers. But she did." Leon pointed right at me. Ryker turned his head and looked at me disbelieving.

"You see, since today is her birthday, she regained her sight but lost her powers. Yet there is a way to get them back." This sparked interest in me but ignored it

"Well, I'm not interested," I spoke, taking long strides towards him.

"Kei," Ryker warned. I saw the look of irritation shot at me, but just I shot him a look in return and passed the wolves, parting in the middle.

"What is up your sleeve, Leon?" I narrowed my eyes at him as I stopped beside Ryker.

"You know me too well," he said with a smile.

"That's what I hate about myself the most," I growled.

"That's about to change," he replied breezily. I opened my mouth to retort a comeback, but the sight of a gleaming silver arrow pointed at Ryker made me freeze. The man was hidden in the trees about twenty yards behind Leon, and I was only able to detect him when a ray of sun bounced off the deadly weapon.

"Maybe you should go to Hell." Ryker snarled and made a step towards him. Just as he did, I could see the arrow move backward before the world froze. In a split second, the arrow was still before it began moving.

"Ryker!" I screamed and pushed him out of the way before the arrow hit him. Instead, it burrowed deeply into my stomach. Time stood still as I began to fall. And I mean it literally stood still. Time froze, and my vision became fuzzy. A familiar bright figure had come into existence before a woman appeared.

"Est... elle." I lay brokenly on the ground, my blood seeping into the ground. She smiled softly and knelt beside me.

"I'm sorry you have to go through with this," she apologized. I shook my head while barely moving. Pain ricocheted in my body.

"No need to apologize. I'm just hoping that I can die in peace." She held my hand in hers, squeezing gently.

"Your life is not going to end here. It's only going to get harder." I rolled my eyes.

"Of course, it's not like I wanted a totally happy and normal life with my mate," I said sarcastically before feeling bad for taking it out on Estelle. "Sorry, I'm just stressed." I began coughing, and it felt like my lungs were doing double time in trying to keep me alive.

"It's fine. But, Kei, when you wake up, you're not going to be the same as before." I frowned.

"What do you mean?" Her expression became somber.

"Kei, you're going to die. But you're also going to come back to life. When you do, you're going to be different."

"How?" She shook her head.

"I've said too much already, but just know that you are loved, and your parents are looking out for you." I felt my conscious waning as my vision started to turn black around the edges.

"You'll... stay with me?" I croaked.

"Of course." I smiled in relief before turning my head. I looked at Ryker's frozen form, his eyes wide and his lips frozen on my name.

"Wait, can you unfreeze, Ryker? I want to speak with him." She nodded and stood up. Walking over to him, she lightly touched his arm.

"Kei!" he shouted my name before blinking. He looked around himself briefly before spotting me on the ground. Horror filled his features, and he came running towards me. He sank to his knees and held my hand.

"Why did you do that?" He sounded angry, but his eyes showed that he was broken. Slowly, I lifted my hand and caressed his cheek.

"Didn't I tell you that I would have your back? Even if I don't have my powers, I still consider it true." I gasped and knew that my time was ticking away too quickly.

"Ryker, listen to me. I'm going to die," I said bluntly, making his eyes widen. "However, I am coming back, but first, you have to let me go."

"You've got to be kidding me. I'm not going to let you go, ever. And you're not going to die. We'll get you help and—" He started to sound more desperate as the seconds ticked by.

"No, Ryker. I'm going to die, and there's nothing that we can do about it." I could feel Death pulling now, asking me to close my eyes.

"Kei, it's almost time for you to go." Estelle looked at me sadly, and Ryker turned his head to look at her.

"No! She's going to be fine, and I'm going to rip Leon to shreds." He snarled. The blood kept leaking out of my wounds, and I knew that Estelle was right. Time had won again.

"Ryker... please promise me you'll let me go." He cradled my head while brushing the hair out of my face.

"I can't."

"Please... let me go... So I can come back..." I felt my eyes droop. "Promise me."

"Kei—"

"Promise me, Ryker." He was silent, and I was so close now.

"I promise." He sounded defeated. Instead of creating peace, I felt sorrow.

"I'll come back... That's my promise... to you." I opened my eyes to look up at his beautiful face one more time. "I love you, Ryker Dare, my King, my love, and my life." My eyes closed one last time. I faintly felt his soft lips brush mine. His tears fell on my cheeks, and his last words warmed me up before I was pulled into the darkness.

"You are my Queen, my light, and my world. I'll wait for you until the end of time, and when you do come back, I'm never letting you go.

"I love you, Kei Valancia."

Color Manual:

**Beige** - *sheepish/embarrassment*
**Black** - *malice*
**Blue** - *uncertainty*
**Copper Brown** - *fear*
**Crimson** - *hatred*
**Dark Brown** - *tense*
**Dark Gray** - *sadness*
**Dark Green** - *mistrust*
**Dark Lavender** - *happiness*
**Electric Green** - *excitement*
**Gold** - *pride*
**Grey** - *focus/concentration*
**Indigo** - *jealousy*
**Light Azure** - *amusement*
**Light Blue** - *calm*
**Light Yellow** - *disbelief*
**Navy Blue** - *confusion*
**Neon Orange** - *confidence*
**Neon Yellow** - *hurt*
**Orange** - *surprise*
**Pale Turquoise** - *relief*
**Red** - *anger*
**Silver** - *possessive*
**Steel Blue** - *irritation*
**Violet** - *desire*
**White** - *hope*
**Yellow** - *curiosity*

**THE END**

Can't get enough of Kei and Ryker? Make sure you sign up for the author's blog to find out more about them!

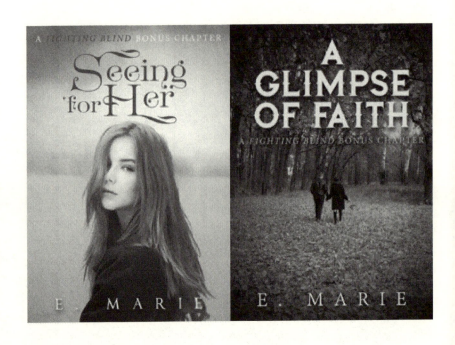

Get these two bonus chapters and more freebies when you sign up at e-marie.awesomeauthors.org!

Here is a sample from another story you may enjoy:

ASHLEY MICHELLE

His to Claim

# 01

**Scarlett**

"—Shift."

I was jolted out of my daydreaming by the sound of a loud voice ringing in my ear. I turned around with raised brows to find Darlene, the shift manager of the small family-owned diner, staring at me expectantly with a tray of dirty dishes in one hand. I had clearly missed the important parts of whatever she had been saying to me.

A sheepish grin worked its way up my face. "What was that?"

She rolled her eyes and blew a stray hair out of her face. "I *said*, do you mind covering the end of my shift for me? My babysitter called. Apparently, Graham is running a pretty high fever."

I nodded my head. "Sure, no problem." It wasn't like I had any plans for the evening anyway, other than obsessively checking the mail. There were only two weeks left before graduation, and I was yet to hear from any of the colleges I had applied to.

Darlene let out a small sigh. "Thanks, Scarlett. I owe you."

I waved my hand. "Don't worry about it. I know how hard it is on you being left to take care of Graham while Troy is away. I'm happy to help lighten the load." Her husband had to travel a lot for his job, and that left Darlene with extra parenting duties.

She gave me a grateful smile as she turned away with the tray of dishes. "You're truly an angel, Scarlett."

I snorted at her comment. "I already agreed to cover you. You don't need to kiss my butt anymore, Darlene."

She gave me a playful wink before turning away, disappearing through the kitchen door. I slowly turned back around with a sigh. This was going to be a long night of nothing but the virtual emptiness of the diner.

I was happy when a familiar face shuffled through the front door of the diner, setting off the little bell that hung above the door. He lifted his hand to his head, ruffling his dark hair which was starting to look shaggy around the edges. This boy would look like a mountain man if it weren't for my constant influence in his life. He met my gaze briefly as he reached out and grabbed one of the cheaply made menus from an empty table. He flipped through the pages quickly before setting it back down.

I pulled the pen and pad from the front pocket of my stained apron. "What can I get you, Wyatt?"

He shrugged as he moved closer toward me. "I think a cup of coffee will be fine. It's been a long day."

"It's going to be a bit longer. Darlene asked me to cover the end of her shift," I commented with an apologetic smile. Wyatt had promised to pick me up after my shift ended while I was running out the door this morning.

He let out a sigh, running his hand through his hair. "Of course, she did. Well, there *is* a meeting tonight. Guess it's going to be extra long for both of us, sweetheart," he replied with a sarcastic grin as I poured him a cup of coffee and placed it on the counter in front of me.

Darlene approached us carrying her purse, her jacket slung over her arm. "You know the coffee here is shit, Wyatt. I don't know why you keep ordering it when you only ever have a sip and leave the rest."

Wyatt ignored her comment. The two of them were always at each other's throats for reasons unknown to me. He pressed his hands to the counter, breathing in deeply. His nose scrunched up a bit, and he looked over at me. "You smell." I frowned at my cousins greeting as he sat himself down on a stool at the breakfast counter, grabbing the coffee.

"Gee, you really know how to compliment a girl," I grumbled, my voice dripping with sarcasm. My cousin and I had a very close relationship, considering that my parents had taken him in after his father ran off and his mother got sick. He returned the favor when my parents died, taking me into his home and raising me like I was his kid sister.

"God, Wyatt..." Darlene remarked as she threw her arms into the sleeves of her jacket, pulling up the collar. "Even if a woman does stink, you shouldn't comment on it. And you wonder why you're still single."

Her words brought a smile to my face, and I gave him a pointed look. I snickered as I turned away from my cousin who was pouting at the blunt reprimand he had received. I could see Winston, our cook, slaving away over the grill through the small hole, singing along to some garbage being gurgled out of the old boom box he kept in the kitchen. The diner was my home away from home, and its motley crew was my self-created wolf pack even if they were only humans.

"Wyatt," she said his name in a flat tone. Darlene had never cared much for my cousin. Maybe it's because he had a knack for putting his foot in his mouth... or maybe because they had gone "grown-up" together and he'd been quite the fool back in his younger years.

"See you tomorrow, Scarlett. Thanks again," she called.

I turned around to give her a quick wave. "See ya, Darlene. Tell Graham I said hello and hope he feels better," I called back as she exited the front door, the bell ringing again.

Wyatt lifted his gaze to mine, staring at me expectantly with wide eyes as if he was waiting for something. I stared back at him, shifting my hands to my hips. "Why are you looking at me like that? Do I have something on my face?" I reached up with a hand and wiped it across my cheek, checking to see if there was any food splatter. It was a hazard of the job.

"Can't you feel it, Scarlett?" he asked me in a soft voice so that no one else could hear. Hell, if it wasn't for my extra-sensitive senses I probably wouldn't have heard him either.

I narrowed my eyes in confusion at his question. "What are talking about? Are you feeling okay, Wyatt?" I reached out and placed my hand on his forehead. He pulled back with a furrowed brow and looked at me as if I had two heads.

"After all the complaining and whining I had to listen to from you… are you seriously telling me that you don't feel even the slightest bit different?" he asked a little louder in an exasperated tone, waving his hand in the air dramatically. I had no idea what he was going on about or why he seemed so upset.

I looked around the small room at the other patrons who seemed content to ignore his outburst. I leaned forward, stuffing my notepad back into the pocket of my apron. "I don't know why you think I should feel different, but I feel the same as I always do. Unless you want to count the fact that my feet feel like I've been walking barefoot on hot coals. These ten-hour shifts have been killing me," I whined at him.

He gave me a slow blink, shaking his head. "Seriously, Scarlett?"

"What?" I questioned with a tired tone.

"Your scent—"

I held up a hand, cutting off his thought mid-sentence.

"I know. I know. I smell, but in my defense, you would smell too if you worked with greasy food all day," I snapped at him, growing tired of the conversation he was having with me. If I wanted to be insulted,

I'm sure I could easily find one of my peers to satisfy that need without a problem. Human or shifter, they were all eager to tear someone else down to elevate themselves.

He shook his head at me. "No, your scent has changed, Scarlett. Your wolf has matured. I can smell her on you now."

I stared at him blankly as I digested his words. Had my wolf finally reached maturity without me noticing? I searched my mind for a sign of my wolf's presence. I had been waiting for this moment since I hit puberty. Most of my peers had already matured, leaving me as an outsider when it came to the pack.

All shifters had to go through two stages of puberty: the natural human one and the beast underneath. It could happen at any time, but basically, it meant that the connection between human and wolf was fully formed. It wasn't until this happens that we were allowed to attend actual pack events. Most of my friends had already matured. I had been left in the group of late bloomers. Sometimes, it happened that a wolf never matured. These people were seen as Omegas. They were still a part of the pack, but they would never be considered true wolves.

I shifted back and forth on my feet, concentrating hard. "I don't feel any different."

Wyatt took a sip of his coffee. "You will, trust me." He pulled the mug away from himself, peering down into the cup with a small look of disgust before setting it down. "But you know what this means?"

"What?" I questioned with a raised brow.

He met my gaze with a knowing look. "You don't have to wait in the car like the other pups during the meeting tonight. You're a true wolf now," he teased as he gave me a wolfish grin. I rolled my eyes at his comment, but on the inside, I felt a bubble of excitement.

* * *

I had only ever seen the pack house from the outside, having never been allowed to enter it before. I found myself getting anxious as I followed Wyatt down the dirt driveway and around the side of the house. In the back, there was another building, about the size of a guest house.

I could hear the sound of happy voices carried on the gentle evening breeze. My palms felt sweaty in the pockets of my sweatshirt as my nerves got the better of me. Wyatt gave me a grin as he opened the door. "So it begins."

I rolled my eyes at him as I walked past him into the large open room. The smells of other pack members overwhelmed me for a moment. My eyes scanned the crowd warily, looking for familiar faces. I found my gaze gravitating towards the front of the room where the stream of bodies seemed to be moving.

That was the first time I saw *him*.

He stood near the front, greeting people with a friendly smile. My heart hammered in my chest as I watched him from where I stood at the back of the room. I had no idea who he was, but I knew he was perfect. His dark hair was shaved close to his head as if it had been shaved bare at some point and was finally being allowed to grow out. My eyes followed the length of his body, taking in every part of him. He had a lean body that spoke of endurance-honed muscles.

Wyatt elbowed my side. "Don't just stand there, Scarlett. People are starting to look at us." He urged me to move forward. I had to force my feet to move from where I had been anchored. My whole world seemed to be shifting on its axis, and I couldn't be sure I was standing on solid ground anymore.

My heart was in my throat as I approached my mate—at least that was what my wolf was telling me. This perfect male specimen was our mate, the one that the Goddess had ordained for us at birth. But what if he hated me? What if I wasn't what he was expecting? Insecurities that I had never felt before began to flood my brain.

I dug my heels into the floor. "I can't do this. Let's go home."

Wyatt grabbed onto my elbow and led me on. "You're being ridiculous. We all had to go through this, Scarlett. Consider it your official initiation into the pack." I gritted my teeth as every step brought me closer to the finality of my situation.

The Alpha and his mate were standing together, greeting the other pack members as they filed into the room, grabbing seats for the meeting. I remembered them from the times they had visited my home when I was much younger, way back when my mother was still alive and my father held a prominent position in the pack. They looked older and a little more worn down, but that had to be expected of people in their positions.

"Alpha Aaron," Wyatt spoke formally as he reached out a hand, a common human greeting. I danced on the balls of my feet, wishing that I hadn't accepted Wyatt's offer to join him. I was still in my work uniform, smelling like grease and probably looking unkempt from the busy workday... not the way I wanted to make my first impression on the pack.

"Wyatt," he replied, shaking the hand that had been offered to him with a firm grip, "it is good to see you again."

Wyatt beamed at the acknowledgment, turning his eyes toward the female beside the Alpha, bowing his head. "Luna Victoria."

She gave him a kind smile. "Wyatt."

Alpha Aaron's dark gaze shifted in my direction, a smile still on his lips. "And who is this beauty?" he questioned, lifting a brow as he examined me further. My cheeks rushed with heat, and I felt the sudden urge to hide behind my cousin like I did back in my younger years where I would cling to my mother's leg.

Wyatt wrapped his arm around my shoulder, pulling me in protectively to his side, and that only made me feel more embarrassed. "This is my cousin, Scarlett."

Luna Victoria gave me a knowing glance as she leaned into her mate's side. "Sweetheart, it's Conrad and Elizabeth's daughter."

"Of course, she is," he replied as if he had already known. My lips twitched with the urge to smile when she looked at me with a playful eye roll at his expense. Alpha Aaron crossed his arms over his wide chest, leaning forward toward me. "I can see it now that I've gotten a closer look. You've got Conrad's eyes."

"And Elizabeth's beautiful face," Luna Victoria remarked. "If I recall correctly, your mother was a late bloomer as well." I felt my head sink a little lower at her comment.

"David..." Luna Victoria called, turning toward my mate with a smile, "come over here real fast."

She glanced back at me. "Conrad helped train David when he was a young boy. I'm sure he will be very interested in meeting you." I felt my nerves spike as he turned in our direction, and I realized that he wasn't an average member of the pack. This was *their* son, the next heir: an Alpha born male.

I wanted to run, but my feet kept me firmly rooted in place. I was afraid to look up from the ground. What would I see staring back at me? I swallowed hard, trying to prepare myself for what was about to happen.

His shoes came into view, and I felt my wolf stirring under my skin. Wyatt elbowed me in the side. "Scarlett..." he hissed under his breath in a warning tone. I lifted my face to meet his gaze with a bated breath.

His dark eyes widened in surprise as we drank each other in. Something in my mind snapped. I could feel it all, everything everyone had tried to explain to me about having a wolf. Her emotions and thoughts surged through me as I watched the corners of his mouth lift upwards into a smile.. a heart-stopping smile that was meant for only me.

I felt my own lips begin to mimic his. There was nothing and no one else in the room for us at that moment. This is what it felt like to have a mate, and I knew he was feeling the same sensations by the look in his eyes.

The moment was broken when a tall dark-haired female placed a kiss on his cheek. "I'm sorry I'm late, David. My shift went into overtime. I had to help Doctor McCarthy deliver the Johnson's twins. Those pups are going to be a handful. I can tell you that now." She finished with a soft chuckle of amusement.

I hadn't even seen her approach us I had been so lost in a different world. My smile faded quickly as my brows furrowed in confusion as I glanced between the two of them. He looked rather stiff as she grabbed a hold of his hand with hers, turning her face in my direction.

"Hello. I don't think I've seen you before." She tilted her head to the side.

"That's because she's only just matured, Eva," Luna Victoria commented toward her, both of them sharing a look of understanding like two people who've already been through it.

"This must be very exciting for you then," she remarked with a bright smile, completely unaware of what had happened between me and the male she was holding onto as if he were hers. My wolf was growling possessively in my mind, struggling to free herself so that she could eliminate the competition.

"David, this is Scarlett," Luna Victoria introduced me. "Conrad's daughter," she supplied as if it were my own special title.

I felt like the rug had been pulled out from under my feet and I was falling without anyone to catch me. My stomach was in my throat, but I forced myself to speak. "Hi…" I replied in a tense voice, finding it hard to hold his gaze.

David pulled his hand free from Eva's grasp and took a step towards me. He lifted his hand slightly like he wanted to reach out to me, but he thought better of it, deciding to stuff it into the pocket of his slacks instead.

"It's nice to meet you, Scarlett." Goosebumps rose on my flesh, and I watched his pupils dilate a bit as he took in more of me. "Your father was a great man. The pack lost a great warrior when he passed away. I lost a dear friend," he added, trying to keep things from getting strange in front of all the onlookers. None of them seemed to know what had transpired between the two of us.

I gave him a small smile that didn't reach my eyes. "Thank you." He looked like he wanted to say something more to me, his lips parted slightly. Alpha Aaron stepped forward, his dark eyes calculating as he glanced between myself and his son. I lowered my gaze to the ground, clenching my jaw tightly.

"Well, we should get this meeting going." He wrapped his arm around his mate and pulled her into his side. "It's wonderful to have another true wolf added to the pack."

Wyatt grabbed my elbow, and I tensed slightly at the touch. Now that I could connect to my wolf, the world seemed too overwhelming. Every sensation moved through me like an exploding bomb. I let him lead me away to some empty seats, but my mind was adrift as I looked around the room. I had matured and met my mate, only to find out that he already had someone at his side. How could I compete with her?

My gaze focused on the female in question, Eva. She was a fully matured female compared to myself, who was still growing into my body, which was mostly knees and elbows. She seemed kind, and she didn't waver under the gaze of all the people in the room. She looked like a queen. I certainly wasn't much compared to her. That was why she was the one standing on the stage, holding his hand.

I sunk down lower in my seat. I could hear Alpha Aaron's voice as he spoke to the group, but none of the words were able to pierce through my racing thoughts.

"We are happy to announce that the mating ceremony of Eva and David will be held at the end of next month," Alpha Aaron said with pride in his voice, clapping David on the back as he stood next to a smiling Eva, hand in hand. My heart dropped, and I sucked in a painful breath. This wasn't how things were supposed to go. I was his mate, not her.

I couldn't sit in that room for another moment and listen to any more words. I leaned over to Wyatt. "I need to go," I whispered. He looked over at me in confusion as I rose up out of my chair and hurried toward the exit. I didn't look back, but I felt David's eyes on me, my body heating up everywhere his gaze drifted to. It was getting hard to breathe as I pushed open the door and flung myself out into the night, letting the cool air wash over me.

I sucked in ragged breaths as I tried to overcome the ache in my chest. No one had warned me maturing would be so painful.

# If you enjoyed this sample then look for
# **His to Claim.**

**Other books you might enjoy:**

King of Beasts
Jamiee Lynne
Available on Amazon!

**Other books you might enjoy:**

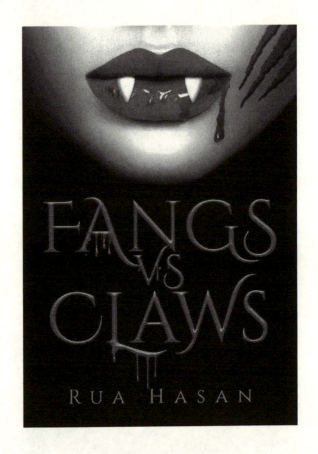

Fangs Vs Claws
Rua Hasan
Available on Amazon!

# Introducing the Characters Magazine App

Download the app to get the free issues of interviews from famous fiction characters and find your next favorite book!

iTunes: bit.ly/CharactersApple
Google Play: bit.ly/CharactersAndroid

# Acknowledgements

I want to thank my family, along with my fans and the people in my community. The support given really pushed me through and it made this whole experience much more exciting. I also want to thank all Blvnp agents and for all of the work that they put in to make this into a reality.

# Author's Note

Hey there!

Thank you so much for reading Fighting Blind! I can't express how grateful I am for reading something that was once just a thought inside my head.

I'd love to hear from you! Please feel free to email me at e_marie@awesomeauthors.org and sign up at e-marie.awesomeauthors.org for freebies!

One last thing: I'd love to hear your thoughts on the book. Please leave a review on Amazon or Goodreads because I just love reading your comments and getting to know YOU!

Whether that review is good or bad, I'd still love to hear it!


Can't wait to hear from you!


AUTHOR NAME

## About the Author

E. Marie lives in a quiet town of Missouri with her parents, loves to play sports such as softball, and enjoys her time hanging out with close friends.

Made in the USA
San Bernardino, CA
24 December 2018